THE
HUNTED

The Bane Island Novels by Lisa Childs

The Runaway

The Hunted

THE
HUNTED

LISA
CHILDS

ZEBRA BOOKS
KENSINGTON PUBLISHING CORP.
www.kensingtonbooks.com

ZEBRA BOOKS are published by

Kensington Publishing Corp.
119 West 40th Street
New York, NY 10018

All Kensington titles, imprints, and distributed lines are available at special quantity discounts for bulk purchases for sales promotion, premiums, fund-raising, educational, or institutional use.

Special book excerpts or customized printings can also be created to fit specific needs. For details, write or phone the office of the Kensington Sales Manager: Attn.: Sales Department. Kensington Publishing Corp., 119 West 40th Street, New York, NY 10018. Phone: 1-800-221-2647.

Zebra and the Z logo Reg. U.S. Pat. & TM Off.

First Printing: December 2021
ISBN-13: 978-1-4201-5022-3
ISBN-13: 978-1-4201-5024-7 (eBook)

10 9 8 7 6 5 4 3 2 1

Printed in the United States of America

Prologue

October 1996

A cry rang out, startling black birds into flight. They rose from the pine trees to form a dark cloud in the sky, casting a shadow over the tall wrought iron gate and the three boys who straddled their bicycles in front of it.

Deacon Howell ducked his head down and murmured, "What the hell was that?" A howl followed the cry as coyotes called out to each other.

"What's the matter? Scared?" Elijah Cooke taunted him. The puny kid wouldn't have been brave enough to do that if his cousin wasn't standing right next to him.

David Cooke was already a teenager while Deacon and Elijah were still twelve. But David was dumb, so he was in their grade even though he was older and bigger. Too much bigger for Deacon to fight the two of them alone. Maybe he was the dumb one for coming here.

"I'm not scared," he lied.

Elijah stared at him with those creepy, pale eyes like he could see right through him. Even though he wasn't as big as his cousin, he was somehow more frightening. It had been his idea to come here. So Deacon was probably getting set up, but it was too late to back out now.

Staring up at the tall, iron gates, he asked, "How we getting in?"

A little smirk curving his thin lips, Elijah wrapped one small hand around a piece of rusted iron and pushed. The gate creaked open.

Damn it.

Now Deacon had no excuse and no escape . . . from the curse. That was the legend—that anyone who set foot on the property of the old insane asylum would be cursed. That was probably why the Cookes were so messed up; their family owned the place, so they had no escape either.

Now they were getting him cursed. He drew in a breath of cold autumn air then pedaled his bike after theirs, down the winding drive. The road was overgrown with pine boughs hanging over them, snagging and pulling at their clothes.

The hospital had been shut down before Deacon was born. But he knew what had been done here. He'd heard all the stories about the people who'd been electrocuted and had holes drilled into their brains. Every time one of those branches tugged on him, he felt like it was a hand reaching out to do those same things to him. He shivered and pedaled harder, passing the Cookes, so they wouldn't have time to set a trap for him. He wasn't bigger than David, but he was faster.

He made it to the building first. All crumbling stone with ivy climbing over it, it looked like a castle and was nearly that tall. Mesmerized, he jumped off his bike and let it drop into the thick weeds. As he stared at the manor, the spooky old building seemed to stare back at him, its broken windows like wide, soulless eyes.

Then the manor called out to him in a high-pitched whisper, "Deacon . . ."

The giggles that followed made him realize it was just the Cookes teasing him, trying to scare him. He would show them that he was no baby. He was brave.

He headed toward the double doors at the front of the crumbling stone building. One door had pulled partly loose from its rusty hinges, so he was able to peel it back and squeeze through the opening. His legs shook as he stepped into the building. It was dark and cold and smelled like something dead.

Probably an animal.

Just an animal.

Animals would have been able to get inside just as easily as he had. Easier because they could have gotten through any of the broken windows. Light filtered through those windows, guiding him toward a staircase in the middle of the front room. The steps wound up a few stories to where long branches broke through the ceiling. Ice or lightning must have dropped a tree onto the roof. Staring up, moving toward the staircase, he wasn't watching where he was going until he tripped, falling across whatever his foot had hit on the floor. He reached out to push himself up, and his hand slid over something, or rather, into it. Something squishy and . . .

He looked down at the person lying beneath him, or what was left of the person. Long, scraggly, light-colored hair framed the decaying face that, like the manor, stared back at him with rotted eyes.

A scream burned in his throat, but it stuck there, unable to come out, just like he was stuck there, unable to move. Trapped in a nightmare.

He knew for certain then that he was cursed, just like this poor person had been.

Chapter One

Present Day

The drive wound between the pine trees, the boughs heavy with snow. A thin sheen of black ice covered the asphalt. That was why he didn't press harder on the accelerator: caution and dread. But despite his slow speed, he reached the parking lot and pulled the SUV into one of the many empty spaces.

More than twenty-five years had passed since the day Deacon Howell had discovered his first dead body at Bainesworth Manor. Even though he wasn't that scared twelve-year-old boy any longer, the same sense of dread and doom tied his guts in knots every time he set foot on the property. He opened the driver's door and stepped onto the slick asphalt. Staring up at the massive stone structure with its snow-covered, clay-tiled roof, Deacon wasn't impressed with the renovations that had been completed a couple of years ago. The gleaming windows looked as soulless to him as the broken ones had so many years ago. Though it had been renamed Halcyon Hall and converted from a psychiatric hospital into some kind of fancy treatment-center spa, it would always be Bainesworth Manor to him.

The curse of his existence . . .

If only he could blame this damn place for everything that had gone wrong in his life.

Just as he had all those years ago, he drew in a deep, shaky breath before walking through the double doors that opened automatically to admit him. Now the foyer was all shiny marble and polished wood, and the air was fresh with the faint traces of leather and sage. He still smelled death though—just as he had all those years ago.

Death hung over the manor just like the dark clouds hung over Bane Island, Maine. The manor dominated nearly half of the big island, leaving the village, its outskirts, and some of the rocky shoreline for the locals. The shore was so rocky that few boats dared to dock there, so no ferry ran. It was a four-mile-long bridge that connected Bane Island to the mainland. Since that rickety, old bridge was rarely passable in the winter, the island was self-contained with a small hospital and a grocery store and other small shops.

Deacon was a local—born and raised here. When he'd left, he'd never wanted to come back, but the curse—and his father's failing health—had called him home.

And his job kept calling him out to the hall.

Elijah Cooke stepped out of the shadows, where he always seemed to be lurking—like one of the ghosts that were rumored to haunt the manor. As the director of Halcyon Hall, Elijah was actually running it, though. "What is it this time, Sheriff?"

Deacon had made quite a few trips to the hall during the past month—to help a woman find her missing daughter. He'd found a dead body instead. Fortunately, it hadn't been hers. But not knowing who he'd discovered had made his job even harder.

"You know why I'm here," Deacon said.

Elijah's pale eyes gleamed eerily from the shadows in which he stood. "You know who she is?"

He shook his head.

"What's taking so long?"

"The body was damaged too badly for fingerprinting." The first corpse he'd found here had haunted him since he was twelve. This one would haunt him until he died. And the one he'd found between those two . . .

He would never be free of her either—especially not of her.

"What about DNA?" Elijah asked.

Deacon knew what he was asking but chose to be as off-putting as the shrink was. "It doesn't match Genevieve Walcott's."

"Of course not," Elijah said. "She's alive. Thank God for that." He arched a dark brow. "Or are *you* going to take credit?"

Deacon shook his head. "Genevieve's a smart girl. She saved herself." With some help from her future stepfather, she had escaped the Halcyon Hall grounds-keeper who'd abducted her. The woman whose body Deacon had discovered had not been so lucky; she hadn't escaped her gruesome fate. Deacon had found her much too late to save her. All he could do now was make sure she got justice.

Elijah stepped closer to Deacon, lowered his voice to a whisper and asked, "What about the other DNA?"

"Which of the other DNA?" Deacon asked. "There's so damn much of it now that it's going to take the lab some time to run it all."

Elijah sighed. "You didn't need to get warrants, you know. I do want to know whose body you found."

"How come you didn't report her missing?" he asked.

His mind was still blown over what Elijah had finally admitted to him. That he was an uncle; his younger brother, Jamie—or as he wanted to be called now, Bode—was a single father. The Bainesworth bloodline continued— maybe even more than anyone had guessed if the other rumors were true. But Deacon, more than anyone, knew not to put too much credence in rumors. He only wanted the facts, like how the mother of Elijah's niece, a personal trainer who'd worked at the spa, had disappeared shortly after the birth of her daughter four months ago.

"She left Bode a good-bye note and resigned," Elijah said.

From her job and from being a mother, according to the note that he had shown to Deacon a few weeks ago.

"Bode thinks it was all just too much for her, and she took off," Elijah continued, in defense of his younger brother. "He doesn't think that body is hers. She'd left months before that woman was murdered."

Elijah was clearly not as convinced. Dark circles shadowed the skin beneath his weird silver eyes. He wasn't getting any more sleep than Deacon was.

"You didn't report Genevieve Walcott as missing either," he reminded him. "Why are you still trying to act as if nothing's going on around here?"

"Whatever was going on—it's over," Elijah said. "The groundskeeper that kidnapped Genevieve is dead. If the woman whose body you found was murdered, then Teddy Bowers must have killed her."

"That's what you want to believe," Deacon said.

"Don't you want to believe that, too?" Elijah asked.

"Doesn't matter what I want," he said. "I have to learn the truth." About everything . . . even that other body he'd found over a year ago. "That's why I asked the state police to reopen their investigation into Shannon's death." Just like the body he'd found a few weeks ago, Shannon had been blond. Genevieve Walcott was also blond. Maybe Bane Island had a serial killer.

"They already ruled it suicide," Elijah said. "Since that made everything easier for you, wasn't that what you wanted?"

"I just told you—I want the truth," he said.

Elijah snorted. "Your truth. You want to blame me and my family for everything that happens on the island—even Shannon's suicide."

"If Genevieve Walcott's kidnapper was telling the truth, your family *is* to blame," Deacon said. "Remember that Teddy Bowers claimed he was a Bainesworth heir. That you and your brother cheated him out of his birthright."

Elijah shook his head. "Teddy Bowers was delusional. If you're just here to antagonize me, you can leave now, Sheriff."

"You call it antagonizing. I call it interrogating," Deacon said.

"I've done nothing to warrant an interrogation," Elijah replied.

Deacon tilted his head and stared skeptically at his old nemesis. "Once again, that's just what you want to believe."

"And once again, you don't want it to be the truth," Elijah replied. "So this conversation is over, Sheriff. The next time you want to come here, you better have a warrant."

Deacon drew a paper out of his pocket. "Look what I happen to have right here . . ."

Elijah cursed. "I don't know how the hell you made friends with the judge."

Deacon wasn't sure either since he had initially treated Whittaker Lawrence, who was Genevieve Walcott's soon-to-be stepfather, with the same suspicion he did the Cookes. Maybe the difference was that Whit hadn't had anything to hide, so he hadn't gotten defensive. He'd realized Deacon was just doing his job.

"What the hell is this warrant for?" Elijah asked as he took the paper. He read it and shook his head. "No. No. No way in hell!"

Deacon chuckled. Elijah wasn't going to win this time—like he had, with the help of his older cousin, pretty much every skirmish of their childhood rivalry. Deacon wasn't the dumb kid he'd once been—not anymore, not after everything he'd lived through . . . and lost.

How long would she be safe here? How long until the press found her—or worse yet—*he* found her?

She glanced around the conservatory. Although sunshine warmed the room, Olivia Smith shivered as a chill chased down her spine. For once, she was the only one using the room, but she didn't feel alone. She felt creeped out, as if someone was watching her. Anyone could have been standing on the other side of the glass walls, hiding among the snow-enshrouded pine trees. Shadows darkened the snow around all those trees. Maybe one of the shadows was of a person instead of a pine. As Olivia peered outside, she caught a reflection in the glass—of herself, with her clothes hanging on her petite frame, of her dark blond hair tangled around her thin face, of her wide eyes staring back at her.

She wasn't dressing to impress anyone. Because of the winter weather and the holiday season, there were few other guests. That was part of why Olivia had chosen now to attend the exclusive spa. Despite the horrifying history of Bainesworth Manor, she had felt safe here at Halcyon Hall. Until the body had been found . . .

It wasn't even so much the body that had scared her but the arrival of the reporter. Edie Stone was legendary for uncovering scandals and secrets. Olivia had both, and she intended to keep them.

That was another reason why, three months ago, she'd checked herself into the exclusive spa. Halcyon Hall promised their guests absolute privacy. The director, Dr. Elijah Cooke, insisted that would not change despite the discovery of a body on the property. Dr. Cooke swore that a reporter would never be allowed access to the hall and especially not to the spa guests. Olivia was still safe.

Wasn't she?

As she stared out the window, she spied another reflection, of a shadow that moved behind her. She jumped and whirled toward the intruder. "What the hell—"

"I'm sorry," the dark-haired teenager said. "I didn't mean to scare you."

Olivia ducked her head down, so her hair slid over to hide her face, and started toward the French doors that stood open to the hallway.

"I won't bother you," the girl said, her voice cracking with emotion. "Just pretend I'm not here."

That was what Olivia had been hoping the teenager would do—ignore her. But every weekend the girl worked, she found some excuse to seek her out, to stare at her. To stalk her . . .

Olivia had enough damn stalkers. She didn't need one here. Not that she was afraid of the girl . . .

In fact, something pulled at her heart as she looked at the kid. Tears streaked down the teenager's full face, and her body shook with the sobs cracking her voice.

"What's wrong?" Olivia asked even though she really didn't want to get involved . . . with anyone . . . with anything. She just wanted to be left alone, but something tugged at her heart when she looked at the teenager.

The girl raised her hand to her face and wiped at her tears. "Do . . . do you really care?" she asked, her deep-set, dark eyes widening with shock.

Olivia had done her best to avoid the girl whenever she worked at the spa. That tug on her heart turned into a twinge of regret that she'd been so obvious about her avoidance. She'd been so intent on protecting herself that she hadn't realized she might have been hurting somebody else. "You're upset," Olivia said. "I want to know why."

The girl sniffled. "For the same reason I'm always upset," she said. "Because of *him* . . ."

Olivia sighed. "Because of a boy?" She shouldn't have been surprised. Teenage angst was usually about hormones unless that teenager had grown up like she had. Then hormones had been the least of her problems.

The girl laughed, but the sound was sharp with bitterness. "Like I could ever have a boyfriend with him as my dad. I'm probably going to lose this job because of him—because he's out there fighting with Dr. Cooke right now, like he's always fighting with someone."

"Fighting?" Olivia asked, and her body tensed with dread. "Is your dad violent?"

The teenager nodded.

And Olivia gasped. She reached out now for the girl, closing her hands over the teenager's shoulders. "Does he get violent with you?" She studied the girl's face, looking for bruises. But she knew, from her own experience, that a smart abuser made sure there was no easily visible evidence.

The girl shook her head, sending her long dark hair across her face. Olivia reached up and pushed it back, and the girl flinched as if anticipating a blow. "I'm sorry," Olivia said as she pulled her hand back. She hated people touching her—for the very same reason the girl had flinched. She shouldn't have reached out like she had.

The girl shook her head again. "It's okay."

"What's your name?" Olivia asked. She'd been told it before; the female shrink, Rosemary Tulle, had mentioned it. But she couldn't remember it now—not with so many other thoughts rushing through her head. So many other memories . . .

"Holly," the girl replied, her voice soft as if she was suddenly shy.

"Holly," Olivia said. "You need to report him. You need to tell someone what he's doing to you."

"Report him?" Holly repeated with another bitter chuckle. "To who?"

"The police."

"He is the police," Holly replied. "He's the sheriff."

Olivia held in the curse burning her throat. She didn't want to add to the girl's fear and frustration. "That doesn't make him above the law. We can report him to the state police. Or to that judge, the one dating Rosemary Tulle." Olivia had met him a couple of times; he'd seemed like someone a person could trust.

"That judge is friends with him," Holly informed her. "And he's already been reported to the state police. They didn't have enough evidence to do anything to him."

"They didn't believe you?" Olivia asked, and anger coursed through her. She'd been that girl—the one nobody had believed.

Holly shrugged. "It's not like that . . ." Tears pooled in her dark eyes again. "He hasn't . . ."

"What?" Olivia prodded her when she trailed off. "What hasn't he done?"

The girl, who was much taller than Olivia's five feet, stared over her shoulder, and those dark eyes widened again as she murmured, "Dad . . ."

Olivia whirled around to the doorway and to the man who nearly filled it. He was tall and broad shouldered and so very dark that it felt as if his shadow swallowed all the sunshine in the conservatory. Her pulse quickened with fear racing over her, as that chill had earlier. She locked her legs that were threatening to tremble, and, summoning all her strength, stepped between father and daughter. Between the abuser and child?

"I won't let him hurt you," she promised the girl.

Beneath the brim of his navy-blue uniform cap, the sheriff's brow furrowed. "Holly, what the hell have you been telling people?"

"I . . . I haven't . . ." Her voice trailed off.

A wave of fierce protectiveness swept over Olivia, and she turned back toward the girl. "You don't have to talk to him. Go," she urged her. "I'll deal with your father."

Like she wished someone would have dealt with hers.

She led Holly toward the doorway where the sheriff stood; Olivia stayed between them, so the girl could slip out without her father touching her. He didn't try, though, not with Olivia there. He didn't even look at his daughter, just shook his head as if disgusted.

Shaking with fury now, she barely held onto her temper until the girl was gone. Then she released her anger. "How dare you!" she said to him. "How dare you act as if she's disappointed you."

She knew how that felt, to be belittled and demeaned— to be treated as less than nothing, as nobody. "How dare you!" she repeated, and she reached out again, stabbing his chest with her finger.

The man was like the hall, built out of rock. His chest was a wall of muscle. He didn't budge except for his mouth, which curved slightly upward in a smirk.

She wanted to slap it off his face, but as if he'd read her mind, he cautioned her, "You should think twice before assaulting an officer, Ms. Smith."

Shocked that he knew her name and that she was touching him, she pulled her finger from his chest and stepped back. "I am not the one assaulting anyone," she said.

He narrowed his dark eyes and studied her face. "Neither am I. I don't know what the hell my daughter has been telling you, but I've never laid a *finger* on her."

Olivia stared back at him, trying to determine if the sincerity in his voice and on his face was genuine or just a thin, handsome veneer he showed the world. "Why are you here then?" she asked. "Harassing her at work?"

"I am not harassing her," he said. "I didn't come here to talk to her."

"Then why are you here?" she asked.

"To talk to you."

Olivia's head snapped back as if he'd slapped her. "Me?"

Why the hell did he want to talk to her? What did he know about her—besides her name? What had he learned?

For the first time Elijah understood the satisfaction of balling his hand into a fist and swinging it. Hard. The force of the blow had his knuckles stinging and a vibration traveling from those knuckles up to his shoulder. He could even feel it in his abdomen.

He probably would have gotten hit in return—if not for his brother grabbing the bag before it swung back and struck him. Bode shook his head and cautioned him, "You're going to break your hand if you're not careful."

That was Elijah's problem. He was always so damn careful—always working so hard to control himself and everything around him. But despite his best efforts, his control was slipping.

"If you want to keep punching the bag, at least let me lace the gloves on you," Bode offered. "Or we can spar, if you want."

Since they'd become business partners in Halcyon Hall, they'd been sparring. Weary of the fight, Elijah shook his head.

Bode grinned. "Don't want to take me on?"

Given that his brother was a world-renowned personal trainer, Elijah would have been a fool to try. Bode was the "body" part of Halcyon Hall. A psychiatrist, Elijah was the "mind" part of the treatment center motto of "total well-being for body and mind."

"I don't want to fight with you," Elijah admitted. "Not anymore."

Bode sighed. "Guess we have taken more than our share of jabs at each other."

Elijah couldn't promise that he wouldn't fight with his brother again; they were business partners after all, who each believed his part of the business was more important. But they weren't enemies. Not anymore . . .

"Instead of fighting each other, we need to fight to save the hall," Elijah said.

Bode tensed. "What's happened?"

"The sheriff is here."

Bode cursed. "He better have a damn warrant."

"He does," Elijah said. "He has a court order that allows him to question our guests."

Bode struck the bag now with such force that, despite the heavy weight of it, it swung up toward the rafters of the open ceiling in the cavernous gym. "Damn it! Now the guests, those that haven't already checked out, damn sure will once he starts harassing them like he's been harassing us!"

That was Elijah's fear, too. "And there's no way they know anything about that body. The sheriff found her a few weeks ago, so she was dead before most of them arrived."

But not all of them. Morgana Drake had been here the longest, coming for a few months at a time since the hall had first opened two years ago. She'd been here for six months this last time, so she was more a resident than a guest at this point.

Olivia Smith had checked in three months ago, and she had yet to inform them of her departure date. Given how she valued her privacy, Elijah suspected that would be soon.

"That's not all he's done," Elijah said. "He's having the state reopen the investigation into his wife's death."

"Why?" Bode asked. "Seems like that's going to come back to bite him on the ass more than it will us."

Elijah shrugged. "I don't know why . . ." Except that Deacon probably didn't want to feel responsible or guilty anymore over the loss of his wife. "But if the state police call that murder too . . ."

"We have to make sure none of this hits the news," Bode said, "or all those bookings we have for upcoming stays will get canceled."

That was Elijah's greatest fear. "I know. I'm meeting with Amanda next." Amanda Plasky was the hall's publicist.

Bode sucked in a breath. "You told me first?"

Elijah nodded. "Of course."

Bode raised his arm again, but instead of swinging, he grabbed Elijah's shoulder and squeezed. "Thanks."

A twinge of regret struck Elijah that their partnership had started out so acrimoniously. "We're in this together," he reminded his younger brother.

Never more so than now.

Unfortunately, they were not the only two partners in the hall. They had a silent one—if only he would stay that way . . .

"Do you want to meet with Amanda with me?" Elijah offered, which was something else he wouldn't have done before, just as coming to Bode first wouldn't have been something he'd have done either.

Bode glanced around at the other people in the gym. "Heather should be finishing up soon," he said of the young female trainer. "I'll have her take my next appointment and join you."

Instead of resenting his involvement, as he would have in the past, Elijah appreciated it until Bode added, "Then we should tell *him*."

Dread clenched the muscles in Elijah's stomach, tightening them more than any of Bode's workouts would have. He groaned.

Bode reminded him, "He's the third one in this partnership."

They wouldn't have been able to renovate and reimagine Bainesworth Manor if their grandfather hadn't given them early access to their inheritance with the stipulation that he had a lifetime lease on the property. If they hadn't agreed to his terms, they would have had to wait until he died to start the treatment center, which Elijah was beginning to believe might never happen.

Had the old man made a pact with the devil? Or was he, as so many of the locals believed, the devil himself? If he was ever proven guilty of all the crimes people suspected him of committing, then Elijah and Bode were the ones who'd made the pact with Satan.

Chapter Two

Gone was the fierce woman who, just moments before, had protected his daughter from him, who'd jabbed her finger in his chest and admonished him. The minute Deacon had handed the warrant to her, she'd seemed to shrink even more than her already petite size. Her slender shoulders sagged and her head tilted forward, her hair sweeping around her face to hide it from him.

As if she was hiding.

Was that why she was here?

Why she'd been here so many months? Only one other person had been here longer than she had. Everybody else had come and gone, staying no more than a month—most of them for just a week or two.

Deacon couldn't understand why anyone would choose to come here, let alone stay. But maybe they hadn't done their research—maybe they hadn't known what this place really was.

Cursed.

She had to know; she couldn't be totally unaware of what had been going on at the manor. Then and now.

That was how he'd obtained the warrant, to seek out

potential witnesses to what had happened to that young woman he'd found.

"I don't understand," she said, and she handed the paper back to him.

"This compels you to talk to me," he said.

She looked up at him, through her thick lashes which she batted a bit as if flirting with him. "Gee, Sheriff, you want to talk to me that badly that you had to go out and get a warrant?"

He chuckled. The first couple of times he'd noticed her around the place, he'd thought she might have worked there with Holly. She hadn't looked much older than his teenage daughter, and she'd dressed like her in her baggy clothes. But up close for the first time now, he could see that she was older. That there were slight lines around her wide, gold-flecked green eyes and her mouth. Like her eyes, her mouth was wide, with the lower lip so full that there was a dimple in the middle of it. There was something so damn sexy about that, so damn sexy about her.

What the hell was wrong with him? He was supposed to be interrogating her, not fantasizing about her. But she'd flirted with him first. Not that she was interested, not after whatever Holly had told her.

What the hell was his daughter saying about him? How much she hated him?

He swallowed a weary sigh. He already worried too much about Holly. He had to focus on Olivia Smith again. Had to find out what she knew.

Her green eyes gleamed with knowledge or maybe wisdom, the kind that came from experiencing life—the good and the bad. Maybe more of the bad since she'd chosen to stay here. It was some kind of treatment center after all.

"Dr. Cooke wouldn't let me talk to any of his guests without the warrant," he told her.

Her wide mouth curved up at the corners. But even smiling, that dimple remained in the middle of her lower lip. There was something about that mouth . . .

Something that pulled at his memory. Where did he know that mouth from?

"Who are you?" he wondered aloud.

"You don't know?" she asked. "Then maybe I'm not who you need to be talking to." She moved as if to step around him and through the doorway to the hall.

But he took a step closer to her, blocking her way.

She sucked in a breath, and her green eyes went dark. "Sheriff . . . ," she murmured his title like it was his name.

He wanted to correct her, wanted her to call him Deacon. But they weren't flirting. Even though he was tempted.

"You are Olivia Smith, and I need to question you," he said, reminding himself as well as her.

"You're wasting your time," she remarked.

He'd wasted too much of that already. If he'd started searching for Genevieve Walcott earlier, instead of thinking she'd just run away, he would have found the other woman's body before the coyotes had.

"I can't help you," she continued. "I keep to myself and have no idea what happens around here."

"You don't know about the body?"

"I wish I didn't," she admitted. "But the new lady shrink, Rosemary Tulle, was worried it might be her daughter." Her breath caught. "Fortunately, it wasn't."

"No," he agreed. "Fortunately for Rosemary and Genevieve, it wasn't. Unfortunate for whoever she is."

"You still don't know?"

He shook his head.

"Neither do I."

"Either before or around the time Genevieve disappeared, nobody else has gone missing? No blond-haired guest or worker?" he asked.

Her slight shoulders lifted in an even slighter shrug. "People come and go at this place all the time. It's a spa."

"People come and go," he agreed. "Not you. You've stayed. Why?"

She looked down again, so that her hair fell all around her face. His fingers twitched with the urge to push it back so that he could see her eyes and that mouth.

"I don't see what that question has to do with the body you found," she said.

"I won't know either," he admitted, "until I get your answer."

"I don't have any answers for you, Sheriff," she said. "I don't know whose body that was. I haven't noticed anyone missing. I can't help you."

He narrowed his eyes and studied what he could see of her face between tresses of dark blond hair. And he wondered . . .

"Can I help you?" he asked. "Are you being held here? Is that why you haven't left?" And why she was acting so damn spooked?

She laughed and shook her head, and the hair tumbled away from her face which glowed now with amusement. "You really do want to think the worst of this place."

Now he knew what his daughter had been telling her. Or maybe Elijah had warned her that the sheriff had it out for the place. How close was she to the director? Was Elijah Cooke the reason she was staying?

"But the answer to your question is no," she continued.

"I'm not being held here against my will. I want to be here."

"Why?" he asked.

"That's my business, Sheriff," she said, "and has nothing to do with your investigation. You asked me all that warrant allows you to ask."

Damn it. She had read it more thoroughly than he'd realized.

He sighed. "Is there anything else you want to tell me?" he asked, hoping she'd offer some information that would help him, at least to understand her better.

She tilted her head and stared at him now. "Yes."

His heart rate quickened, and his breath stuck in his lungs for a moment. Unlike his late wife, who wouldn't have been, and hadn't been, caught dead with no makeup, Olivia Smith wore none—nothing to enhance her green eyes or hide the freckles sprinkled across her nose—but she was really beautiful. Naturally beautiful.

And somehow oddly familiar.

His voice just a rasp, he asked, "What do you want to tell me?"

She straightened up now, her shoulders back, her chin up, and the fire in her eyes. And that finger stabbed his chest again. "You better not be hurting your daughter—because I will make sure you never hurt her again."

He sucked in a breath, feeling like she'd struck him harder than that finger had poked him. He felt like she'd knocked him to his knees. "I would never . . ."

But he had, just not in the way Olivia Smith meant. He hadn't been able to protect her from the pain and the loss she'd suffered. He'd let her down, and she hated him now.

"You better not," Olivia said. Then she pushed past him

and stalked out of the room, leaving him reeling and not from her threat.

That amused him—that she'd threatened an officer of the law.

No. He was reeling because he felt something, something he hadn't felt in so damn long.

Attraction.

He was attracted to Olivia Smith, which was crazy since he wasn't even sure that was her real name.

Who was she?

And why the hell was she really staying at the manor?

Why did her dad want to talk to Olivia?

What was he doing here again?

Even if she asked him, he wouldn't give her any answers. He never did. So she sought out someone else who might know what her father was up to.

But at the door to the security office, she paused before she raised her hand to knock. Her dad was already upset over what she'd said to A—

To Olivia.

That was what she wanted to be called here, what the privacy rules required her to be called. To say her real name would be a violation, which would get Holly fired for sure, unless her father got her fired first.

If he found out she talked to the head of security about him, he would try even harder to get her fired. Or he would force her to quit. He hadn't done that yet. And he could have.

He could have threatened to take away her driver's license or her phone. He hadn't done that.

Why not?

Was he trying to get along with her? She wouldn't know because she never tried to get along with him. In fact she tried just the opposite, so why was she hesitating now?

Her arm shot up and she knocked hard on that closed door to the security room. It opened quickly to Warren Cooke. Warren ran the security team here as well as worked as a deputy for her dad. Or as a spy as her dad suspected.

And as a spy, Warren would know what was going on.

He grinned when he saw her. "Hello, Holly," he said in that slimy tone that unsettled her.

He was old, but not as old as her dad or Dr. Cooke. He was probably closer to her age than theirs. But her dad and Dr. Cooke were in better shape. Warren was flabby and already losing his hair, but for some reason he acted like he was hot. Maybe he'd never looked in a mirror before.

Or maybe he just had no idea what hot was, since he always treated her like she was. And Holly looked in a mirror. She knew what she saw in it. She was chunky with greasy skin that always broke out, and her hair and eyes were just plain dark brown. She didn't look anything like her mom. Or like Olivia Smith. Or like Genevieve Walcott.

"What do you need?" he asked, obviously surprised that she'd sought him out.

He probably thought it was work related, and maybe she should have just let him think that. But she had to know . . .

"I want to ask you about my dad."

He stepped back and gestured for her to join him in the already too-small room that was crowded with computer monitors and steel filing cabinets. While she hated to admit it, she did listen to her dad and all his dire warnings of doom. She knew not to be alone with a man behind a closed door. So she shook her head and remained in the hall. "I just have a minute," she said. "I need to get back to the kitchen."

She worked there as a dishwasher and assisted the maids with cleaning up the common areas like the dining rooms, conservatory, and lobby.

"But if this is a private conversation, we should have it in privacy," Warren said, still holding open that door.

"It's just a quick question," she said. "I'm wondering why my dad is here. And why he wanted to talk to Miss Smith."

"Smith?" His brow furrowed.

How had he noticed her and not Olivia?

"Olivia," she added, even though the name felt strange coming out of her mouth. She'd felt even stranger when Olivia had talked to her, had touched her. She shouldn't have flinched when Olivia had pushed back her hair, but for just a second a memory had flashed through her mind of the last time a woman had touched her. That memory of a stinging slap . . .

She drew in a shaky breath as if the pain was still fresh, as if her cheek still stung. But that slap had been long ago.

Before her mother died.

Except for her dad trying to hug her, nobody had touched her since then, not like that.

"Olivia . . . ," Warren murmured, and his blue eyes lit up with amusement, as if he knew something nobody else did.

Holly knew. But she wasn't going to risk her job or Olivia's privacy to talk about that. "I just want to know why my dad wants to talk to her."

"He got a warrant to talk to the guests," Warren explained. "He's asking about the body he found."

Holly shuddered before tensing. "But Miss Smith doesn't know anything about that." How could she? Until Rosemary Tulle had started working at the hall, Olivia hadn't ever talked to anyone. Until today, she'd never talked to Holly. With her dad harassing her about a dead body, Olivia would probably never speak to her again.

Or she'd leave.

"It won't be the first time your dad has wasted his time and everybody else's," Warren said. He stepped out of the room now, joining her in the narrow hallway.

"He's investigating a murder," she said. He was good at helping other people. It was his own family he couldn't help. Not that they were a family anymore. Not that they had ever really been a family in that loving, trusting, no-fighting kind of way.

"He's trying to destroy the hall," Warren said, "out of spite. Thanks to a trooper I know, I found out he's even asked the state police to reopen the investigation into your mother's death."

She sucked in a breath as a jab of pain struck her heart. "Why would he do that?"

Warren shrugged. "Like I said, spite."

"I heard him fighting with Dr. Cooke," she admitted. Now she knew why; Dr. Cooke was obsessive about protecting the privacy of the guests as well as his own.

"He fights with everybody," Warren said. "But you know that better than anyone."

She'd said something similar to Olivia, but now she wondered if it was true. Other people liked her dad. Rosemary Tulle and her boyfriend, the judge, and a lot of the locals.

Just not the Cookes.

Warren stepped closer, so close that his body brushed against hers. She moved as far away as she could, but the wall behind her stopped her. She tried sliding along it, but he took a shuffle step to the side, moving with her.

"I . . . I have to get back to the kitchen," she said.

"You don't have to rush off right away," Warren said, and he closed his hand around her arm so she couldn't slide any farther along the corridor.

She was stuck—between him and the wall. Panic pressed on her lungs, making it hard to breathe. "I do," she said. "I don't want to get in any trouble."

His thin lips curled into a smirk. "Getting in trouble can be a lot of fun," he said, and he wriggled his bushy eyebrows at her. He had more hair on his face than on his head.

She shuddered.

"Let the girl go," a male voice said.

It sounded a lot like Warren's, just a little deeper. Probably because David Cooke was so much older than his brother. Warren jumped back, like he was scared—like he'd been scaring Holly.

"Don't you have cameras to watch or something?" David asked.

"You're not my boss," Warren said, and now he sounded like a little kid.

David must have thought so, too, because he snorted. "We both know better than that," he replied.

Confusion replaced Holly's relief. David had nothing to do with security. He was the contractor who had renovated the hall.

"One of us knows better," Warren said, as he glared at his brother. "Or should I say—more?"

David reached out, and his brother must have thought he was going to hit him because he jumped into the security room. And David pulled the door closed on him. "Sorry about that," he said to Holly. "Just ignore him. He's messing with you to mess with your dad."

He wasn't the only Cooke who liked messing with her dad—if everything she'd heard about David was true. But if she believed gossip, she'd have to believe terrible things about her dad, too. Terrible things . . .

"My brother would never hurt you," David assured her. But now he stepped closer to her, and he stared at her in such a weird way that she felt more creeped out than she had with Warren.

"I . . . I wasn't worried about that," she lied. "I just have to get back to work." And before he could touch her, like his brother had, she turned and rushed off down the hall.

Maybe her dad was right about Halcyon Hall. Maybe it wasn't safe for her to be here. Or maybe she'd just let him get inside her head with all his suspicions so that now she was suspecting everyone of something. He was going to make her crazy, just like he had her mother.

She'd gone crazy, like all those women whose families had committed them to the hall back when it had been Bainesworth Manor. Olivia had tried to ignore the rumors, but it was hard when one of the other guests claimed she was a medium who communicated with the ghosts of those dead girls. Morgana Drake talked so often about hearing them crying that sometimes Olivia thought she heard them, too.

She'd definitely gone crazy, even more so since she'd just

threatened an officer. Like she would be able to actually follow through on that threat . . .

The man was big and muscular and carried a gun. Just being around him had made her feel weak and vulnerable again.

Still . . .

She had money now. More fame than she'd ever wanted. But the money and fame hadn't changed anything. It had actually made her more vulnerable.

That was why she couldn't stay here—not now. She straightened away from the door she'd been leaning against since she'd rushed up to her suite. Once she'd unlocked it and stepped inside, she'd nearly collapsed against that thick mahogany. Her knees had been shaking, her heart pounding, and she wasn't even sure why.

What was it about the sheriff that had rattled her so much? She really didn't know anything about that body he'd found. She didn't want to know anything about it either.

She had enough problems of her own. And maybe talking to him had reminded her of that, that she couldn't hide forever. The story about that body, about the hall, was bound to leak out soon to the media. She was surprised it hadn't already since that scandal reporter had shown up on the island. Maybe Edie Stone was waiting until the body was identified before she filed her story about it.

Once the news got out and more reporters descended on the island, someone would identify Olivia. She wasn't worried about the paparazzi finding her, though.

She was worried about *him* finding her.

Her legs began to shake again, as she crossed the suite to the desk beneath one of the many windows. The drapes were closed, but even when they were open, shadows remained in the room. Shadows remained in Olivia's life.

She couldn't escape them. She couldn't escape *him*. Even though he hadn't found her, Olivia felt his presence. She opened one of the desk drawers and pulled out a stack of letters. None of the envelopes accompanying those notes bore the address for Halcyon Hall or a postmark of Bane Island. He hadn't found her here. Yet.

There were no new letters, just all the old ones with surreptitiously snapped photos of her. In those letters, her stalker promised that no matter where she went or who she was with, he would find her. And he would kill her . . .

Chapter Three

How many girls had died at Bainesworth Manor?

Edie Stone closed her eyes, which stung from the strain of studying all the death certificates she'd been pulling up online. She couldn't look at the computer anymore. Not because of the glare of the screen but because of all those deaths. Those senseless deaths.

Maybe her eyes weren't stinging just from the strain . . .

But from frustration. How had that gone on for so many years before the state had finally shut down the psychiatric hospital? That was just one of the many things she wanted to learn before she ran her story. She was the kind of reporter that took her time, that got all the facts right. And more than that, she tried to get justice, too.

Justice for those dead girls.

And justice for the living ones.

Like the librarian on the island. Edie had met her when she'd first come to Bane Island and had tried researching Bainesworth Manor. The woman hadn't been very forthcoming in the beginning, but then she'd admitted to what she knew about the manor and the Bainesworth family. And it hadn't been the secondhand knowledge or gossip

Edie had initially learned. The librarian had shown Edie
the scars she'd received while she'd been committed to the
former asylum. The hospital had left more than physical
scars on their former patients, though.

A squeak of metal drew Edie's attention to the doorway
between the dining room, where she sat, and the kitchen.
The swinging door creaked open on old hinges, and a
head poked through the opening. White hair framed a pale
face smooth of wrinkles. Bonita Pierce was older than
she looked and much older than she acted. Despite being
more than sixty years old, she was so childlike, even more
so than the teenager she'd been when her parents had committed her to Bainesworth Manor.

Edie curved her lips and forced a bright smile. "Hello
there."

The head poked back through the opening and the door
swung shut.

Despite her best efforts, she wasn't able to put Bonita
at ease with her. But after what the woman had endured
as a teenager, she had every reason to be fearful and mis-
trustful.

The only thing the woman had ever talked about with
Edie was the curse. The curse of Bainesworth Manor . . .

A chill chased down her spine. Maybe she was sitting
too close to the leaded glass of the bay window where she'd
set up her desk at the smallest round table in the dining
room. The glass rattled from the force of the wind whip-
ping around icy snowflakes, making it sound like someone
was pounding on the window, trying to get in, trying to get
to her.

She wasn't superstitious. She didn't believe in curses.
Or ghosts.

That was why she needed to find more survivors from

the asylum. Even though those things had happened decades ago, Edie still wanted to get justice. She knew the curse hadn't killed those girls or gotten them pregnant and forced them to give up their babies. People had done that—people who hadn't yet been held responsible. To find out who those people were, Edie needed to find more survivors who could speak for themselves, and for the dead.

Because the dead could not talk.

"You hear them, too, Sheriff," the woman said. "I know you do. You wouldn't find them if they weren't talking to you."

His head had begun to pound, which was probably better than the way his pulse had pounded when he'd been talking to Olivia Smith. He didn't need that complication; he didn't need to be attracted to a potential witness. He had no such problem with Morgana Drake. She was probably older than his father, but it was hard to say beneath the layers of brightly colored makeup she'd slathered onto her wrinkled face.

"Wouldn't find who?" he asked, trying to pick up the thread of their conversation again.

"The dead," she said with a weary sigh, as if frustrated with him. "You hear the dead, too."

He sighed now—with just weariness. "I wish I could, Ms. Drake," he admitted. "Then I would have the answers I need." Then they could tell him who they were, how they'd died, and who had killed them. But it wasn't that easy for him.

Nothing had ever been.

Especially not parenting. What had Holly told Olivia Smith about him that had made the woman threaten him about hurting his own daughter? He would never hurt Holly—at least not intentionally. But he knew she wasn't happy, and that was probably his fault.

He would talk to Holly later. Since he'd dropped her off that morning, he was also her ride home. Fortunately, her four-hour shift should be ending soon, like he should be ending this interview. Outside all those windows of the conservatory, snow was falling again. Actually it wasn't falling so much as being hurled around, bits of ice hitting the glass. The weather was the reason Deacon had given his daughter for driving her to work, but it wasn't the only reason.

"What answers do you need, Sheriff?" Morgana asked, making him wonder if she'd heard anything he'd said.

He swallowed another sigh and repeated his questions. "Have you noticed anyone missing?"

She smiled at him. "No. In fact there are more ghosts making themselves visible to me than ever before."

Summoning all his patience, he clarified, "I'm asking about living people, Miss Drake. Have you noticed anyone living who's gone missing from the hall?"

Beneath her brightly colored poncho, her shoulders lifted and dropped in a shrug. "Not really. People check in and out all the time. But for me and that other woman, the unfriendly one."

"Olivia . . . ," he murmured.

"Is that her name?" she asked, then shrugged as if Olivia was of no concern to her. Morgana was obviously only concerned about the dead, not the living.

Deacon was concerned about both. He had to find out who had killed that woman so that nobody else would die. Unlike Morgana Drake, he didn't want any more ghosts.

"So you don't have any idea whose body I found?" he asked her.

She shook her head, which sent her bright red curls bouncing. "She hasn't spoken to me, but I might have heard her crying. I hear so many of them cry."

The body he'd found had had a weird hole in her head, like from an ice pick or maybe whatever the hell had been used to perform the lobotomies they used to do at the manor. Many young women had died during those botched lobotomies. And even those who'd survived had never been the same, like Bonita Pierce who *helped* her sister Evelyn run the local boarding house.

But nobody was supposed to be performing lobotomies anymore. The archaic practice had been stopped in the sixties except at the manor where they had illegally continued them. That was why it had been shut down. Elijah wouldn't risk that happening again. And this place was supposed to be a cushy spa—not an insane asylum. So how had that woman died?

And how had his wife died? Had Shannon really hurled herself off one of the many cliffs on the hall property or had someone pushed her?

"Do you remember a woman who stayed here shortly after Halcyon Hall opened?" he asked.

Her heavily powdered nose wrinkled. "Halcyon Hall?"

Was she so out of it that she didn't even know where she was?

"It'll always be Bainesworth Manor," she murmured. "To them . . ."

To everyone on the island. To everyone who had ever heard of the manor. Maybe Morgana wasn't as out of it as he'd thought.

Shannon had been. She'd believed that changing the

name had changed everything about it, that it was no longer cursed. But then Shannon had been cursed before she'd even checked into the hall.

Like him . . .

Their whole relationship had been cursed.

"Shannon Howell was her name," he continued. "Like you, she was one of the first guests to stay at the hall." Except Shannon had never left, unlike Morgana who'd come and gone over the past couple of years.

She wrinkled her nose again. Maybe she didn't recognize Shannon's name like she hadn't recognized Halcyon Hall. But then she said, "She was even less friendly than the woman who's been here so long. At least she was with me. With the men she was very friendly."

He flinched, but she wasn't telling him anything he hadn't already known. "Do you know what happened to her?" he asked.

She shook her head, sending those red curls bouncing around her face again.

"You haven't heard anything?" Like Shannon's ghost?

"Some people think her husband threw her off the cliff," she said.

He flinched again.

But she didn't notice. She'd tilted her head as if she was listening to something. "She says he didn't," Morgana said. "That it was all her fault."

He swallowed a laugh. She definitely wasn't "talking" to Shannon's ghost then; she'd never taken responsibility for anything she'd done. He wasn't going to get any answers from Morgana Drake.

But what about Olivia Smith? Did she know more than she'd told him?

When he'd questioned her, he'd suspected she'd been

keeping something back—some secret. About what had been happening at the manor? Or about herself? Who the hell was she really?

An hour later, when Holly jumped into the passenger's seat of the SUV, he asked her, "Who was that woman you were talking to earlier?"

Her face flushed—probably with anger. She was always mad at him. Or maybe the snow and wind had chafed her skin when she'd walked from the employee entrance to where he'd parked in the front lot. He would have driven around to the back if he'd known she would be as late as she'd been coming out. Had she really been working late or had she made him wait out of spite?

"*You* shouldn't have talked to her at all!" she exclaimed.

"Neither should you," he said. "You obviously weren't telling her the truth. She thinks I abuse you."

Her face flushed a deeper red now. He hoped it was with embarrassment or shame.

"Why would you say that to anyone?" he asked. Some people already thought the worst of him because of the lies his late wife and her lover had spread. Knowing he couldn't control gossip, he hadn't let that bother him too much. But for some reason, he didn't want Olivia Smith to think the worst of him.

"I didn't tell her that," Holly said defensively. "She just assumed."

"But why would she jump to that assumption?" Knowing how dramatic his teenage daughter could be, he could guess how Olivia had.

"Haven't you heard her—" She slapped her hand over her mouth, as if to hold back the words.

"Heard what?" he asked.

She shook her head and turned away from him.

"Heard what?" he persisted. He'd suspected that Olivia had been holding something back; apparently his daughter knew what it was. "If you know anything about her, you need to tell me."

She turned back to him, her eyes narrowed in a glare. "Why? You can't believe she has anything to do with that body you found on the property."

No. He didn't really. So why did he want to know?

Why was he so damn curious about Olivia Smith?

Damn it!

What had happened to the days when Sheriff Deacon Howell hadn't been allowed on the property without a warrant? Apparently—thanks to his new friendship with a judge—he'd had one this time, but even without it, he seemed to come and go as he pleased now. And he pleased a hell of a lot.

Too much . . .

Eventually he was going to put it all together.

Eventually he was going to find some evidence— something that had been overlooked, something that might point to—

The real guilty party.

And this damn guilty party was not about to let Deacon Howell arrest him for anything—let alone murder. Deacon's investigation had to be stopped.

Deacon had to be stopped.

And there was only one way to stop Deacon once he got this determined . . .

To kill him.

Chapter Four

A smile lit up the shrink's face as Olivia walked into Rosemary Tulle's office. The woman's smile and her blue eyes were the only bright things in the dark-paneled space. "You want to see me?" Rosemary asked, as if she didn't believe that Olivia had actually called for an appointment.

Since starting her job at the hall, the psychologist had been trying to get Olivia to talk to her about her problems. Hell, everybody had been trying to get her into therapy or the gym. Halcyon Hall took their motto seriously about total health of the body and the mind. The place was famous for it, and for the personal trainer to the stars who was one of the partners. The other partner, Dr. Elijah Cooke, a psychiatrist, was more quietly known for discreetly treating addiction and stress.

But an issue with her body or her mind wasn't the reason Olivia had checked herself into the place. Sure, she'd been physically and mentally exhausted but more than that—she'd been scared.

Of that damn stalker and all his threats.

She'd been hurt enough in her life; she hadn't wanted

to risk more pain. But now she wasn't scared just for herself.

That was why she'd sought out the dark-haired psychologist.

"I do want to talk to you," Olivia said.

And Rosemary's smile widened even more.

"But not about myself," she clarified.

Rosemary's smile slipped away, and she dropped back into the chair behind the shiny mahogany desk. With a heavy sigh, she asked, "So you want to talk about a *friend*?"

Olivia dropped into the seat in front of Rosemary's desk; her knees were a little shaky from earlier—from the encounter with the sheriff and from reading all those threats again. "I wouldn't call her a friend," Olivia said. "I barely know her."

That was her fault, though. The girl had intently been trying to get her attention since Olivia had checked in, and Olivia had been just as intent on avoiding her—because she'd known what she was. A fan, which was probably what that stalker had started out as being.

The stalker was no fan anymore.

"I can't discuss another guest with you," Rosemary said, "if you're here to talk about Morgana."

Olivia chuckled at the mention of the self-proclaimed medium. "I'm not sure even you can help her. And I'm not here to discuss another guest with you. I'm here to discuss an employee."

Rosemary narrowed her blue eyes and studied Olivia's face. "Have you been having an issue with an employee? If that's the case, you need to talk to Dr. Cooke, unless . . . is he the problem?"

Olivia shook her head. "No." Despite his efforts to *help* her, she'd barely spoken to the director of Halcyon Hall. "And I don't have an issue with an employee. I am worried that she's having a problem with someone else." And Olivia couldn't leave the hall or Bane Island until she knew that Holly Howell was in no danger.

Rosemary's face flushed with color. "Are you talking about me?" she asked. "Because you don't need to worry about me anymore."

Olivia smiled. "I'm not—although I do worry that you need a shrink as much as Morgana does, since you've chosen to stay here."

"You stay here."

She shook her head. "Not anymore . . ."

Rosemary tensed and leaned forward, over her desk. "You're leaving?"

The thought of stepping outside that tall, wrought iron gate, of exposing herself to her stalker again, filled her with dread. But the thought of reporters descending on the hall, of her face being all over the news again . . .

She shuddered and nodded.

"Are you sure you're ready to do that?" Rosemary asked. "You haven't talked to anyone about why you've come here. You haven't let anyone help you."

Olivia chuckled. Nobody had ever helped her. That was why she hadn't reported the stalker's threats. The police hadn't protected her when she'd been in danger before; she didn't trust them to protect her now.

"I don't need help," she said. She'd learned long ago to take care of herself.

"That's right," Rosemary said. "You've come here to talk about a friend."

"You said that, not me," Olivia reminded her. "I'm here to talk about Holly Howell. Before I leave, I want to make sure she's in no danger."

Rosemary's brow furrowed. "What danger are you worried that she's in?" The color drained away from her face now, leaving it even paler than usual. "The kidnapper who abducted my daughter is dead. He can't abduct another girl. Or are you talking about the other girl—the body the sheriff found when he was looking for Genevieve? Even though he denied it, the kidnapper probably killed her."

Olivia figured the thought must have gone through Rosemary's head that he also could have killed her daughter because her body trembled. And Olivia reached across the desk to squeeze her hand. "Genevieve is fine," she assured her.

"Is she?" Rosemary asked, then sighed.

"She will be," Olivia said. "She has you to help her through everything. That's what I want you to do for Holly. Help her." Because Olivia couldn't; she had to leave.

"Help her with what?" Rosemary asked.

"Protect her from her father," Olivia said.

Rosemary sighed again and shook her head. "I didn't think you were susceptible to gossip."

"Gossip?"

"A lot of people say things about Deacon," Rosemary said. "But I don't believe those rumors. I believe the man. He's a good man."

Now Olivia furrowed her brow. She'd thought the shrink was in love with a judge, but she obviously had a soft spot for the sheriff as well. "I'm not concerned with what kind of man he is," she said. It wasn't as if she was interested in him, at least not for herself, although her pulse had quickened when she'd stood so close to him, when she'd flirted with him and he'd flirted back.

But her reaction had probably been fear. Just fear that he was harming his child. She wasn't actually attracted to him—although she couldn't deny that with his dark hair and eyes, he was good looking. Damn good looking.

But that didn't make someone a good person. "I'm concerned about what kind of father he is," she said.

"A single one," Rosemary replied. "Dealing with a surly teenager."

"Holly didn't seem surly to me," Olivia said in defense of the girl. "She seemed scared."

"Of her father?"

Olivia nodded.

But Rosemary shook her head. "He loves her so much. He would never hurt her."

"Has he hurt someone else?" Olivia asked. "Is that the rumor you don't want to repeat?"

"Won't repeat," Rosemary said. "It doesn't bear repeating because it's not true."

"What?" Olivia asked, her head beginning to pound with frustration. "What are you talking about?"

"I'm not talking about Deacon," Rosemary said. "I'm not repeating unsubstantiated, vicious suspicions."

"Whose suspicions?" Olivia asked. "Holly's?"

Rosemary shook her head. "I don't know what Holly thinks about all of that . . ."

"She's the one you need to talk to," Olivia urged. "You need to make sure she's okay."

"You're very concerned about her," Rosemary said, and

now her eyes narrowed with speculation. "I've never seen you even speak to her before."

"I . . . I haven't until today," Olivia admitted.

"What was different about today?"

Olivia smiled. "You are such a shrink."

"Psychologist," Rosemary said. "Licensed counselor. I'm not a psychiatrist like Dr. Chase or Dr. Cooke."

Olivia ignored the correction the same way she had every other time Rosemary had made it, just as she ignored Dr. Cooke and the even more creepy Dr. Chase every time they'd tried to talk to her about her problems. At least Cooke backed off, but Dr. Chase kept trying. For someone who could have probably retired years ago, he was really persistent about doing his job. A little too persistent.

"What was different about today?" Olivia repeated the counselor's question. "Holly's tears."

"She was crying?" Rosemary asked with concern. "What was she crying about?"

"Her father," Olivia said. That hadn't been all though. There had been more to it.

Rosemary sighed. "Children often cry over their parents, especially teenage children."

Olivia couldn't argue about that. "They often have a reason to cry over them."

Rosemary leaned farther over her desk, closer to her. "Did you have a reason?" she asked.

Olivia jumped up from the chair. "How many times do I have to tell you that I'm not here to talk about me?"

Rosemary leaned back now, but she continued to study Olivia through narrowed eyes. "I've listened to your songs, you know . . ."

Not heard. *Listened . . .*

She'd paid attention, too much attention from the way she was staring at her. Olivia wrapped her arms around herself. Despite the oversized sweater she wore, she felt naked.

"Autobiographical?" Rosemary asked.

Olivia forced a chuckle. "Platinum," she said. "Record breaking."

"Then why are you here?" Rosemary asked. "How come you're not still making music?"

"I am making music," she said. More than she had when she'd been forced to perform it. Now she was able to focus only on writing. "But please, stop pushing me to talk about myself." She hated doing that, hated all the interviews her manager had talked her into doing, hated all the paparazzi that had followed her everywhere she'd gone, shouting invasive questions at her while they snapped photos she hadn't given them permission to take.

Just as she hadn't given the stalker permission to take all those photos he had when she'd been on tour. Six months of letters and photos and threats.

Rosemary nodded. "I'm sorry. I know. You want to talk about Holly."

"And Sheriff Howell, but you refuse to answer my questions about him," Olivia said. "Why are you protecting him?"

Rosemary chuckled. "Deacon doesn't need protection." Then her brow furrowed, and she murmured, "Or maybe he does . . ."

"I don't care about him," Olivia said. "I just want to make sure he's not hurting his daughter."

"I told you that he's not," Rosemary said.

But she was obviously the sheriff's friend, so Olivia

didn't trust her. Hell, she didn't trust anyone. She needed to hear from someone else that Holly Howell was in no danger. Once she had that assurance, she would feel free to leave. Free but not safe.

She wondered if she would ever be safe.

Elijah pulled at his tie, loosening what suddenly felt like a noose tightening around his throat. The reporter kept calling; the messages from Edie Stone were piling up.

"Eventually I'm going to have to talk to her," he said.

"No, you're not. Handling the press is my job. Let me handle Ms. Stone," Amanda Plasky said, and she reached across his desk and squeezed his hand. Maybe she'd meant the gesture to comfort him, but her long, manicured nails scratched his skin.

Elijah pulled his hand from beneath the publicist's as he leaned back in his chair. It creaked slightly with the re-distribution of his weight. "I hired you to promote the hall," he said. "Not to handle investigations like this."

"You warned me about this when you hired me," she reminded him. "You told me about the manor and about how people have a problem letting go of its history."

He was one of those people. But hell, the history of the manor was his history, too. His damn legacy. "The sheriff's investigation isn't about history," he said. At least not ancient history. It had nothing to do with the manor and everything to do with that body he'd found on the property.

"The reporter's story is," Amanda said. "She's digging up the past."

Then she was bound to find more bodies. Even his

grandfather had warned him that there were more, although he'd later denied making that admission. James Bainesworth was a liar, though. And probably, although nothing had been proven, so much more . . .

Was Elijah capable of more than he realized? Was his brother?

What was the legacy of the Bainesworth blood? Torture? Murder? Greed?

Elijah wanted nothing to do with that legacy or with the curse. Once he'd left Bane Island for college, he'd vowed to never return. But something had called him back here.

His desire to change his legacy. To make up for his family's past.

He sighed. "It doesn't matter."

"It does," Amanda insisted. "You've worked so hard. I'm not going to let anything jeopardize that. Don't worry about the reporter. I will get rid of Miss Stone."

He furrowed his brow and studied her face. Despite how cold and gloomy the weather had been this winter, her skin was tanned. Since she never took a vacation, her golden hue must have been from a tanning bed or spray. Highlights streaked her hair and thick lashes framed her eyes, so thick that they probably weren't real. Not a lot about her seemed real, but then that might have been an occupational hazard of being in the publicity business. Amanda was a few years older than he was—with a well-earned reputation for being one of the best publicists in the business. Promoting her clients was more than a job to her; she was known to take it personally.

Maybe too personally.

When Bode had left the meeting earlier, he'd wriggled his brows at him and grinned. Bode thought the publicist had a crush on Elijah—which made no sense. Bode was younger and in better physical shape due to all his working out. He was also famous. Elijah was only infamous because of his family, because of this place.

But Amanda had dismissed Bode from their meeting, assuring him that she and Elijah could handle the situation without his input. Obviously thinking that she'd wanted to be alone with his older brother, Bode had chuckled. Elijah would have liked to prove his little brother wrong, but Bode hadn't been gone long when Amanda had reached for his hand the first time. Maybe she was just a tactile person, but, feeling a little uneasy, he'd pressed the button that opened his office door to the hall.

"Thank you, Amanda," he said now as he stood to dismiss her. He had other things that needed his attention. But then he found himself admitting, "I'm not as worried about the reporter as I am the sheriff. I don't want him scaring off any of our guests."

"The reporter could scare off some of them, too," Amanda said. "That's why we need to get rid of Edie Stone."

Edie Stone would probably scare off at least one of the guests, the one who'd probably come to the hall to escape media attention. The one whose gasp drew his attention to his open doorway. Olivia Smith stood there, her eyes wide with shock, her mouth hanging open. She must have over-heard the publicist mentioning the reporter. If she hadn't come here to check out after the sheriff had interrogated her, she probably would now because of Edie Stone. She certainly left quickly now, turning around and rushing off down the hall.

He didn't want to lose any guests, but at least she wasn't leaving like the other woman Deacon had found on the property or like Deacon's wife. Olivia Smith wasn't leaving in a body bag.

As Deacon rushed down the sidewalk, he pulled his phone from his pocket and glanced at the screen. Snowflakes melted and ran across it, but he could still see the time. He was running late, but he'd already sent Whit a text to warn him. So instead of hopping into his SUV, he continued down the sidewalk toward the pub which was a block down and across the street. The wind whipped more flakes into his face and down the collar of his jacket.

The bar wasn't far, but he still might freeze to death before he got there. Whit was probably already at the pub, warmed up and sipping on a drink.

Deacon owed the judge a drink and then some for helping him get the warrants he'd needed. After those warrants hadn't gained him any new information, Deacon needed a drink himself. Not that he often drank anything more than coffee and water.

He'd learned at a young age that alcohol never helped solve anyone's problems; it usually just added to them. At least it had for his father.

Orange neon glowed through the falling snow as the sign for the pub flashed on the other side of the street. Tonight he might actually have a drink or two or three.

Nothing could make Deacon's life any worse. He'd already lost his wife and Holly hated his guts. Unlike the judge, Deacon would be lucky to get any votes in the next election, so he was unlikely to keep his job much longer either. He had nothing left to lose.

The thought flitted through his mind just as he stepped

off the curb to cross the street. Tires squealed and bright lights flashed in his face, blinding him so that he froze in the road—in the path of the vehicle, that instead of stopping, revved its engine and bore down on him.

He was about to lose the only thing he had left: his life.

Chapter Five

Pulse pounding, Olivia pushed open the door to her suite. What the hell had she just overheard Dr. Cooke and that woman discussing? It had almost sounded like a murder plot.

Was the reporter's body the next one the sheriff would find on the property of Halcyon Hall?

Or would it be Olivia's?

She drew in a deep breath to calm the panic pressing on her chest. She was probably overreacting. Reading those threats again had unsettled her. No. She'd been unsettled before that—since the sheriff had questioned her about that body. Somebody had died here.

But that could have been an accident; she was just letting the sheriff's suspicious nature bring out hers. She doubted that Dr. Cooke and that woman really intended to get rid of Edie Stone by killing her. Olivia had wanted to get rid of reporters herself, but she'd never plotted to kill any of them.

She hadn't even wished her stalker dead—just that he would leave her alone. Thinking about him made her shudder. She closed and locked the door to her suite, making sure that she was alone now. But she wasn't alone—not at the hall. In the past, that had given her comfort—that the place was so hard to get inside that her stalker wouldn't be able to get to her. But would she be able to get out?

She'd laughed at the sheriff when he'd asked if she was being held against her will. Maybe she was just letting his comments get to her now.

A chill chased down her spine, and goose bumps lifted on her skin beneath her heavy sweater. She would have pulled the comforter from her bed and wrapped it around herself, but it was rumpled beneath her half-packed suitcase. She needed to put the rest of her things into that bag and that bag into her car.

She glanced toward the windows, which were like black holes in the wall. Darkness wrapped around the building. Not so much as a sliver of moon or spark of a star lighted the sky. Despite the dark, the urge to run burned inside her. Just as it had when she was young and had felt so helpless.

But she wasn't helpless anymore. She was able to take care of herself—to afford to stay in a place like this, a place that had once felt so secure with its stone walls, and beyond those walls the rocky cliffs that gave way to the icy waves of the ocean.

But now she didn't feel safe anymore. And it wasn't just because of the body or even the reporter. It was because of the sheriff and not just what he'd said, but what he might have done . . . to his daughter. She couldn't leave until she knew for certain that the girl was safe. So she'd intended to talk to Dr. Cooke about it. But now she wondered if the sheriff had been right not to trust him.

Olivia didn't trust him now either. And he'd seen her.

He knew she'd overheard whatever he'd been talking

about with that woman. Hopefully it hadn't been as bad as it had sounded.

A knock rattled her door, and rattled even more, Olivia let a cry of alarm slip through her lips. "Ms. Smith," a deep voice called out. "It's Dr. Cooke."

He hadn't needed to announce his presence; she'd known he would seek her out after he'd noticed her standing outside his open office door.

"I'd like to come inside and explain the conversation you overheard," he said.

Was that really what he wanted to do, though? Did he intend to explain himself to her? Or get rid of her like they intended to get rid of the reporter?

Even if she was overreacting, she needed to be careful. If she hadn't been cautious, she wouldn't still be alive. But as always, fear silenced her. She couldn't speak out against it. That was why she wrote instead, and when she was strong enough to conquer the fear, sing.

"Ms. Smith, please," Dr. Cooke implored through the door. "I want to assure you that you're safe here. That the reporter won't bother you."

The fear that surged through her now wasn't for herself but for the woman she'd never met. That compelled her to move across the room to the door which she jerked open. "I know. You and your employee intend to get rid of her."

A tall man, he easily glanced over her head toward the bed and her open suitcase. "You are leaving."

She nodded. "Yes, I am, once I'm certain that Holly Howell *and* Edie Stone are safe."

His brow furrowed beneath a lock of thick black hair. "Why wouldn't they be safe?"

"You tell me," she said. "You're the one determined to

get rid of the reporter." And what about the girl? Was she in danger from her father or from her employer?

"You did misunderstand what you heard," he said, as if confirming his own suspicions.

Of course her running off when he'd spotted her standing in his doorway had probably offered all the confirmation he'd needed. But her instinct to run was probably the only thing that had kept her alive all these years.

She needed confirmation now that she'd actually misunderstood anything. "Really?" she asked. "It sounded like you were plotting with that woman to get rid of the reporter. How did you mean to get *rid* of her?"

"That woman is the publicist for the hall," he said. "She was assuring me that she would handle Edie Stone. She didn't want me talking to the reporter myself."

She narrowed her eyes and studied his face. "That wasn't what it sounded like." It hadn't sounded that innocent at all.

"Ms. Plasky is very fervent about handling all interactions with the media herself."

"But her handling Ms. Stone made it sound like she intended to get rid of her permanently."

"That is her intention," he admitted. "To make sure that Ms. Stone stops harassing us with requests for interviews."

"How does she intend to accomplish that?" Olivia asked skeptically. "By killing her?"

He gasped now and shook his head. "No, of course not. She would never harm anyone."

Olivia arched a brow. "She wouldn't? What about you?"

He sucked in a breath as if she'd slapped him. "I would not. And I don't understand why you would jump to such wild conclusions, why you would think that I would put either Ms. Stone or Holly Howell in danger. Why are you so paranoid all of a sudden? Have you taken something, Ms. Smith, something that's affected your thinking?" He stared intently into her eyes, probably checking to see if her pupils were dilated.

Of course he would think she'd taken something; if anyone found out she'd checked herself into Halcyon Hall, the whole world would think she was an addict. That was another reason she needed to get out of here before the reporter realized who she was.

"You had my bags searched when I first arrived," she reminded him. "I couldn't take anything even if I wanted to. But I haven't wanted to. That's not why I came here."

"Then what's wrong? Why do you seem so frightened?" he asked.

"I talked to the sheriff," she said.

He expelled a ragged breath. "Of course. I'm sorry about that," he said. "I had no idea he would be granted a warrant. If that's why you're leaving, you don't need to worry about continued harassment from him. He had to realize that you had nothing to do with the body he found on the property."

Maybe he had. But even though she'd told him she knew nothing about that body, he had continued to question her. He'd been too interested in her, in her secrets. The reporter would be, too, if she got inside the hall and recognized her.

"I still think it's best if I leave now," she said.

He glanced at the dark windows. "I hope that you'll at least wait until morning," he said. "It wouldn't be safe for you to leave now. This time of year, the roads are usually icy and treacherous, which make them especially dangerous at night when it's difficult to see the black ice on them. And sometimes the bridge to the mainland is closed because it gets impassable."

Born and raised in Florida, Olivia didn't have much experience driving in wintry conditions. When she'd arrived at the hall, summer had just ended and, with it, the tourist season. Everyone else had left; shops and hotels had shut down.

Maybe that was why she'd felt so safe on the island, because it was so secluded. Now she felt uneasy, trapped. Scared.

She glanced around the director toward the door. Fortunately, he hadn't shut it tightly. If she screamed for help, someone might come to her aid. But then, everyone worked for him, so maybe they would come to his aid rather than hers.

Even Holly Howell?

As if he'd read her mind, Elijah said the girl's name aloud. "Why do you think she's in danger?" he asked, concern in his deep voice.

Concern for her or for himself?

"She was upset earlier," Olivia said, "when she heard that her father was arguing with you."

Cooke sighed and rubbed one of his hands around the nape of his neck. "Then she must be upset a lot."

"You argue with the sheriff that often?" she asked. "Why?"

Cooke sighed again. "History," he murmured. "We've known each other since we were kids."

"Why would the two of you arguing upset his daughter?" she asked.

He shrugged. "Maybe she's worried that I'll fire her because of him."

"Why would she even want to work here?" Olivia wondered aloud. "For someone her father doesn't like?" And obviously didn't trust.

Cooke shrugged now. "I don't know teenagers that well."

Olivia did. They were her biggest fans. She also remembered how she'd felt as a teen—all the pain and fear.

"You're a psychiatrist," she said. "You must know that it's a way of acting out against her father. Why would she want to do that? And how would she know that working for you would bother her father so much?"

"He blames me for something that happened at the hall," Dr. Cooke admitted. "And I think Holly knows where the blame really lies—with her father."

After overhearing Dr. Cooke's conversation with the publicist, Olivia wasn't certain she could trust him, but she felt compelled to ask him the question she'd come to his office to pose to him. "Is she in danger from her dad?"

A curse drew Olivia and Cooke's attention to her door, which had been pushed fully open. She gasped at the sight of the sheriff, looking so disheveled, his hair mussed, his jacket and jeans torn.

"What happened to you?" she asked.

Sheriff Howell looked from her to Dr. Cooke. "Ask *him* that question," he said. "Ask him why he had someone from the hall try to run me down in the street."

Cooke shook his head. "You need to stop making all these unfounded accusations, Deacon. You're embarrassing yourself."

Was he? The sheriff's face was flushed but that appeared

more with anger than embarrassment. There was also a painful-looking scrape on one side of his face.

"Are you okay?" she asked.

"If you were really run down," Cooke said, "you should be at the hospital, not here."

"You should get checked out at the ER," she agreed as she moved closer to that open doorway and to the sheriff and studied his scraped face. He might have been hurt more than he was willing to admit. "You could have hit your head." He'd definitely hit his face. "You could have a concussion."

"I'm fine," he said, dismissing her concern.

"I can attest that he has a hard head," Cooke said. "And I'm sure nobody tried to actually run you down. As I was telling Ms. Smith, the roads are treacherous right now. Someone might have been unable to stop and accidentally struck you."

"This was no accident," Deacon Howell said. "And you damn well know that."

"No, I don't," Cooke replied. "And I don't know why you're here either. A traffic mishap has nothing to do with the hall."

"I'm sure it was one of your vehicles," Deacon insisted. He touched the shoulder of his torn jacket. "And now one of those vehicles has a broken mirror."

Cooke stepped around her then and grasped the sheriff's arm. Despite being bigger than the psychiatrist, the sheriff flinched. He was hurt. But before Olivia could urge him again to seek medical attention, Cooke pulled him into the hall.

"We shouldn't bore Ms. Smith with your false allegations," he said.

Her pulse racing, Olivia doubted the sheriff would ever bore her.

Frighten her . . .

Excite her . . .

Never bore.

But she didn't argue when Dr. Cooke pulled the door to her suite closed, shutting her inside with the two of them in the corridor. She resisted the urge to go to the door and listen. While she wanted to know what had happened to the sheriff, she was afraid to get any more involved in the situation at the hall than she already was. She didn't know anything about the dead body the sheriff had found. But if another one turned up, like the reporter or his, she might know too much.

Or hell, hers might be the next dead body if Cooke had lied about what she'd overheard. Maybe he really intended to kill the reporter. And maybe the sheriff was right that someone from the hall had tried to kill him.

She needed to get the hell out of here.

Now.

His gloved hands gripped the steering wheel as he sat in the dark, his heart pounding at how close he'd come. But not close enough . . .

The sheriff had jumped out of the way before the bumper had struck him. Only the side mirror had caught his shoulder and sent him tumbling into the street. A man had rushed out of the pub then, or he would have turned around. He would have gone back to finish what he'd started.

Deacon Howell was going to be difficult to kill. He'd already known that—the man was strong.

He was even more stubborn than he was strong, though. It was that stubbornness that kept him coming back to the manor, that stubbornness that kept him investigating.

He wasn't going to stop—not until he was dead. The next attempt could not fail.

Sheriff Deacon Howell had to die.

Soon.

Before he discovered the truth . . .

Chapter Six

Maybe Deacon had hit his head. Why else would Olivia Smith's concern have affected him so much? Or maybe it was that the numbness from the cold and the initial impact was just finally wearing off.

He suspected his numbness hadn't been just from his recent near miss. He'd been numb for a long time when it came to attraction, the kind of attraction he felt for Olivia Smith. The open suitcase on her bed told him that he was going to lose out, just as he'd lost out on Rosemary Tulle. Not that he'd ever felt the kind of attraction for her that he felt for Olivia.

Olivia didn't trust him, though. She was worried about his daughter, worried that he was hurting her. He'd even heard her ask Elijah about Holly. Remembering that numbed him again, numbed him to anything but the rage coursing through him.

"So who did you send?" he asked Elijah as the other man tried to lead him down the hall, away from what must have been all guest suites like Olivia's.

"Send who where?" Elijah asked with confusion.

"To run me down," Deacon said. "Who did you send to kill me?"

Elijah spun around and glared at him. "Ms. Smith is right. You do need medical attention. You must have hit your head to think that I would send anyone after you."

Deacon sighed. "I must have hit my head to think that you'd actually have the balls to admit that you did."

Elijah turned away from him and continued down the hall and down the wide stairwell to the reception area. Deacon followed him, anxious for answers. But the other man said, "You need to leave. Now." He must have pressed some button on the reception desk because the double doors opened. Cold air blasted, sending icy chunks of snow swirling over the marble floor of the foyer. "I don't even know how you got inside the gates."

Deacon ignored the snow and the cold. He had on a jacket, torn though it was. Elijah was the one with no coat. "I had a warrant," he reminded the hall director.

"Earlier," Elijah said. "And that warrant only allowed you to talk to the guests who might have been here when that woman, whose body you found, died."

"Murdered," Deacon corrected. "She was murdered. She didn't just die." Like Elijah wanted everyone to believe. "And someone here must either know who did it or at least who the hell she was."

"No wonder Ms. Smith is packing," Elijah said. "She's leaving because of your harassment."

He hoped she heeded Cooke's advice and didn't try to leave tonight. With the snow continuing to blast in through those open doors, the weather was only getting worse, the roads even more treacherous.

"I didn't harass her," Deacon said, just as he'd had to defend his questioning of her to his daughter as well. "I am trying to investigate a murder, Elijah. A murder that someone obviously doesn't want me investigating."

And that person was so damn determined to stop him that he or she had tried to murder him.

"You're not investigating right now," Elijah said. "You're trespassing." He must have pressed another button because a door opened somewhere down the hall and a security guard rushed toward them. Another man, in a suit, followed him. Warren Cooke. It wasn't the uniform he wore as Deacon's deputy.

Warren sighed and shook his head. "I knew I shouldn't have told you where he was."

Elijah turned on his younger cousin. "You told him I was with a guest? What were you thinking?"

Warren's chubby face flushed with color. "I was thinking that he had a warrant to talk to her, so he already knew she was here."

"But he didn't want to talk to her. He wanted to talk to me."

Deacon had wanted to talk to her but not about his being run down earlier. He'd wanted to talk to her about her; he couldn't remember the last time he'd been so interested in something other than solving a crime. On the mainland, he'd been damn good at it, so good that he'd made detective early in his law enforcement career. But back home, he struggled to even prove something was a crime.

"We've talked," the director said as he turned toward Deacon. "So now you need to leave."

"I'll leave," Deacon agreed. "Once you let me inspect all the Halcyon Hall vehicles."

Elijah groaned. "Not this again. And your warrant to do that expired weeks ago."

This wasn't the first time that Deacon had demanded to inspect the vehicles that were all a shade of gray specific only to the hall. Elijah or his brother, Jamie, or Bode as he now called himself, must have had the vehicles custom painted.

"Why would you want to inspect them?" Warren asked. "You already know that it was the groundskeeper, that Teddy kid, who tried running Ms. Tulle off the road all those weeks ago."

"I know that," Deacon said. "Now I want to know who tried running me down tonight."

Warren sighed. "You're claiming someone tried running you over? When did this supposedly happen?"

"Less than an hour ago," Deacon said. "And there was nothing *supposed* about it. I was on my way to the pub—"

Warren snorted. "Sure you weren't on your way *from* the pub, like your old man would've been?"

Deacon curled his fingers into his palm, but he resisted the urge to throw the fist into Warren's weak chin. The guy would definitely press charges against him.

Drawing in a deep breath for patience, Deacon replied, "There is a witness." Whit Lawrence had stepped out of the pub just as the mirror of the vehicle had knocked Deacon down. But the judge had been so focused on checking on him that he hadn't made note of the license plate or anything else about the vehicle or the driver.

"I should take his statement," Warren said. "You shouldn't be investigating this yourself."

"Neither should you," Deacon said. "You obviously have a conflict of interest."

Warren's face flushed a deeper shade of red. "Do you suspect me? I don't need to kill you to get your job. I just need to wait until the next election. There's no way you're winning it." Despite the dimwitted deputy's bravado, maybe he'd decided not to take any chances.

"Not if I'm dead," Deacon agreed. "Were you the one driving the Halcyon Hall vehicle that nearly ran me over?" Because how had Warren known the witness was male— since Deacon hadn't identified him?

Warren narrowed his already beady eyes and glared at his boss. "I'm not the only one who drives a company vehicle."

"Let me see it," Deacon challenged him.

Warren shrugged. "Sure. Even if you found damage on it, you wouldn't be able to prove I was driving it when it happened. I've loaned that SUV out to other employees at the hall. Even your daughter. And we all know how she feels about you."

Elijah stepped between the two men just as Deacon lost control of his temper and began to swing. Elijah must have seen that Deacon's hand was already fisted, or even he knew that his cousin had gone too far. The usually calm shrink raised his voice, but Deacon's name wasn't the one he yelled. "Warren!"

The younger man stepped back, as if he was more afraid of his older cousin than he was of Deacon. "Yes, Elijah."

"Get back to work."

Deacon let a bitter chuckle slip out. "Glad I'm not the only one who needs to tell him that." The deputy was never available when he needed him.

"I'm surprised you haven't fired him," Elijah admitted.

"Ditto." Deacon believed in keeping his enemies close; that was why he hadn't fired his deputy. He was also convinced that the guy knew what his cousins and brother were up to at the hall, and that he was dimwitted enough that Deacon might be able to get that information out of him someday. That day had yet to come, though, and Deacon's patience was wearing thin. Apparently, so was Elijah's.

"Your security chief hasn't done a very good job of protecting your guests," Deacon pointed out. "A girl got kidnapped—"

"She left willingly with the groundskeeper," Elijah corrected him.

"Because she wanted so badly to get out of this place," Deacon said, "I can relate."

"Then go."

Deacon ignored him and the open doors. "And a woman was murdered on the property as well."

"You don't know that she was murdered—"

"The coroner—"

"—here," Elijah continued as if he hadn't been interrupted.

"So somebody dumped a body here?" Deacon asked.

"It wouldn't be the first time."

That was what James Bainesworth and Deacon's own father had claimed when Deacon had found his first body in the manor all those years ago. He glanced toward the stairwell leading up to the second story. Light funneled down, not from a hole in the ceiling, but from the mammoth, crystal chandelier dangling over the stairwell. He shuddered again at the memory. Other people had suggested that she'd come here to kill herself.

Was that why Shannon had checked into the place?

"Go home, Deacon," Elijah urged him. "Or better yet, go to the hospital. You're hurt."

He was lucky that was all he was. Somebody wanted him dead.

* * *

Warmth flooded Rosemary's heart as she joined her daughter and Whit in the front parlor at the Pierce sisters' boarding house. This was the family she'd always wanted but had accepted long ago would never be possible . . . for so many reasons.

She'd never been so happy to be proven wrong.

"Are you really okay?" she asked Whit.

He stood in front of the fire with Genevieve at his side. Her daughter stared at him with as much concern and love as Rosemary did. Genevieve didn't have the biological father either she or Rosemary wanted for her, but she had already claimed Whit as her true father—because the man was true, full of honor and integrity and caring.

A twinge of guilt struck Rosemary that she had taken so long to realize that. But now she knew and if she needed any reminders, he proved it to her every day. Like how he understood that she wanted to stay working at the hall because she believed she could help Morgana and Olivia and all the other guests who arrived struggling with stress and addiction or mental disorders. Whit was even looking for a house to buy or property on which to build a house for them, but he had yet to find anything suitable for sale. Fortunately, the old Victorian boarding house was so big that there was plenty of room for all of them to stay with the sisters who ran it.

Whit wrapped his arm around Rosemary's shoulders and pulled her close to his side, and when he looked down at her, love glinted in his green eyes. "I'm fine," he assured her. "Just got a little cold standing outside with the sheriff." His golden hair was damp, but this time it was from his shower—not the snow like it had been when he'd first come home from his meeting with Deacon Howell. "Deacon's the one that vehicle struck."

"He wouldn't let you call an ambulance or even take him to the ER?" Genevieve asked.

Whit shook his head, and a droplet of water slipped over his brow and trailed down his temple. "No."

"He's stubborn," Rosemary said.

"That stubbornness is going to be his downfall," Whit said. "He was going back out to Halcyon Hall."

Genevieve shuddered with revulsion. "That place will be his downfall."

"It's everyone's downfall," Evelyn Pierce said as she walked into the parlor, carrying a tray of steaming mugs and a plate piled high with cookies that steamed a bit as well.

Rosemary suppressed a sigh of frustration. Only Whit understood her decision to remain on at the hall. She believed that the place had changed with the renovations and new leadership. Dr. Cooke and his brother really were doing good work, helping people achieve physical and mental wellness. Her mentor, Dr. Chase, also worked there. Although her mother had made some horrible claims about his character when last they'd seen each other, Rosemary had found no proof of those claims. She wasn't surprised; all her mother had ever done was lie to her.

Rosemary reached out to help Evelyn with the tray. "I would have gotten that," she said. "You didn't need to bring it in."

Evelyn smiled at her. "It's my job to take care of all of you."

Rosemary shook her head. "I hope you don't feel that way." When they hadn't found anything for sale, she and Whit had also tried to find a house to rent on the island, but most of the properties were only summer cottages that had no heating sources.

"It's also my honor," Evelyn said, and after she placed the tray on the coffee table, she reached out and squeezed Rosemary's hand.

"Thank you," Rosemary replied. "For everything." Evelyn had become the mother to Rosemary that she'd never had—caring and honest and concerned. Maybe too concerned sometimes . . .

But she had reason.

Bonita skipped into the room behind her sister. A smile lit up her face and even cleared a bit of the cloudiness from her blue eyes. "Everybody's home!" she exclaimed with childlike excitement and acceptance.

Acceptance of Rosemary, Whit, and Genevieve anyway. Bonita had still not accepted Edie. Where was the reporter? Whit had said the roads were getting bad. Once he'd made it across the bridge from the mainland, the state police and the road commission had shut it down as impassable. Before Rosemary could ask if anyone had heard from Edie, the doorbell rang. As a boarder, Edie had a key; she wouldn't ring the bell.

"It's probably Deacon," Whit said. "He was in such a hurry to get to the hall that he didn't take a full report from me. Not that I really saw anything."

"Sheriff Howell!" Bonita exclaimed with even more excitement, as if the man was a celebrity or a superhero. To her, maybe he was. He often found her when she ran off to search for her baby.

Rosemary and Evelyn had thought she was talking about a doll until they'd realized that she'd given birth all those years ago during the time she'd been committed to Bainesworth Manor. And someone from the asylum must have taken her baby. The older woman was as spry as a child when she sprinted out of the parlor to rush to the front door.

Seconds later Deacon walked in with Bonita, snow melting in his dark hair.

"Speak of the devil . . . ," Whit murmured with a chuckle.

Bonita gasped, and the smile slipped away from her face. "No, don't talk about him—not here."

"I was just teasing the sheriff," Whit assured her.

What devil was Bonita talking about? The one who'd hurt her all those decades ago? The one who'd stolen her baby? Bonita didn't trust Edie Stone, but the reporter was determined to help her and the other survivors like Bonita get the answers and the justice they deserved.

"I could use a laugh about now," Deacon murmured as he dropped onto one of the small sofas in the parlor. The antique must have been tougher than it looked because it held beneath his weight.

Rosemary glanced at her daughter, who was also tougher than she looked. At seventeen the girl had already survived so much. "Are you all right?" Genevieve asked the lawman.

He nodded. "Just pissed as sh—" He cut off his curse as if just remembering that he was addressing a kid.

But Genevieve was no kid anymore, not after her ordeal. She chuckled now. "I've heard all the bad words before, Sheriff," she assured him.

He glanced at Bonita. "Maybe it wasn't you I was worried about."

"Good," Genevieve said. "Nobody needs to worry about me anymore." She looked at Rosemary. "They've already worried enough."

"So you want me to worry about someone else now?" Rosemary teased her.

Genevieve nodded. "Yes, worry about the sheriff. Someone tried running him down just a short while ago. Did you find out who?"

His jaw tensed, as if he was biting back another curse, and he shook his head.

"Did you happen to see Edie on your way here?" Rosemary asked as concern for the reporter niggled at her.

He glanced around the room as if he was looking for her. "Her Jeep is parked in the driveway. She must be here."

"She's upstairs," Evelyn said. "She came in through the kitchen when I was taking the cookies from the oven." As the sheriff had moments ago, she glanced at her sister with a pointed look. "She decided not to join us."

Because Bonita wouldn't have been comfortable with her being in the parlor with all of them.

"Good," Deacon said. "I don't need her getting in the way of my investigation."

"Edie could help you," Whit said.

He shook his head. "No. I have no problem with her going after Bainesworth Manor, but this . . ."

"It's not related to Bainesworth Manor?" Whit asked. "You rushed off to confront Cooke, so I thought . . ."

"Elijah Cooke wouldn't have tried to run you down," Rosemary assured him. The hall director was not the villain Deacon thought he was.

"Not himself," Deacon agreed. "But he never did his own dirty work."

"Who do you think would have done it for him?" Whit asked. "His security staff?"

"The head of which is also my deputy," Deacon replied. "And has already announced his intention to run against me for sheriff at the next election."

"Warren?" Genevieve shuddered. "That guy's super creepy."

Deacon groaned.

"What?" Rosemary asked with concern.

"He claims he's loaned his Halcyon Hall vehicle to my daughter."

"Tonight?" Whit asked.

"He didn't specifically say," Deacon admitted. "But apparently she has access to his vehicle or to the other company vehicles."

"That's why you're here," Rosemary realized.

He nodded. "I'm here to ask you if you think . . ." His throat moved as if he was struggling to swallow. "Does she hate me that much?"

"I really can't tell you anything," Rosemary said.

"Is she your patient?" he asked—almost hopefully. "Is that why you can't tell me anything?"

She shook her head. "I can't tell you anything because she doesn't tell me anything."

"She told Olivia Smith something," Deacon said. "Something that had the woman threatening me."

Rosemary sighed and admitted, "Olivia asked me if I thought you were hurting Holly."

His face flushed a dark red. "What the hell did Holly tell her?"

Rosemary shook her head again.

"What?" he asked. "Is Olivia Smith your patient?"

"No," Rosemary said. "Just a guest."

"Not for much longer," Deacon said. "She was packing tonight. She's leaving . . . even though Elijah was trying to talk her out of it."

"Good for her," Genevieve said, and she turned toward Rosemary now with a pointed look, her eyebrows raised.

"I don't understand why anyone would want to stay in that house of horrors, or work at it either."

Deacon sighed again. "I agree."

"This Olivia woman won't get off the island," Whit said. "The bridge has been shut down."

"So now Olivia Smith is trapped in that house of horrors," Deacon murmured, but instead of sounding concerned, he almost sounded relieved. Did he want her to stay?

Edie hadn't joined the group in the parlor, but that hadn't stopped her from listening in on the other side of the pocket doors that separated the parlor from the dining room.

Someone had tried running down the sheriff tonight. Someone from the hall.

Because of his investigation?

She hoped that was the case and that it hadn't been his own daughter. For his sake . . .

And for hers.

If he was right about someone at the hall being responsible, then someone there had something to hide. Something Edie needed to uncover for her story.

And now she had a couple of names to gain access to the place. The sheriff's daughter . . .

And Olivia Smith.

Who was she?

The name sounded like an alias. And usually the only people who used aliases were the people who had something to hide.

"Why are you hiding in here?"

Edie jumped at the question and whirled around to find the pocket door open, Evelyn standing in the space between the two rooms. She wasn't alone. While the sheriff had left and Whit, Rosemary, and Genevieve had gone upstairs, the Pierce sisters had remained down. Bonita stood behind her sister, as if using Evelyn's body to shield her from Edie.

Edie wanted to promise that she wouldn't hurt the fragile woman, but she couldn't guarantee that she wouldn't—when she kept bringing up what must have been horrible memories for her. Maybe it would have been more humane to let the past die, like all those women had died.

Bainesworth Manor had been shut down forty years ago, but shutting down the asylum wasn't really punishment or even acknowledgment of what had happened to those women. And now it could be happening again . . .

"Are you okay?" Evelyn asked her, and she stepped closer, peering at her with concern.

Edie forced a smile. "I know. I'm usually not this quiet."

"You sure aren't," Evelyn heartily agreed. "And you usually don't miss an opportunity to harass the sheriff whenever you see him."

Edie sighed. "I already know what the sheriff knows." She needed to know what Bonita knew. The woman, still clinging to her sister, had come closer, too. She glanced at Edie, her blue eyes looking more cloudy than usual. It was too late to get her memories.

Not just tonight but maybe forever . . .

She forced a smile for the older woman, trying to put her at ease. "And I didn't want to intrude."

To her surprise, Evelyn reached out and grasped her arm. "You're staying here, too," she said, although she'd only begrudgingly allowed Edie to rent a room. And that was a cramped dormer room in the attic. "So you're welcome anywhere in the house."

Except Bonita's memories . . .

"I don't often get welcomed places," Edie admitted.

"I bet," Evelyn said as she pulled her hand from Edie's arm. A twinkle lit up her eyes as she teased, "You do have a tendency to make a pest of yourself."

"Occupational hazard," she remarked. Which was why she wasn't often welcome.

Like at Halcyon Hall.

How the hell was she going to get inside there? How was she going to get to the remaining Bainesworths? Unlike the sheriff, she couldn't get a warrant to talk to anyone.

She had to find another way to get them to talk.

Was Olivia Smith that way?

Chapter Seven

Olivia awoke to a blinking light on the phone beside the bed in her suite at Halcyon Hall. The suitcase lay open on the floor, its contents spilling onto the plush carpet. She'd pushed it off before crawling, exhausted, into the bed. If the roads hadn't been so bad, she would have left.

At least that was what she'd told herself last night. If fear hadn't frozen her in place, the weather conditions probably would have. The wind had howled all night, and ice had pelted the windows so hard that they'd rattled in their frames. She wouldn't have made it far from the hall if she'd tried to leave last night.

Just as that woman whose body the sheriff had found hadn't made it far from the hall either. She'd been found somewhere on the grounds. Had she been staying at the hall? Or had she worked there?

And what about the sheriff? Had someone really tried to run him down? Someone from the hall?

Had he even made it home last night?

Concern gripped her, tightening the muscles in her empty stomach. She was used to her stomach being empty; she wasn't used to feeling this concern for someone else, at least not for someone like the sheriff. Someone who might be harming his own daughter.

She drew in a deep breath, but it wasn't enough to fill that emptiness inside her, wasn't enough to push away that concern. She turned toward the phone.

Who could have left her a message? Knowing there was only one way to find out, she reached out and pressed that blinking button. "Ms. Smith, this is Dr. Cooke. I would like to speak to you before you leave the hall."

She sighed. Of course he wanted to speak to her.

He wanted to get her to stay.

Or to at least keep her mouth shut about what she'd heard he and his publicist discussing.

And he confirmed that when he continued, "We need to talk about Edie Stone."

If she had misconstrued what she'd overheard, why was he so concerned about it? Maybe she should have risked the roads and left last night when the sheriff was here. Would she be able to get out now? Or would they treat her like they had Genevieve Walcott, denying her the choice of checking herself out?

Genevieve was a minor, though.

Olivia hadn't been one for a long time. She could check herself out of the hall anytime she wanted, and she sure as hell wanted to now. She jumped up from the bed and gathered up the suitcase from the floor. Dumping all the worn jeans and oversized sweaters and her underwear back into the case, she snapped it shut. There wasn't much else she cared to bring, but her guitar and notebooks.

Those went with her everywhere . . . even when she'd had no place to go. Growing up, she'd lugged them around from shelter to shelter and a few foster homes where police and social services had tried to place her. The notebooks and guitar were the reasons why she could now afford to stay at an exclusive place like Halcyon Hall. But maybe she had been safer in those shelters than she'd really been here.

A knock at the door rattled her even more than she already was, especially when a deep voice called out, "Ms. Smith, as I said in the message I left for you, we need to talk."

How did he know she'd played that message? That she was awake now? Were there cameras even in the rooms at Halcyon Hall? She glanced around, searching the walls and furniture for sight of a lens. But she'd done that when she'd checked in—because she'd learned to look for cameras. After all those photos of her had started showing up with the threatening notes . . .

Had she missed one?

"We talked last night," she said through the door. "There's nothing more to say."

"Yes, there is," he persisted.

She wasn't about to open that door to him, not now, not with her pulse hammering with fear. She did not want to be the next person the sheriff found dead on the grounds. "Please leave me alone."

A deep sigh drifted through the door. "I don't want to bother you," he assured her. "I just wanted to warn you."

"About what?" she asked. "The roads? I don't care how bad they are, I'm leaving." She did care, though, since she didn't have any experience driving in snow. It was only a few years ago that she'd finally taken the time to get her driver's license.

"What I want to tell you about the reporter is that she knows you're here."

Shock had her unlocking and pulling open the door. "How? How did she find out?"

She hadn't trusted anyone with her whereabouts. So someone here, who had realized who she was, must have told the reporter. Someone like Holly Howell or Rosemary Tulle or . . .

"I'm not sure that she knows who you really are," Dr. Cooke said, "but she called this morning and asked to speak to Olivia Smith."

So the reporter knew her alias. Well, it was a real name, just not hers. She'd borrowed the name and identity of one of her backup singers. But over the past couple of months, she'd begun to feel more like Olivia Smith than she ever had herself.

She blew out a ragged breath. "Well, that confirms that I need to check out today. No matter how damn bad the weather is."

He shook his head. "I think that would be a mistake. The reporter might be waiting outside the gates. It could be a trap to draw you out."

Or he could be lying in order to get her to stay.

She didn't know who to trust, but that was nothing new for her. She hadn't completely trusted anyone for a very long time.

"That's a chance I'll have to take," she said. Because she couldn't stay here now.

If the reporter did a story on her, the stalker would find her for certain. And he was far more dangerous than the weather on Bane Island.

Snow fell so densely that it was as if a white blanket had wrapped around the vehicle, around the island itself, hiding it from the ocean, from the rest of the world. That was how isolated Holly felt. Only a rickety, old bridge connected the island to the mainland, and that was long and often impassable in the winter. Not that Holly was ever allowed to travel that bridge. She was stuck here—with her dad.

Holly gripped the armrest of the SUV as the police vehicle swerved across the snow-covered road. She would have been more scared had she been behind the wheel, but she wasn't about to admit that to her father. "I could have driven myself," she said, as she always did whenever Dad acted like she was helpless and stupid.

"Your car wouldn't have made it out of the driveway," he said.

And with as deep as the snow was, he was probably right.

"That's why I need a better vehicle," she said.

"With as much as you've been working, you should be able to afford one soon," he said.

She only worked weekends. But to her father, any time spent at the hall was too much time. "I'm not going to spend my money on that," she said. She was saving for college, so that she could go to one far, far away from this place.

"Why?" he asked. "Because you can use Warren's anytime you want?"

"What?" she asked.

"He said he loans you his company vehicle whenever you want," he said.

Warren Cooke? Despite her heavy jacket, goose bumps lifted on her skin. "Yeah, whatever . . ."

She'd used it once to pick up something from town that the chef had needed for dinner. Since she was just a dishwasher, she was the only one the chef had been willing to send on his errand, but he hadn't been willing to trust her with his vehicle. And that had been another day her dad had insisted on dropping her at work.

"You know he's a lot older than you are," Dad said with his disapproving dad tone.

Then again, he disapproved of everything about her and especially about Halcyon Hall.

"Duh . . ."

"Holly!"

"Why are we talking about Warren?" she asked. She could think of a million other people she'd rather talk about—like Olivia Smith. But then he'd only get mad at her about that, too, about letting Olivia think that he abused her or something. She should have made it clearer to Olivia that her dad just upset her because he was so strict and so suspicious of everyone. But Olivia had jumped to conclusions, that it was like the songs that she wrote . . .

Listening to those songs made Holly feel less alone, made her feel like at least someone's life sucked more than hers. She reached out and flicked on the radio, and Olivia's voice emanated from the speakers. But Olivia wasn't her real name—at least it wasn't her stage name. AKAN was, which meant Also Known As Nobody.

That was what Holly felt like here on Bane Island. Like nobody.

She had no identity of her own. She was the sheriff's daughter. The child of the crazy woman who'd jumped off the cliffs.

That was why she would rather focus on the music than her real life. But before she could lose herself in the song, like she always did, her dad reached out and shut off the radio.

"Dad!" she cried back at him.

"I am trying to have a conversation with you," he said as he pulled the SUV up to the gate to the employee entrance of Halcyon Hall.

Like at the front entrance, there was a camera. The receptionist watched and monitored the front gate, while the back gate was manned by a security guard. Warren? If it was, he must have noticed her inside the truck, too, because the gate opened, and her dad drove through it.

"A conversation about what?" She snorted. "Warren's company vehicle? Why are you asking me about that?" She turned fully toward him now and studied him with suspicion.

He took his attention from the drive and glanced over at her; the suspicion was on his face, too.

"What are you talking about?" she said.

"Someone—driving a Halcyon Hall vehicle—tried to run me over last night," he said.

Pain jabbed her heart like he'd plunged a knife into it. "And you think it was me?"

"No, of course not," he said. "But it sounded like Warren was going to blame you—"

"And you believe him over me?"

"You said you have access to it, too," he reminded her.

And she bit her lip to hold back the regret that she'd let him think that. But if she backtracked now, he would think she was lying, that she was trying to cover up. But . . .

That pain jabbed her again. And she had to ask, "How can you think that I would do something like that?"

"I don't," he said. "I just wanted to make sure that you

didn't come back out and use his vehicle last night. I want to make sure he can't lay the blame on you."

"You want to make sure I didn't do it," she said. "Why do you think I would?"

"I don't," he said. "I really don't . . ."

"But you have doubts." Her stomach churned, and she felt like throwing up. "Just be honest with me."

He expelled a ragged breath. "You tell me all the time how much you hate me."

She opened her mouth, but she couldn't deny that she had said that. But she hadn't really meant it. At least not all the time. Just some of the time. When he made her angry. Or when she just felt angry.

She waited for the rush of it now, for the heat and the pounding pulse and the rage. All she felt was that pain stabbing her heart over and over again. Tears stung her eyes, but she furiously tried to blink them away. She wasn't going to cry—not again. Not over her dad.

But she couldn't believe . . .

"How . . . how can you . . . interrogate me . . . like I'm just some suspect?" she asked, and her voice quavered with the tears she tried to choke down. "Like a criminal . . ."

"Holly . . . ," he said, and his voice cracked again. "I'm not interrogating you. I'm just trying to protect you."

She shook her head. She couldn't talk to him, couldn't look at him. She peered through the windshield instead. Fortunately, the dark stone structure of the hall appeared through what seemed like a wall of snow falling in front of the SUV. Holly didn't wait for him to pull up to the door of the employee entrance. "Drop me off here!" she yelled, and she was already pushing open the door. She couldn't spend another second in the SUV with him—not without dissolving into tears.

"Holly!" he yelled back.

But she'd already opened the door, jumped out, and slammed it shut.

He rolled down the passenger window. "We need to talk about this."

"I'm going to be late for work," she said. He'd driven slow and maybe not just because of the snow but because he'd wanted to interrogate her.

"Holly—"

"No," she yelled. "I don't want to talk to you."

"Holly, we need to—"

"No!" she screamed at him through that open window. She ran then, the rest of the way across the parking lot toward the back door. It wasn't that far, but the snow— falling so densely—made it hard for her to see. Maybe the lot had been plowed, but her boots sank into the snow and slipped on the icy asphalt beneath it. The falling snow clung to her hair and face and slipped down the back of her coat, and it was so cold that it burned her skin. More tears stung her eyes, tears of pain. But she couldn't shed them. She couldn't give in, to the tears or to the pain.

She had to keep going . . . away from him. So he couldn't see her cry. So he couldn't know how badly he'd hurt her. Her fingers numb from the cold, she pulled her employee badge from her pocket and swiped it through the keycard door lock. Then she jerked open the door and ducked inside the building. Her legs shaky, she leaned back against that door. And she waited.

Was he going to come after her? Was he going to try to talk to her? Or had he just driven off, believing that she might have tried to kill him?

* * *

Deacon watched until the door closed behind her, until his daughter had made it safely inside the building. The snow was falling so hard that even going that short distance, she might have gotten lost.

He didn't want the next body he found to be hers. He couldn't even imagine the pain of that, but yet, he could—because he'd seen the pain on her face, the pain he'd caused with his accusation. What the hell had he been thinking?

He never should have let Warren get to him like that, never should have let him get inside his head and make him doubt his own daughter. Now she hated him even more than she already had. That was exactly what Warren wanted—to make Deacon's life even worse than it already was.

But Deacon was used to Holly hating him. He just couldn't handle hurting her. And he had. So badly.

He stared at that closed door, tempted to go after her—to apologize. But he doubted she would listen to him. Hell, he doubted he'd get inside without a warrant. Just as he eased his foot off the brake pedal, though, that door opened again. And the unbearable pressure on his heart eased slightly. She was coming back to him.

But it wasn't Holly who stepped out into the swirling snow. This woman was smaller, and the hair that whipped around her face was lighter and longer. Olivia. He'd known she wouldn't have been able to leave last night, not with the bridge having been shut down. But she was obviously trying again. She wore a long jacket, but it was too thin to be a true parka. And where was her hat? Her scarf?

"What are you doing?" he called out to her through the passenger window he'd left open, snow already beginning to accumulate on the seat.

Olivia Smith approached the open window and stared at him through it. "I'm going to check out of the hall."

"You can't!" He protested at the thought of her on the treacherous roads as much as her leaving Bane Island.

"During your interrogation yesterday, you didn't tell me that I couldn't, Sheriff."

He would have if he'd considered her a viable suspect. But she'd checked into the hall alone and had no apparent connection to anyone on the island. What would have been her motive?

"You can't leave because it's too dangerous. The roads are snow covered and slippery," he said. "The bridge to the mainland was shut down last night because it was impassable." It had been reopened this morning after the plows had tended to it. If the snow kept falling like this, though, they wouldn't be able to keep it clear, and it would need to be closed again.

"It sounds more dangerous to stay here—after what happened to you last night and what you claim happened to that body you found," she said.

"Are you worried about being the next victim?" he asked.

Her eyes widened as if the question had startled her, and she shook her head.

"Then why the rush to leave in such bad weather?" he asked. Why would anyone check out unless they were worried about being in danger or maybe being exposed? He didn't believe she was a killer, but was she something else? Or someone else? Someone famous? "Or are you worried about reporters showing up?"

"A reporter has already shown up on the island," she reminded him.

And that seemed to concern her more than the murder.

"Who are you, Ms. Smith?" he wondered aloud. And why, even though he didn't believe she was involved in the murder, was he so fascinated with her? She was beautiful with her gold-flecked, green eyes and that dimple in her full lower lip. She was also a mystery to him, and he'd never been able to resist trying to solve a mystery.

"I'm not the killer you seek," she said. "Or the person who tried running you over last night. So who I am doesn't matter to you, Sheriff."

She'd basically confirmed that her name was an alias, that she was hiding her identity for some reason. That mattered to him; he wanted to know what she was hiding and why—even if it had nothing to do with him and the case he was trying to solve.

She leaned through that window, her gaze intent on his face. "And the only thing that matters to me is that you're not hurting your daughter."

He flinched. He had hurt her.

Olivia's beautiful eyes narrowed. "What did you do? I saw her rushing toward the kitchen, but I just thought she was running late."

"She was." But that had been his fault, too. "I don't know how to talk to her without upsetting her," he admitted. But asking her if she'd tried to kill him? There was no way he could have asked that question without upsetting her. And he never should have. He shouldn't have let Warren get to him . . .

"But I would never lay a hand on her," he promised. And he hoped she believed him. For some reason, it was really important to him that Olivia Smith didn't think as badly of him as his own daughter did.

She studied his face for another long moment before

she stepped back, away from the SUV. But he wasn't sure if she believed him or not. He suspected she wasn't either.

"Go back inside," he urged her.

"Do you want me to check on her?"

"No." If Holly told her what he'd done, she would think even worse of him than she already did. And that bothered him . . . too much. "Go back inside so you don't freeze and stay there until the weather clears up and it's safe to travel."

And he hoped that would be a long while because he didn't want her to leave. Not yet . . .

But maybe she was right; maybe it was more dangerous for her to stay, and not just for her sake but also for his. He couldn't afford any distractions right now—not if someone had seriously tried running him down last night. And Olivia Smith, with her vulnerable beauty and her secrets, was entirely too distracting. With the bridge cleared and open at the moment, this was probably her only chance to escape before the snow accumulated and it closed again.

"Good-bye, Sheriff," she said with an air of finality.

She was leaving. And he had no legal reason to stop her. "Be careful," he advised, and he forced himself to roll up the window and drive away. Once the security guard manning the camera at the employee gate opened it, he drove through and onto the slick street. Olivia Smith was leaving, and Holly was furious with him. He needed to make it up to his daughter for doubting her. But how, when she refused to talk to him?

His cell rang, startling him. Was she calling him? Not Olivia. She didn't have his number. But Holly? Had she changed her mind about talking?

But the number lighting up his screen wasn't his daughter's. It was his dad's. The dread, that Holly probably felt whenever he called her, gripped him now. But he had no choice; he had to take the call. He pressed the accept button. "Hello?"

"Deacon? It's Helen . . ."

The dread gripped him more tightly, twisting his stomach into knots. Helen was his father's nurse. "Is it time?" he asked.

The old man had been given just six months to live after being diagnosed with pancreatic cancer . . . over three years ago. That was one of the reasons why Deacon had brought his wife and daughter back to Bane Island. Now he wished he had never returned.

Helen chuckled. "No."

Of course not. Sam Howell was too damn stubborn to die.

"He received something for you," Helen continued. "A box was delivered here at the house, but it's addressed to you."

Deacon sighed. Since he never knew whether or not his deputy was showing up, he needed to go straight to the station. But he hadn't been to see his father for a while.

Not that interactions with his dad ever went any better than interactions with his daughter.

But his day couldn't get much worse than it already was, with Holly mad at him and Olivia leaving, so he might as well stop in and pick up his package now. His father's cottage wasn't far from the grounds of Bainesworth Manor, which was fitting, since old man Bainesworth had probably paid for it with bribes for the former sheriff to look the other way all those years ago.

That dread settling heavily in the bottom of his stomach, he drove the short distance to his father's place. Too short . . .

Within minutes he pulled into the driveway, the tires of

his SUV slipping and spinning on the icy gravel. His brakes barely stopped his vehicle behind the nurse's snow-covered truck. It hadn't been snowing long enough yet to cover it this morning, so she must have spent the night. His dad was getting worse. Until now he'd only needed her to come and check on him throughout the day. She was the only one who did.

Deacon's mother had left his father long ago. And the man had never had a true friend—because he'd never been a true friend or a good father. Deacon had vowed to be nothing like him, but he was . . . too damn much. His daughter hated him as much as he'd hated his old man.

He hesitated before shutting off the SUV and pushing open the driver's door. His foot slipped on the ice when he stepped out. He caught himself on the door, caught himself from falling on his ass.

But he'd already done that . . . with Holly. Would she forgive him?

Not damn likely.

She hadn't been able to forgive him anything else.

Even things that hadn't been his fault.

He forced himself to release the door, slam it shut, and walk toward the front door of the cottage. It opened before he could knock; the nurse must have been waiting for him.

"I'm glad you came," Helen said. "He will be, too."

Deacon wasn't so sure about that; like his conversations with his daughter, they usually ended in an argument. Or started with one . . .

He smiled at her, or at least he tried; it probably looked more like a grimace because the older woman chuckled. She was in her sixties, and after retiring from the small hospital in town, she'd become a home health nurse. She had the experience and the patience to care for someone like his father. Whereas the younger nurses—male and female—that Deacon had hired first had all quit within weeks.

"He will be," she insisted, and shivering over the cold, she pulled him inside and closed the door. "It's freezing."

The cottage wasn't that warm inside either. But it wasn't well insulated and had only a woodstove and space heaters for warmth. Maybe his father should have held out for some bigger bribes from old man Bainesworth.

Sam Howell sat, propped up, in a hospital bed close to the woodstove. When Deacon was a kid, he'd thought his father was a giant. As he'd gotten older, the giant had shrunk, but he'd never looked as small as he did now and as frail.

Concern drew Deacon closer to the bed, closer to his father. "Hey, Dad," he said, his voice soft so he wouldn't startle him.

Sam's eyes were closed, but he must not have been asleep because they were clear when he opened them. Clear and sharp with annoyance. "What the hell do you think my home is—your personal post office box?"

Deacon chuckled. Sam might have lost most of his body weight, but he hadn't lost his wit and belligerence. "I didn't ask to have anything delivered here, Dad," he said.

"It's to Sheriff Deacon Howell," the old man said, his voice raspy either with weakness or annoyance.

That was his father's real problem—that he was no longer the sheriff. That killed him more than the cancer was killing him. That he'd lost the job that had mattered so much to him. He hadn't lost his job when the state police and the attorney general's office had come to Bane Island to investigate and shut down Bainesworth Manor forty years ago, even though he should have.

The locals had been scared of him then. Just like they'd been too scared of James Bainesworth—or maybe of the scandal—to testify against him. So the old man had escaped punishment and so had Deacon's father. It was only later that he'd finally lost his job, and that because all the years of drinking had begun to ravage his body.

"Where is the package?" Deacon asked. "I can get it out of your way."

"You're not going to open it here?" his dad asked.

Deacon furrowed his brow. "You want to know what's in it?" The old man usually had no curiosity about his life, had barely ever had any involvement in it at all . . . until he'd gotten sick and needed Deacon.

His dad was a couple of decades older than his mom; he'd been forty-two when Deacon was born. Not that Deacon had ever spent much time with him. His mom had divorced his dad when Deacon was young, and she'd raised him mostly on her own at a house in town while his dad had moved to his cottage.

"Obviously you don't want anyone at the police department to know," his father said, "so you wouldn't have had it delivered there."

"I didn't have anything delivered anywhere," Deacon said.

The old man shrugged shoulders so skinny that the bones nearly poked through his thin skin and flannel shirt. "Then why the hell would someone send it to you here?"

Deacon shrugged now. "I don't know. But I have to get to work, so I'll just take it with me." The old man might have been bored but Deacon didn't have time to entertain him.

"Don't trust me with whatever it is?" Sam asked with

even more belligerence. "Think it's something related to Bainesworth Manor?"

He hadn't . . . until now. But everybody at the hall knew where he lived, except maybe old man Bainesworth. He might think Deacon lived with his dad.

"Do you still have contact with anyone there?" Deacon asked.

Sam glared at him. "You don't trust me."

Deacon sighed, and his already frayed patience drained away from him. "No. I don't. You were on the Bainesworth payroll before."

"What would they pay me for now?" his dad asked. "To die? That's the only thing I'm capable of doing anymore."

What had he been capable of doing before? What the hell had he done for Bainesworth Manor?

Deacon didn't want to know anymore. And whatever it was, the guy was already being punished for it; pancreatic cancer was his death penalty.

"Here's the box," Helen said as she carried in a large carton from the kitchen.

Deacon rushed over to take it from the older woman's arms. The block letters on the shipping label addressed it to Sheriff Deacon Howell at his father's address, but there was no return address and no sign of postage attached to the label.

"Did you see who brought this?" he asked.

She shook her head. "I don't even know when it was dropped. I went out this morning to shovel the front walk and collect more wood, and it was sitting next to the door."

"What's with the inquisition?" Sam asked. "Why the hell don't you just open it?"

Because Deacon didn't want to spend any more time

with the bitter old man than necessary. "It's addressed to the sheriff," Deacon pointed out. "It must be police business."

"And I'm not the police anymore," Sam said.

He had never been a true man of the law—since he'd never gone after the real criminals. Just the petty ones.

Sam must have read his mind because he snapped at him. "You think you're so damn much better than I am."

He hoped he was, but he had his doubts. He wanted to do a better job protecting Bane Island than his father had, but people were dying during his term in office, too.

"I'm just busy," Deacon said. "I need to take this and leave."

Helen took mercy on him and rushed ahead to open the door for him. He clicked his key fob and opened the hatch on the back of the SUV. The box wasn't heavy, but the weight was odd, slightly uneven. He settled it into the back of the SUV. Helen stood yet at the cottage door, holding it open for him, waiting for him to come back and say a proper good-bye to his father.

He didn't owe him one, and he doubted it would be the last time he'd see the old man. Sure, Sam was getting worse, but he was still too ornery to die. A sigh burned the back of Deacon's throat, and he released it to freeze into a cloud in front of his face. If he didn't go back inside, the old man would keep complaining to Helen. To save her the hassle, he started back toward the cottage, clicking the key fob to close the hatch. The metal hinges creaked in the cold but just as it snapped close, lightly rocking the SUV, the vehicle exploded. Glass and metal blasted out from it, knocking Deacon to the ground, knocking him out cold.

Chapter Eight

With thick snow swirling around, James could not see anything outside his window on the second story of the carriage house. He could only see his own reflection in the glass—that of a frail-looking old man slouched in a wheelchair. It was hell to get old. And James Bainesworth knew hell.

Many people actually believed he was the devil; sometimes he even believed it himself. The worst thing about getting old, though, was that people didn't fear him like they used to. A ninety-two-year-old man fairly crippled with age didn't intimidate anyone. Not anymore . . .

That was what he hated most. People treating him like he was feeble-minded as well as feeble. But he was stronger than he looked. And he was always smarter than everybody else—even than that damn self-righteous grandson of his.

Elijah wasn't his only problem though.

There was the sheriff, too.

If Elijah and Deacon Howell ever put aside their egos and their rivalry long enough to work together . . .

Then James might have a problem. But even then,

he would figure out how to take care of it. Just like he always had.

He still ruled Bainesworth Manor; they just didn't know it anymore. They'd moved him out to this cottage on the outskirts of the property not realizing that it sat on the highest point on the island, so from his second story window, he could see everything. It was the old caretaker's cottage, and he was the old caretaker.

Finally the snow abated, and he was able to see over the property—almost over the entire island. Suddenly a plume of smoke rose above the pines, and he smiled. Then he caught the reflection in the glass of someone coming up behind him, and he whirled his chair around to confront him.

The big man jumped like a scalded cat, and all the color drained away from his face, leaving just dark circles beneath his eyes. With his burly build and crooked nose and beady eyes, Theo Collins looked more like a prize fighter than a nurse.

"Don't sneak up behind an old man," James advised him. "Might scare him to death." He wasn't the one who was scared, though.

Theo was scared—scared that someone might find out the truth. James already knew it—just like he knew everything else.

"I was coming up to check on you," Theo said. Taking care of an old man in a wheelchair probably entailed more than the nurse had bargained for . . .

Or maybe he'd known all along . . . since he'd had an agenda of his own.

"I'm fine," James said. "You're the one who looks like hell."

Theo smiled slightly. "Maybe you've been working me too hard."

"We both know that's not the problem," James said. "It's your son. That's why you can't sleep."

"I don't have a son." At least not one that had used his last name. Teddy Bowers had been his illegitimate son.

"Not anymore," James said. "But you did. You got Teddy Bowers a job at the manor as a groundskeeper. Then he had to go and abduct that girl . . ." James knew everything, especially about Theo. He'd known him a long time. The man had grown up on the island.

"Teddy didn't abduct that spoiled little rich girl," Theo said defensively. Like there was any defending Bowers holding that Walcott girl. "She asked him to help her escape."

"Escape—not stay with him," James said. "He held her against her will. That's an abduction or at the very least a kidnapping. Did you help him keep her?"

Theo's face flushed with color, and he shook his head. "I had nothing to do with that."

"Then there's the other body the sheriff found . . . ," James murmured as he studied the nurse's face. "Of course, it wasn't the first body he found here." And probably wouldn't be the last.

"You know my son had nothing to do with that," Theo said.

"Maybe he should have," James said. "Maybe then the sheriff would stop coming around here." Deacon Howell was nothing like his father; he actually wanted to solve cases and punish the guilty. He wouldn't accept money to look the other way.

Theo looked out the window in the direction from which James had seen the smoke. "Maybe he will . . . ," he murmured.

What the hell had happened? Elijah peered out his office window, which moments ago had seemed to rattle. Had a plane flown low over the building? Had there been some kind of accident on the grounds?

He could see nothing beyond the snow-covered pine trees. Maybe if he went up to the second or third floors . . .

He turned and pressed a button on his desk to open his office door, and Warren stepped through it like he'd been waiting outside. "I was just leaving to investigate what that noise was," Elijah told his cousin.

"Me, too," Warren said, his voice quavering slightly with what sounded like excitement. "Except I know what it was."

Elijah narrowed his eyes and studied his cousin. His face was flushed, but then Warren's face always seemed flushed. "What was it?"

"An explosion," Warren said.

That made sense then.

"On the property?" Elijah asked with alarm. "What blew up?"

"Not our property," Warren said.

Elijah narrowed his eyes more at his cousin's possessiveness. The property belonged to the Bainesworth side of his family, not the Cooke side. Before he could comment, his cousin continued, "It was at the sheriff's dad's house."

Elijah gasped. "Was anyone hurt?"

Warren nodded. "That's why I have to leave. I have to lead the investigation."

Elijah doubted Deacon would allow that, especially after last night and his obvious doubts about his deputy— doubts that Elijah was beginning to share. "Are you sure the sheriff will want you investigating?"

"I don't think he has a choice," Warren said. "He was at his father's when the bomb went off."

"Bomb?" An explosion could have been an accident. Maybe the result of a gas leak, if the cottage had gas. But a bomb? Deacon hadn't been paranoid, then. Someone must have been trying to kill him. Had he succeeded? "You think Deacon's dead?"

Warren nodded. "Margaret—the dispatcher—was pretty hard to understand when she called, but it sounds like it."

Elijah gasped again as a sudden pang struck his heart. He'd never been a fan of Deacon Howell's, but he'd never wished him harm. Well, at least not since they'd grown up.

"What about Holly?" Elijah asked. "Has anyone talked to Holly?"

Warren shook his head. "I don't have time to look for her. Can you?"

He didn't want to, but maybe it was better that he talked to her rather than Warren, who was clearly happy that the sheriff was out of his way. Had he set that bomb?

She hadn't heeded the warning the sheriff had given her less than an hour ago. She'd waited until he'd driven away, and then she'd brushed off her car and started the engine. It hadn't started easily, but with a rumble of protest and a rattling noise coming from the engine. She'd left it to warm up, and hopefully melt the snow off it, while she'd gone to retrieve her things.

Her legs shook slightly as she carried her suitcase to her car. It was her third trip to the vehicle. On her second, when she'd brought out her guitar and backpack, it had felt as if the ground shook beneath her, and she'd heard something like a boom of thunder. The snow had stopped—finally—so she tipped back her head to peer up at the sky. Dark clouds hung low over her, over the entire island, but she caught no glimpse of lightning. Was another storm coming—following up all the snow that had fallen? Should she leave now?

She had to—if the bridge was open. She had to leave before that reporter tried again to speak to her. Before the stalker found her . . .

The roads were probably plowed by now. Or so she hoped.

While she'd retrieved her things, the snow had melted off her car, which idled quietly now. The engine must have just needed to warm up. As long as the bridge was open, nothing would prevent her from leaving. And she had no reason to stay. Yesterday, Rosemary had assured her that the sheriff was not harming his daughter. Olivia hadn't quite believed that until she'd asked him earlier this morning, and he'd looked so tortured. He and Holly didn't have an easy relationship, but it wasn't because he didn't love his daughter. Holly was safe from her father. He was the one who seemed to be in danger. If someone had really tried running him down . . .

Why would someone do that? Because of the body he'd found? Because they didn't want him investigating?

None of it was her business, though. She didn't want to get involved, and she certainly didn't want to be put in any more danger than she already was. But as she reached out for the door handle, someone grabbed her.

"You can't leave!" the teenage girl protested.

The sheriff had told her the same thing just an hour ago. Why was everyone so determined that she stayed?

Olivia had thought that all of Morgana Drake's crazy ghost stories had been just that, just urban—or not so urban considering the remoteness of the island—legends about all those girls who hadn't been able to leave the hall. No. Not the hall. Bainesworth Manor. The asylum . . .

All the stories about the place had reminded her of the old Eagles song. *You can check out any time you like, but . . .*

But Olivia had long ago stopped letting people tell her what to do. She shook the hand off her arm and opened her door. Only after tossing her suitcase inside next to her guitar and backpack did she turn around.

"You can't leave!" Holly Howell wailed again, her dark eyes brimming with tears.

First the father had tried to get her to stay; now the daughter did.

All these months Olivia had probably been right to trust her instincts and avoid the girl. The last thing she needed was another stalker. "I can, and I am leaving," she said.

"Then take me with you!" Holly implored. "Dr. Cooke is probably going to fire me. I was ordered to go to his office, but then I saw you walking out with your suitcase. If you can't stay, then take me with you. Because I can't stay here—not without you."

"You don't even know me," Olivia reminded her.

"I know who you are—who you really are," Holly said.

Olivia had already guessed as much, but now she narrowed her eyes and studied the girl's face. "Is that why you want to leave with me?" she asked. "Because you think I'll give you money or a recording contract? What do you want from me?"

Because everybody always wanted something . . .

Holly sucked in a breath and sucked up some of her tears. "I . . . I don't want anything from you."

"You said you want to leave with me," Olivia reminded her.

"Because I can't stay here," Holly wailed again. "I can't stay with my dad."

"Are you going to try to tell me again that he's hurting you?" Olivia asked.

The girl's face reddened with embarrassment and she said, "I never told you that he was. You just assumed that's why I hate him." Her voice cracked with fury. "I hate him!"

"Why?" Olivia asked. She understood hating someone if he was abusing you. But . . .

"He killed my mom!" Holly exclaimed. "That's why I hate him. He killed her. He killed her!"

Olivia's head began to pound from the volume of the girl's voice and from the confusion over what she was claiming. "Is that body he found your mother's?"

Holly shook her head. "No. Not that one. But he did find my mom here—on the property, nearly two years ago."

"I don't understand," Olivia said. "What was she doing here?" Had she worked here too?

"She'd checked into the hall when it first opened," Holly said. "She wanted some time away from my dad because all they ever did was fight. She was under so much stress . . ." Holly raised her hand to her own face, cupping her cheek in her palm.

And Olivia remembered how the girl had flinched when

she'd brushed her hair back. Was her mother the one who'd hit her—because she'd been stressed? At least she'd bothered to make an excuse. The ones who'd hurt Olivia had always blamed her.

"What happened to your mother?" Olivia asked.

"My dad found her at the bottom of the cliffs at the edge of this property. It was ruled a suicide, but . . ."

"But what?"

"Some people think he pushed her," she said.

That must have been the rumor that Rosemary Tulle had refused to repeat because she hadn't believed it. Olivia didn't either. "Surely, someone else investigated besides him? He wasn't allowed to rule on his own wife's death?"

Holly shook her head. "No. The state police came in, but . . ."

Rumors persisted? All anyone on this island ever seemed to talk about was the past. Olivia wanted to keep it that way, though. She'd rather they all talked about themselves than talk about her. But then a pang of guilt struck her. She didn't want Holly or the sheriff contending with all the horrible speculation about their lives either.

"So there you have it," Olivia said. "They must have determined he didn't push her, or he would be in jail right now." And Holly would probably be in foster care. Olivia could attest that sometimes that was almost as bad. But not quite . . . because those people weren't supposed to love you like your family was.

"It doesn't matter if he didn't physically push her," she said. "He did in other ways. Just like he's pushing me!"

Maybe Rosemary had been right about Holly being just an overly dramatic teenager. But then the girl had lost her mother; she had a right to be however dramatic she felt.

"How is he pushing you?" Olivia asked.

Tears brimmed over her dark eyes again, running down her already cold-chafed face. Olivia should have had her get into the car with her, out of the elements. But she was afraid that if she let her inside her vehicle, Holly wouldn't get out again.

"He accused me of trying to run him down!"

Olivia tensed. That must have been what he'd done that he'd admitted had upset his daughter, the thing he'd been obviously tortured over. Now she understood.

"Oh, my God, you know about that," Holly said. "You know he suspects me." More tears flowed. "Do you?"

"No, of course not." But then she didn't know the girl very well—not like her father knew her. If he suspected . . .

Having once been a teenager for what felt like forever, Olivia knew what they were capable of . . . but Olivia had only ever hurt herself.

"Then let me go with you," Holly implored her. "I won't be a burden to you. I just have to get off this damn island."

So did Olivia . . .

"If I take you with me, your father could have me arrested for kidnapping," Olivia said. Or worse . . .

She could wind up like the last person who'd abducted someone from Halcyon Hall. Like Teddy Bowers, she could wind up dead.

The thought had just crossed her mind when the rear window of her vehicle shattered as a shot rang out, echoing off the snow and rocks and ice.

Then another shot followed it and another and another . . .

Chapter Nine

A soft hand clasped his and squeezed, drawing him away from the darkness that engulfed him. Deacon struggled against the pain throbbing inside his head, struggled to open his eyes, as he murmured, "Holly . . ."

She was so mad at him that he was surprised she was here. Maybe she'd forgiven him.

"Holly . . . ," he murmured again, and finally he managed to pry open his eyelids.

But the face peering down at him didn't belong to his daughter. Rosemary Tulle leaned over him, her brow creased with worry. "Are you okay?" she asked.

Disappointment flooded him, making his eyes sting. Or maybe that was the pain that blinded him from the light hanging over his bed. Bed . . . ?

"Where the hell am I?" he asked.

"The hospital," she said. "Don't you remember what happened?"

He closed his eyes, to shut out that light and to search his memory. "I stopped by my dad's . . ." He'd been going back to him, to say good-bye, with the hatch of his SUV closing. "The explosion . . ." He opened his eyes again as concern shot through him. "Helen? Is Helen okay?"

"Who's Helen?" Rosemary asked.

"My dad's nurse," he said. "And my dad . . . are they okay?"

She nodded. "Nobody was hurt but you. The doctor says you have a concussion from the blast knocking you to the ground."

He remembered flying forward—back toward the cottage he hadn't wanted to go to in the first place. But somebody had sent that damn box to his dad's . . .

With a bomb inside? That must have been what had gone off.

"What was it?" he asked.

She shrugged. "Warren is investigating—"

He shook his head and sent an explosion of pain reverberating inside his skull. "No . . ."

"Margaret already called the state police," Rosemary assured him. "She told me to tell you that if you woke up."

If . . . ?

Had there been some doubt that he might survive? How the hell badly was he hurt?

He looked down at his body lying beneath a thin sheet. And as he stared, he moved things—his arms, his legs. Everything moved, albeit with some grunts of pain slipping through his lips. "I . . . I didn't lose anything?"

"It's all there," a deep male voice assured him.

And he glanced back at Rosemary and saw a man standing behind her, his arm around her. He'd been disappointed that Rosemary wasn't Holly, but he was happy that he had friends. When he'd moved back to Bane Island, he'd left them all behind, and despite the promises to keep in touch, nobody had. Neither them nor him.

"Whit, why aren't you in court?" he asked the judge.

"It's Sunday," Whit reminded him. "And the court's not in session during the holidays. Even if the bridge hadn't been shut down, I planned to be here for a while. But maybe you shouldn't be. Seems like it's getting pretty dangerous here for you all of a sudden."

"Why is that?" Rosemary asked. "What's going on, Deacon?"

He shrugged and grunted at the ache in his shoulders. Hell, he ached all over. "You know me—I have a tendency to piss people off," he said. "You hated me before you got to know me better."

She didn't laugh like he'd meant for her to do.

He narrowed his eyes and studied her face, which was oddly pale. Had she been that worried about him?

Or was she calling him on his lie? Familiarity with him didn't breed love, but contempt. Nobody knew him better than his daughter and she hated him most. But then maybe Holly didn't really know him at all. She only knew what her mother and the Cookes had told her: lies.

"Deacon," Rosemary began, her voice soft as she spoke slowly. "Holly's here . . ."

So she had actually come to the hospital. Or maybe Rosemary had forced her to come. Either way he uttered a sigh of relief and murmured, "Maybe she doesn't hate me."

Rosemary's already pale face turned even paler. Deacon glanced behind her to Whit, but the judge looked as confused as he was.

"What?" he asked. "What's going on? What aren't you telling me?"

"Holly's here with Olivia Smith."

His pulse quickened, and he checked to see if any machines had registered his reaction to just the mention of the petite blonde's name. If that was actually her name . . .

Who was she? And why was she the one who'd brought his daughter to the hospital for him? He studied Rosemary's face, which was surprisingly closed for her. "What aren't you telling me?" he asked. Because he knew there was something. "And why aren't you telling me?"

"You have a concussion," she said. "I don't know if I should upset you right now."

"You're pissing me off," Deacon said.

"Just tell him," Whit said. "Tell me, too, while you're at it."

Rosemary reached for Deacon's hand again, wrapping her fingers around his palm. "Holly is okay," she said.

"Good . . ."

Then he remembered what Rosemary had told him moments ago. "But you said she's here with Olivia Smith?" And as much as he might like to think so, he doubted that Olivia was here to see him. "Why is she here?"

"She's being treated in the ER."

Deacon's pulse leaped again—with concern for the mysterious woman. "For what?"

"Just some cuts from broken glass," Rosemary said. "When she was getting ready to leave the hall, someone fired some shots at her. They hit the rear window of her car."

"Damn it!" He'd told her not to leave because of the weather; he hadn't realized that she might be in danger of another kind. "And Holly?" he asked. "Why is she with her?"

"Because she was with her when the shooting happened," Rosemary said. And she squeezed his hand again, reassuringly. "But she doesn't have a scratch on her. She's fine."

For now. But she could have been hit with the glass, too, or a bullet. And if she'd been with him . . .

He shuddered to think what could have happened to her. He knew he was lucky he hadn't been hurt worse. Despite Rosemary's assurances, had Olivia?

"She's really okay?"

"Holly is fine," Rosemary assured him.

"And Olivia?"

Rosemary glanced back and exchanged a significant look with Whit. What the hell was significant about it?

"Somebody shot at her," he reminded his friends. "I need to get out of this bed and investigate." But when he tried to sit up, his head pounded, and he flinched at the pain.

He wasn't just in physical pain. He was hurting over everything that had happened starting with that horrible argument with his daughter, one he'd caused with his unfounded suspicions. Obviously, Holly had had nothing to do with any of this. Even if she'd been tempted to hurt him, she would have never hurt Olivia Smith; for some reason she seemed to idolize the woman.

But what the hell was happening on Bane Island? A bombing and a shooting on the same day? Was he looking for one assailant or two? It had to be two because why would the same person be after both him and Olivia Smith? Unless she knew more than she'd told him the day before . . .

He'd suspected she'd been hiding something from him. He needed to find out what—for both their sakes and maybe his daughter's as well.

* * *

Sharp metal pierced her skin, then stretched it before piercing another spot, pulling the two sides of the cut together. Olivia flinched and bit the inside of her cheek, holding in the cry of pain.

"You should have let me numb you," the ER resident said.

"You're not numb?" Deputy Warren Cooke asked, and finally that was a question she could answer.

"No, I'm not," she said. Years ago she'd stopped wanting to be numb . . . and had vowed to never let it happen again.

"But why not?" Warren asked.

"Because it's just a scratch," she said.

"It's a deep cut," the doctor corrected her. "And I'm not sure if I got all the glass out of the wound because you're not numb." And, as he'd told her, he hadn't wanted to push his tools any deeper into her flesh.

She smiled at him. "I'm sure you got it all."

His brow furrowed, and he stared oddly at her, as if he almost recognized her but couldn't quite figure out from where.

She was used to that. Warren hadn't had any such look cross his pudgy face. But maybe he already knew who she was.

"Miss Smith, you need to answer my questions," he said, sounding more like a whiny child than a police officer.

Fortunately, she had only one to deal with right now, but a pang of guilt struck her over comparing Holly to the deputy. She was so much sweeter than he was. She'd gone off to find Olivia a candy bar, thinking that chocolate might help with her pain. Maybe it would; it certainly couldn't hurt any more than the needle pulling her skin together.

"Done," the doctor said.

"Good," Olivia said. "Now I can leave."

The doctor nodded. "Agreed. I'll have a nurse come back with wound care directions and your discharge papers." He glanced at the deputy as he left, as if wondering if he should have left her alone with the man.

She wondered the same. Warren Cooke might have been an officer of the law, but for some men, being in that field made them think they were above the law.

"You can't leave until you answer my questions," Warren persisted.

She sighed. "I already did. I didn't see anyone. I'm not sure where the shots came from—just that they hit close." Too damn close. Fortunately, Holly hadn't been hurt as well.

"Those shots might have just been a warning," he suggested. "The next time they might not miss."

She narrowed her eyes now and studied his face. Had he just threatened her? "There won't be a next time," she said. "I'm leaving Halcyon Hall and Bane Island."

He shook his head. "You can't leave now—not in the middle of an investigation. You're a material witness."

"I didn't witness anything," she said. "And you can't keep me here." Was that why someone had taken those shots? To prevent her from leaving? If so, they'd failed. She was even more determined to get the hell off Bane Island.

"I can keep you here until you answer all my questions," he insisted.

"I have," she snapped at him. Now she felt like wailing at him. What an idiot . . .

Or was he? Maybe it was all just an act, and he was something more than he appeared, something worse.

"But who would have a motive to shoot at you?" he asked. "Don't you have any idea?"

"No," she lied. "But I have a question for you."

He quirked an eyebrow. "You do?"

"Where were you when the shooting happened?" Because he'd appeared fast, like he'd already been outside with them.

His head snapped back, and his mouth dropped open. "How dare you," he sputtered. "I'm not going to answer that."

"Yes, you are," a deep voice informed him.

Olivia turned toward the doorway of the small exam room and the man filling it. Sheriff Howell leaned against the jamb as if it was all that was holding him up. His face was more scratched than hers with bruises that were already turning from red to blue and black. His dark hair was disheveled, and his clothes were torn.

"What happened to you?" she asked with horror and concern.

"I got blown up," he replied.

"Blown up?" she repeated incredulously.

Even his deputy stared at him as if he'd come face to face with a ghost. Deacon chuckled as he studied the man's dumbfounded expression. "You look surprised to see me," he murmured.

"I . . . I . . . uh," Warren stammered.

"I thought you were off duty this weekend," Deacon continued, "at least for Bane Island."

"Margaret called me in to investigate—"

"By all means, investigate," Deacon interrupted him, his voice sharp with anger. "Although Ms. Smith might be better at it. She asked you a great question."

Warren's brow furrowed. "What do you mean?"

"Where the hell were you when she was shot at?"

"He came right after the shooting stopped," she said. "Like he was very close."

Deacon looked at her then for the first time, and when their eyes met, she felt a strange jolt to her very core. Something about him, about his dark eyes and all the passion in them, pulled at her—pulled her out of herself in a way she hadn't felt in years, if ever . . .

But that passion in his eyes wasn't romantic. He was angry. And she damn well didn't blame him; she was angry, too. Angry about always being a victim. She wanted to attack someone now—the person who'd shot at her.

"That is a strange coincidence," the sheriff agreed in an almost conspiratorial tone.

Awareness rippled through her. All his passion might have been anger; hers was not.

Warren stepped closer to the sheriff, probably to recapture his attention. With him between them, the connection was broken. Disappointment chased away the awareness, making Olivia's shoulders slump.

"I was just leaving the hall to investigate the explosion when I heard the shots," he told his boss. "That's why I was outside then."

"But, aren't you head of security for Halcyon Hall? How does a girl get kidnapped a few weeks ago, another one gets murdered, and now Ms. Smith gets shot at—all under your watch?"

"You're the sheriff. It's all your watch, too," Warren said. The deputy pushed past Deacon, leaving just the two of them together. And now the fear was all Olivia's . . .

He'd levered himself away from the doorjamb when Warren had passed him; now he moved closer, his dark gaze intent on her face. "Are you okay?" he asked.

"Just a scratch . . ." She touched her fingers to the stitches on her forehead and nodded. "How about you?"

He shrugged. "I was lucky."

"Me, too . . . ," she murmured.

He glanced around the room. "I thought Holly was with you."

Disappointment jabbed her in the heart. He hadn't come to check on her; he'd come for his daughter. "She'll be back soon," she promised him. "She's fine. She's not hurt at all."

"Thank God," he murmured, and a shudder of relief shook his muscular body.

"Deacon—" Olivia began, and she wasn't certain what she might have said because the nurse came back then with those release papers. But she wasn't alone; Dr. Cooke came into the room with her.

"You look like hell," Elijah told the sheriff.

"I'm alive," Deacon said. "That must disappoint you."

Elijah shook his head. "Surprisingly not."

The nurse started talking to Olivia then, and the two men stepped into the hall. She couldn't hear what they were saying, but moments later only one of them returned.

Holly blinked, trying to clear away the tears burning her eyes so she could see the vending machine. She reached out, blindly pushing buttons. When a bag of chips, instead of the candy bar, fell to the bottom of the machine, she burst into sobs, letting them rack her body.

Somebody had tried to blow up her dad. Warren hadn't told her that until after he'd questioned Olivia, when just minutes ago he'd passed her standing by the vending machine. He'd claimed he hadn't told her earlier because he'd forgotten about it because of the shooting. Somebody had tried to kill Olivia too. Or her?

Who had those bullets meant to strike? She'd been frozen—with cold and fear—when it had happened. She hadn't thawed until just a short while ago when Warren finally told her about what else had happened . . .

About the explosion.

An arm slipped around her, turning her, pulling her into an embrace. She wanted it to be her dad holding her. But it was a woman. Not Olivia, since Holly dwarfed her. This woman was her size and strong and warm.

"It's okay," Rosemary Tulle assured her. "Everything's okay."

Holly pulled back and sucked up her tears. "I thought that shrinks aren't supposed to lie."

Rosemary smiled. "I'm not. For the moment—everything's okay. Olivia Smith is okay. And your dad will be fine."

"Somebody tried to blow him up," she said, her voice cracking with another wave of sobs. She shook with fear just thinking of how close she had come to losing him.

When he'd told her that someone had tried running him down, she hadn't realized what that meant. She'd just been angry that he had been questioning her about it.

Now she got it; someone was trying to kill her dad, trying to take away from her the only parent she had left.

And Olivia . . .

She'd been standing right next to her when those shots had rung out, shattering the rear window so close to Olivia's face. She shuddered, and Rosemary reached for her again. But Holly stepped back and shook her head. "You shouldn't be near me," she said. "Nobody should. It's all my fault . . ."

Rosemary's brow creased. "What are you talking about? None of this is your fault."

"It is," she insisted. "My dad was right. The hall is cursed, and now so am I." Cursed to lose everyone she cared about . . .

First her mom had died at that place. And she'd blamed her dad. Now she realized he'd been right, though.

It was the hall. Or Bainesworth Manor.

That was what it really was.

That was why her mom had died there—like those other women had.

Like Olivia nearly had when she'd tried to leave it.

Holly shouldn't have tried to stop her. But Olivia was sure to leave now—the hall and the island and Holly, too.

And if whoever was trying to kill her dad succeeded, Holly would be all alone.

Chapter Ten

"Why are you here?" Olivia asked Dr. Cooke. And where had the sheriff gone?

He was the man she'd wanted to stay. Hell, he was the man she just wanted. And she wasn't sure why. She didn't even completely trust him. But then she didn't completely trust anyone. She couldn't. That was why she hadn't told anyone about the threats and why she hadn't let anyone know where she was.

She hadn't even brought along a bodyguard for protection. Because she'd wondered . . .

Could it have been one of them? Because of all those photos, it might be someone close to her.

"You're going to need a ride back to the hall," Dr. Cooke told her. He was the one who'd insisted that an ambulance bring her to the small hospital on the island. At the time, with her head wound bleeding profusely, she hadn't been able to argue with him. There was no way she would have been able to drive herself, and everyone else had agreed that it was best to call an ambulance.

Dr. Cooke had rushed out to the parking lot not long after Warren Cooke. He could have been the shooter, too.

"I don't want to go back," she said. And she certainly didn't want to ride with him anywhere.

"I'll make sure you're safe at the hall," he assured her.

"Somebody shot at me there," she reminded him as she touched her fingertips to those stitches.

"I think it must have been an accident. That it was just a hunter," he said. "Or maybe the new groundskeeper firing at a coyote or something and the shot went wild. Nobody has any reason to purposely shoot at you or at Holly Howell."

She wondered if he was trying to convince her or himself. He probably didn't want the news getting out that someone had shot at a guest at Halcyon Hall. That wouldn't be good for business. Neither was finding a dead body on the property, though.

"So nobody's after me or Holly—just the sheriff?" she asked.

Dr. Cooke's pale eyes narrowed as he studied her face. "Nobody has taken shots at the sheriff."

Maybe that was the only thing that hadn't happened to him. "No," she agreed, "they just tried to run him over and blow him up."

"So as long as you stay away from him, you'll be safe," Dr. Cooke said with a slight grin.

"You think it's funny what the sheriff is going through?" she asked, appalled.

"Of course not," he said. "I am just aware that Deacon Howell tends to make more enemies than friends. Whatever is happening with him has nothing to do with Halcyon Hall."

"He doesn't believe that," Olivia said, and neither did she. But it was clearly what Dr. Cooke wanted her to believe. Had that many other guests already canceled? Was

THE HUNTED 121

that why he was so desperate for her to stay? Or did he want her to stay so that she couldn't talk to reporters about what had happened to her there?

"I told you why the sheriff harbors ill will against the hall," Dr. Cooke said. "It's much easier to lay the blame on someone else or someplace else than accept it yourself."

She snorted. "You do sound like a shrink."

He sighed. "I haven't felt like one for a while," he murmured. But then he blinked, as if surprised at himself for letting the admission slip out. "I'm sorry. You've been discharged, and I'm keeping you here talking. Let's get you back to the hall."

She nodded in agreement but only because her car was back at the hall. She needed it and her things so that she could find a new place to go. A safer place . . .

Why the hell was someone trying to kill him? Was it over the body he'd found? He'd found her weeks ago. Why were the attempts happening now?

Was it because he'd reopened the investigation into his wife's death? If so, then Shannon must have been murdered.

No matter what the cause, he knew the source. The hall . . .

Someone here wanted him dead.

Maybe it was a conflict of interest but he damn well wasn't trusting this investigation to anyone else. Not even the state police who'd showed up at the hospital to question him.

Fortunately, Rosemary had promised she would take care of Holly for him. He hadn't wanted to see her yet—not

after how he'd blown it with her that morning, before nearly
getting blown up.

Once the police and the doctor had let him leave, he'd
ignored the doctor's warning not to drive and had headed
straight to the hall in his personal truck he'd had a deputy
drop at the hospital. The security guard operating the
camera at the employee gate must have recognized him
because the gates had opened, and he'd driven to the back
parking lot where crime scene tape fluttered around a small
white hatchback. If not for that tape, he might not have
even noticed the car since it blended in with the snow
falling all around it. The snow fell onto the woman who
approached the vehicle.

"You can't go in there," Deacon said as he stepped out
of his truck that he'd parked next to it.

Startled, she jumped and nearly slipped on the icy asphalt. He reached out and clasped her arm. Despite his
gloves and her jacket, a strange little jolt passed through
him when he made that contact with her. From the look in
her eyes when she turned toward him, he could tell she felt
it, too. It wasn't just him.

She jerked her arm from his grasp, though, and stepped
away from him. "You're trying to stop me from leaving now,
too?" she asked.

Was there some hopefulness? Did she want him to beg
her to stay? He wanted to—wanted her—but his life was
too crazy to inflict on anyone else.

He pointed toward the vehicle. "You can't leave with
the evidence."

"Evidence?" she asked.

"Your car," he said. "The state police lab is sending a
tow truck for it. They're going to pull bullets out of it and

run them through databases to find out who took those shots at you."

At least there was evidence left from the attempt on her life.

There probably wasn't much from his. But the state police were at his father's now, collecting whatever was left from the scene. They needed a flatbed to haul away his SUV since there probably wasn't enough left to tow. He hadn't gone back there yet, not after having been taken away from the scene in an ambulance.

He'd wanted to come here instead, to where Olivia and his daughter had been put in danger. Where they could have died . . .

He shuddered at the thought of having nearly lost his daughter. And Olivia.

He couldn't lose what he hadn't had, though, and he hadn't had more than a few conversations with the mysterious woman.

"You should go inside," Olivia said. "Your jacket is all torn. You must be freezing."

He wasn't cold. His anger pumped hot blood through his veins, warming him up. But it wasn't just anger making his heart race. It was her.

"You need to go inside," he told her. To get away from him before he did something unprofessional, something stupid . . .

"I'm fine," she said.

"No, you're not," he argued. "Not if you think you're driving off anywhere in that vehicle with no back window and all the bullets from the crime scene."

"Dr. Cooke thinks it was just a hunter missing his target," she said.

Deacon snorted. "That makes no damn sense." He

gestured at the broken back window. Shattered glass lay scattered across the cargo area where the back seats had been lain down to accommodate a suitcase, guitar case, and a backpack. "Doesn't look like any shots missed." Not if someone had meant to take out that window and scare the crap out of her.

Or out of Holly?

Someone was going after him, and maybe to make sure he got the message, they'd threatened his child as well. But Holly hadn't been harmed; Olivia Smith had.

Snow on the asphalt near her car had turned red from the blood she'd shed when she'd been struck earlier. From her wound . . .

"And you were hit," he pointed out as concern and anger surged through him.

She shook her head, sending her dark blond hair fluttering around her thin shoulders. "Not by a bullet. A piece of glass hit me."

With all of it lying around, he wasn't surprised.

"So you don't think it's an accident like Dr. Cooke does?" she said.

He couldn't rule out that a shot had gone wild. But he doubted it. "An investigation will determine that," he said. "Not Dr. Elijah Cooke. He's just trying to save his ass and salvage his business."

"You really hate him," she mused.

"The feeling's mutual."

"I'm not so sure about that," she said. "I think he's just resigned himself to how you feel about him."

He chuckled. The man was good; he'd fooled her. That was why she should leave the hall, why Deacon should be driving her to the airport on the mainland instead of trying to get her to stay. But he didn't want her gone.

Not yet.

And not just because he needed to question her.

The snow started coming down more heavily, the flakes big and wet so it was more slush than snow. She let out a little cry and pulled open the back door.

"I can't leave my guitar in there," she protested. But that wasn't the only thing she pulled from the hatchback. She dragged out a backpack, too.

He shook his head. "You can't take them until they're inspected for bullets."

"I can't let them get wet," she argued. "They'll get damaged."

The guitar case was already pretty battered, and the backpack was threadbare in spots. "Not sure it would be such a great loss," he teased.

But her full lips pulled together into a tight frown of disapproval. "You don't know anything about me."

"No," he agreed. "I don't." But he wanted to. He had to. "But I need to in order to investigate what happened here today."

"You were hurt today—far worse than I was," she said. "You should be home, resting. Or still in the hospital."

But he ignored her argument and reached for the guitar case. The hard plastic was battered but it bore no holes. He doubted there were any bullets inside it. Then he reached for the backpack, but she held tightly to a strap, refusing to turn it over to him.

"Olivia," he cautioned her. "You can't interfere in an ongoing investigation."

"And you can't seize my property without a warrant," she argued back.

His lips curved into a slight grin even though he wasn't

particularly amused. He was just prepared. "Already have one."

Actually the state police had it, but as the sheriff, he could help them enforce that warrant, to make sure she didn't remove evidence from the scene. He tugged harder on the bag, and the strap she held tore free, tearing the pack open, too. Notebooks, envelopes, and sheets of stationery slipped through the rip and spilled onto the snow-covered parking lot.

She gasped in horror. And so did he when he saw the threat scrawled across one of those pieces of stationery. *You're going to die . . .*

"What the hell is this?" he asked.

"Personal," she said. "This is all personal."

He shook his head. "No." He pointed out that threat. "This makes it my business."

She grabbed up the notebooks from the snow and clasped them against her chest. "This is my business," she insisted.

He'd guessed she was hiding something. But he'd had no idea that she was in danger. That someone had been threatening her. He reached for her arm again, and this time he didn't let her shrug off his grasp. "You're coming with me, and you're going to tell me everything."

He had no more time for secrets or lies . . . because he had a feeling that time was running out . . . for both of them.

Chapter Eleven

Olivia had expected the sheriff to take her to jail, so that he could continue his interrogation in some little room with a two-way mirror. Or maybe even a jail cell. The hall had begun to feel like a prison, though, and that was where he'd taken her—upstairs to her suite. She stood in front of the windows, and as she stared out the leaded glass, she felt like she was staring out bars. It was easier to look out over the snow-covered grounds than it was to look at the sheriff.

She knew he was looking at her; she could feel his scrutiny. And she'd never felt so exposed. He hadn't just seen the notes and the photographs from the stalker; he'd seen her notebooks, had flipped through the songs she'd been writing.

"You didn't find any bullets," she said, because she knew he hadn't. She'd only heard the sound of paper rustling, not the thump of a bullet dropping out, as he'd gone through the things she'd removed from her car. Before they'd left the parking lot, a forensic van for the state police had pulled up, and he'd had them search the items as well. So she'd been allowed to bring up her suitcase as well as her backpack and guitar case.

"I found the smoking gun," he said.

She whirled around then. "What are you talking about? I don't even own a gun, and I couldn't have fired the shots at myself."

He shook his head. "I meant motive." He held up the letters she'd received. "You have a crazy stalker who wants you dead. This is probably who fired those shots at you."

She shook her head. "There is no way that stalker knows where I am. I made certain of that." Nobody knew where she was—because she trusted nobody.

He studied her through narrowed eyes. "Really? You're famous, aren't you?" He held up one of the notebooks now. "AKAN? What the hell does that even mean?"

"Also known as . . ."—she swallowed hard, choking on the emotion that overwhelmed her when she thought of her old life, how she'd grown up—"nobody."

He gasped in surprise. "You're not nobody," he assured her. "Not to Holly anyway. She idolizes you."

"She doesn't know me," Olivia said.

"All anybody has to do is listen to one of your songs to know you," he said.

And he was right. She exposed herself in every lyric. That was why she hadn't wanted to sing them herself, but when she'd played them for someone else to buy, the man who'd become her manager had insisted that only she could do them justice.

He was wrong, though. Her backup singers had better singing voices than she did. She was a writer. Not a performer.

Over the past few months at the hall, she'd realized that she didn't want to perform anymore. Now if only her manager, Bruce, would let her out of her contract. He'd refused to let anyone else out of their contracts with the tour, holding the dancers and backup singers to their contracts even though she'd told him she wasn't going back anytime soon. Now she didn't intend to ever go back. But she wasn't sure where she could go and be safe.

For six months of the tour, with security all around her, she'd received those notes and photographs. If she hadn't been safe there or here at the hall, where would she be safe?

She wound her arms more tightly around herself, trying to chase away the cold. But it had penetrated deeply, chilling her to the bone.

"Did you come here to hide from your stalker?" the sheriff asked. "Or to hide from everyone? From the paparazzi, from your fans?"

"Everyone," she admitted. "Including the stalker."

"What are the police doing to find him?" he asked.

"Nothing."

He cursed. "This person is making serious threats—death threats. Why aren't they doing anything?"

"Because I haven't filed a report," she admitted.

"What? Why not? You're clearly in danger."

"A lot of people receive threats," she said, trying to downplay them for him, even though she didn't believe what she was saying. "Most of them are empty." And despite all those threats, nobody had tried to physically hurt her. Certainly nobody had taken shots at her. "I didn't want to waste anyone's time." And she hadn't trusted anyone to actually help her anyway.

He closed the short distance between them and reached out, stopping just short of actually touching her. But she could feel the heat of the hand he'd raised to her face, feel the closeness of his fingers to the wound on her forehead. "You were shot at," he reminded her. "That's not an empty threat. That's a serious attempt."

She shook her head, and her skin brushed his for just a moment, a moment that made her catch her breath. Then she stepped back, away from him. "Nothing like that has happened until now. And it was an accident. That's what Dr. Cooke believes."

"That's what he wants you to believe, so you'll stay," Deacon said. "No hunter accidentally fired those shots, not unless he was drunk. And I doubt any hunter would have been drinking that early in the morning."

"Some people do," she insisted. She'd known some of them. But she didn't believe, any more than he did, that those shots had been fired by accident. She just wondered if maybe she hadn't been the target. Had someone been trying to hurt his daughter to hurt him?

He sighed. "Yes, some people do start drinking in the morning, and then they wind up dying a slow painful death from pancreatic cancer . . ."

"Who are you talking about?" she asked.

He shook his head. "Nobody. Nothing."

"That's my line," she said. "What's yours? Who are you talking about?"

He sighed. "My father. That's where I was when the bomb went off."

"Is he okay?" she asked.

"Except for the pancreatic cancer, I think so."

"Deacon . . ." She recognized the pain in him that she'd experienced herself—the pain of having a parent that hurt you. She moved toward him now, and she was the one reaching out. But she didn't pull back; she let her finger-tips glide along his jaw, along the ridge of it that felt like chiseled stone covered in coarse stubble. Her skin tingled, and her breath caught again, trapped and burning, in her lungs. "Deacon . . ."

He leaned down, closing the distance between their faces, and his mouth glided over hers. Her lips tingled now and parted on a gasp of surprise and pleasure. And he deepened the kiss.

Passion overwhelmed her. Maybe she'd hidden away too long, not just from the world but from herself, from her wants and needs. She wanted him. But before she could throw her arms around his neck, he pulled back, panting for breath.

"I'm sorry," he said, and he pushed one of his hands through his disheveled hair, pushing it back from his bruised forehead. "Maybe I do have a bad concussion."

"What?" she asked. "You'd have to have a head injury to want to kiss me?"

"To lose control," he said. "I shouldn't have lost control. I had no right to kiss you."

Except that she'd wanted it. She wanted him. And if he'd truly lost control, they'd be in bed right now—tangled up in her sheets, tangled up in each other. Because she had no control when it came to him . . .

No common sense either, apparently.

"I . . . I need to get back to the investigation," he said, as if trying to remind himself.

She shook her head. "You shouldn't be investigating the attempts on your own life."

"The state police are handling that investigation," he assured her. "I'm going to handle this one." He raised the sheaf of threats she'd received. One from every stop on her last tour, with those candid shots of her that even the paparazzi couldn't have managed to snap—not unless they'd had unlimited access to her.

And she'd made certain—she'd thought—that no one had unlimited access to her. "You're injured," she said. "I don't expect you to be investigating anything right now."

"I want to," he said. "I want to keep you . . . safe."

"But I'm not safe," she said. "I need to get out of here." Just in case those shots *had* been meant for her, just in case the stalker had found her.

"Your car is probably gone now, on its way to the police lab," he said. "So you can't go anywhere."

"I'll call a cab."

He chuckled. "On Bane Island?" He shook his head. "There are no cabs based on the island, and I doubt you'd be able to get one from the mainland to come across that bridge in this weather, even if the state police haven't shut it down again. You need to stay here."

"Where someone shot at me?" The stalker hadn't done that before. Except for the pictures and the threats, she hadn't been harmed . . . physically.

"The shooting was outside," he said. "Not in your room. You're safer in here—where there are too many witnesses."

She wasn't so sure about that, and she didn't think he was either.

"Give me a little time," he implored her.

Moments ago she'd been ready to give him more than that, but he was the one who'd pulled back, who'd exerted control.

She was still struggling to find hers.

"Let me investigate this before you leave," he said. "I'll give these letters to the state forensic lab, have them run them for prints or DNA, anything that might track down who your stalker is."

She shrugged. "Some crazy fan . . ."

"A fan doesn't want to kill you," he said. "And this person clearly does."

She shivered again, but when he reached for her, as if to comfort her, she found her control and stepped back. Because she knew that if he touched her again, she might wind up begging for more. She'd vowed long ago to stop pleading with people to want her.

She wouldn't waste any more time looking for love.

Maybe Deacon should have listened to the doctor. Obviously, he had a serious concussion, or he wouldn't have stopped kissing Olivia just a short while ago. He wouldn't have pulled away from her, and he wouldn't be standing outside the door to her suite right now. He would be inside—with her.

But he'd forced himself to walk away from her. Exerting that much willpower had exhausted him, making his legs a bit shaky, so he leaned against the wall outside her room. Just a few minutes . . .

That was all he needed. Then he'd be able to ignore all the aches in his body and walk out to his truck. Instead of having one of his deputies drive his personal pickup to the hospital for him to use, he could have taken over one of their vehicles. Warren's—it wasn't as if that guy was ever really on duty. For the Bane Island police department or apparently even for Halcyon Hall.

Deacon needed to talk to him. And to Elijah.

But the shrink had found him. Elijah waited for him at the top of that elaborate stairwell leading to the second floor. "What the hell are you doing up here?" Elijah asked.

"I'm looking for a killer," Deacon replied.

"In Olivia Smith's room?" Elijah asked, a dark brow raised in skepticism as he glanced at the door to the celebrity's suite.

Deacon knew who she was now, the pop singer who protected her privacy at all costs. That was probably why she'd come out here during the winter. Sure, some celebrities frequented the place year-round because of the famous personal trainer on staff, but hardly anybody stayed over the holidays. And Christmas was fast approaching now.

When Deacon didn't answer his question, Elijah continued, "Do you think she was the one who tried to run you over last night?"

The attempts on his life had made Deacon so paranoid that he was beginning to suspect everyone and anyone. He'd even questioned his own daughter, but he'd just wanted to make sure Warren couldn't lay the blame on her. After his interrogation that morning, Holly undoubtedly hated him even more than she already had. She'd been at the hospital with Olivia, but she hadn't come to see him. She was here. Somewhere.

Rosemary had texted him that she'd driven the teenager back to the hall. He would have rather had her take Holly home—not to his home, but to where Rosemary was staying at the boarding house. Holly would probably be safer there with the Pierce sisters than she would be with him. They had saved Genevieve from Teddy Bowers.

"I think Olivia Smith is in danger, too," Deacon said. "And my daughter."

"Maybe you're overreacting," Elijah said. "I told her it might have been the stray bullets from some hunter that struck her car."

"And very nearly her," Deacon reminded him. "And my daughter."

Elijah flinched. "Holly wasn't hurt. And Ms. Smith wasn't seriously injured either. Nobody has any reason to want to hurt them."

"Unlike me?" Deacon asked.

Elijah shrugged. "I don't know what enemies you've made, Deacon."

He damn well knew because he was one of them, his family, too. But Deacon wasn't concerned about himself right now. "Some people don't need to have reasons to hurt people," he said. "And Ms. Smith has been hurt." And not just by that glass. If the songs that Holly constantly played were at all autobiographical, she'd been hurt a lot. Anger churned in Deacon's stomach at the thought. "It wasn't a hunter who fired those shots, and you know that," Deacon said, calling Elijah on his bullshit like he had since they were kids. "You just want Ms. Smith to think that, so she won't check out."

"Do you want her to leave?" Elijah asked, and his pale eyes narrowed as he studied Deacon's face like he probably did his patients. The psychiatrist was astute, too damn astute to actually believe the shooting had been an accident.

"Not with her stalker out there," Deacon said.

"Stalker?"

"You don't know about him?" Deacon asked, and he raised the sheaf of papers, photographs and envelopes he clasped in his hand.

Elijah shook his head. "I suspected she had a reason for coming here and for staying so long, but she never said . . ."

Deacon doubted she would have told him had he not discovered the threats on his own. "She never reported it to the police either," he said. She'd just run away from her problems.

That reminded him of someone. Two people actually. His wife and his daughter.

He'd been right to pull back from Olivia, to stop himself after just that kiss. That had been one of the hardest things he'd ever done, though, and Deacon had had to do a lot of hard things in his life. Like tell his daughter her mother was dead . . .

He couldn't get involved with another woman like Shannon, one who refused to deal with her problems. One who would run away every time the going got tough. "What happened to her?" he wondered aloud.

Elijah shrugged. "I don't know why she wouldn't report a stalker," he said. "Maybe she didn't want the press to get a hold of the story."

"I wasn't talking about Olivia," he said, although Elijah's theory made sense with how closely Olivia had guarded her privacy despite the paparazzi always hounding her. "I was talking about Shannon. What happened to her?"

"You know," Elijah said. "That's why having the investigation reopened was stupid."

"No," Deacon said. "I thought I knew. I thought she did it, but after finding that other woman, a blonde like Shannon, I started to wonder if someone helped her over that cliff."

"I've always thought that," Elijah admitted and arched a brow as he looked pointedly at Deacon.

He cursed. "It wasn't me. I wish you and your damn cousins would stop spreading those lies." He glared at his old nemesis. "But I can think of one reason why you would, to deflect your own guilt."

"Isn't that what you're doing now?" Elijah asked.

"Because you feel that, whether it was figuratively or literally, you pushed your wife over the edge."

Deacon had managed to control himself earlier—with Olivia. But it took much more effort now, to stop himself from swinging his fist into Elijah Cooke's smug face. "You son of a bitch!"

Elijah shrugged. "The truth doesn't bother me, not like it bothers you."

"You don't know what the truth is, do you?" Deacon asked. "You've spread so damn many lies that you don't even know anymore. . . ."

"Neither do you," Elijah said.

"That's why I requested the new investigation," Deacon said. "Shannon's body has already been exhumed. I'm going to get to the truth once and for all."

"Or implicate yourself," Elijah shot back at him. "I thought you were smarter than that, Deacon. Guess I thought wrong."

"You did if you thought you could keep secrets like your damn family has for so many years," he said. "It's not happening anymore. The truth is going to come out."

He hoped that it would only hurt the guilty though—not the innocent. Not his daughter.

He probably should have talked to her before he'd talked to the state police and to Elijah Cooke. But he'd thought this would be better for her . . . to know what really happened to her mother. Then maybe she would stop blaming him. Maybe she would stop hating him so damn much.

They were going at it again. The two of them. Her boss and her father.

Even from the foyer, she'd heard every word they'd said to each other in the hallway on the second floor.

This time Holly didn't necessarily care if her dad got her fired. All she cared about was learning the truth, like he'd promised. About everything . . .

But when he walked down that wide stairwell, leaning heavily on the railing, she focused instead on his face—on the bruises and the scrape on his cheek that was already scabbing over. He'd been hurt. Someone was trying to kill him. Why?

Because of his investigation? Or because of what he'd done?

"What is the truth?" she asked when he limped off the last step and joined her in the foyer.

Her dad blinked and focused on her, but his expression was blank. "What is what?" he asked.

Frustration tightened her muscles. She hated when he acted like this, like he was trying to hide something from her. He wasn't good at it. Unless he was responsible for her mother's murder. Then he was damn good at it.

"Did you do it?" she asked. "Did you push my mother like everybody thinks?"

"Not everybody thinks that," he replied. "Only the Cookes. You're letting them poison you against me. That's why I didn't want you working here. It's why I didn't want you anywhere near them. They're the ones you can't trust—just like your mother shouldn't have trusted them."

"Your mother felt safe here," Elijah Cooke said as he joined them. "With us. Safer than she did with your father."

"But yet she died here," her dad countered. "With you and your backstabbing cousins and your younger brother. Which one of you did it? Which one of you pushed her?"

Holly gasped as the visual popped into her mind—of her mom struggling, fighting for her life . . . but not being able to save herself. The image taunted and terrified her, and she ran—from it and from her father.

She headed down the corridor that led to the employee entrance, and without stopping to grab her coat, she pushed open the door and ran out into the snow. She ran and ran but she could hear someone behind her, hear the sound of snow crunching beneath their feet, the snap of twigs breaking as they ducked under the same branches she had.

Snow drifted down, falling onto her hair and her lashes, blinding her. And the farther from the hall she got, the deeper the snow was. Her feet sank in deep, and she stumbled and fell.

Big hands closed over her shoulders. And she turned expecting to find her father over her, but it wasn't her father holding her. He must not have cared enough to go after her.

Someone else had chased her down across the estate.

A scream burned in her throat, but she never got the chance to utter it.

Chapter Twelve

From inside her room, Olivia had listened to the argument between the two men. Holly joining in had drawn Olivia out of her room and to the top of the stairs, so she'd heard and seen it all. And when Deacon had started after his daughter, she'd stopped him, her hand on his arm. "Let me go," she'd said. "She'll talk to me."

From experience, she knew that Holly would keep running from him. He must have known it, too, because he nodded in agreement. So she'd started off, but the girl was younger and faster than Olivia and had already disappeared from sight by the time Olivia pushed open the back door.

Holly had left tracks in the snow, though, so she was easy enough to follow . . . until other tracks trampled hers, bigger footprints obliterating Holly's smaller ones.

Olivia gasped in surprise. Who was chasing after the girl?

Deacon and Elijah were inside the hall still. Or even if they'd left it after she had, they wouldn't have gotten in front of her. Someone else was following Holly. Someone big . . .

Through the snow-laden boughs of a straggly pine tree,

Olivia caught sight of a dark shadow looming over the girl sprawled in the snow. Afraid for the girl, she began to push through the branches when she heard the man's voice and recognized it. Surely, he was no threat to Holly, so Olivia waited for a moment before interrupting them.

He was related to Dr. Cooke just like the security guy was. He must have been another cousin. Maybe Warren's brother. He was older, though, than all of them. His hair had quite a bit of silver mixed in with the black and snow that had fallen on it.

"Don't be scared," he told Holly. "I didn't mean to frighten you. I just saw you running away from the hall, and I wanted to know what's wrong. What's happened?"

The teenager allowed him to help her up from the snow. But when he reached out to brush it off her, she stepped back, and Olivia felt a flash of pride in the girl. She might have been impetuous to run off like she had without her jacket, but she wasn't too trusting.

But then, maybe like Olivia, she'd learned to trust no one. Not even her own father.

Holly shook her head. "Nothing. I'm fine."

"Don't lie to me," he chastised, but gently, with a soft voice. "I could always tell when your mother was lying. I was probably the only one who really knew her."

"How . . . how did you know her so well?" Holly asked, and her dark eyes narrowed with well-placed suspicion.

"We went to school together. She was my girl before your father . . ." He trailed off as if biting back what he really wanted to say. "She was mine." The possessiveness in his voice was in his eyes when he stared at Holly.

A chill chased down Olivia's spine that had nothing to do with the cold. Was this man wanting to replace the mother with the daughter?

She pushed through the branches then and called out, "Holly! There you are!"

"Olivia!" Holly exclaimed, and she tried to step around the man, but he reached out again and grasped her arms.

"Wait," he said. "You might fall again."

"I'm fine," Holly said, and she tried shrugging off his grasp, but his big hands remained wrapped around her upper arms.

"Is there a problem?" Olivia asked. And hoped like hell there wasn't. This man was so big, so strong.

And the way he looked at her chilled her even more than she'd already been. His eyes were so cold, his face so hard.

But then he tilted his head, smiled, and stepped back. "Of course not. I was just making sure she didn't fall again."

Or he'd been reluctant to let her go until he'd heard what she heard now, the murmur of voices as two men approached. From the depth of those voices and the volume, they had to be Deacon and Dr. Cooke.

"She's going to freeze out here," Olivia said, and she reached out for Holly's hand, pulling her around the man so that he no longer stood between them. The teenager's skin was icy and damp. "Let's get out of the cold."

Holly nodded, as if she couldn't speak, and maybe she couldn't. Her jaw clenched; she appeared to be trying to keep her teeth from chattering, but they snapped together anyway.

Olivia wrapped her arm around her, trying to warm her up, but since she'd run out without a jacket as well, she was also freezing. Still clutching Olivia's hand, Holly hurried away from the man who'd professed he was only helping her. They ducked beneath the pines and hurried back toward the hall, following the path forged into the snow. They hadn't walked far when Deacon and Dr. Cooke appeared.

Deacon's face was tight with concern for his daughter. The minute he saw her, he lifted a blanket he carried and wrapped it around her. "You must be freezing."

Olivia's teeth began to snap together, too. Dr. Cooke held out a blanket toward her, which she eagerly let him wrap around her. But she didn't lean into him, like Holly leaned against her father. Her entire body was shaking. With cold or with fear?

"I'll carry you back," Deacon said and reached for his daughter, to lift her.

But she jerked away from him. "No, Dad."

He flinched as if she'd slapped him. "I just want to help you," he said, his voice gruff with concern and frustration.

"You're hurt," she said. "I can walk. I'm fine." And as if to prove it, she rushed ahead of him, back toward the hall. But Deacon stuck close to her, as if unwilling to let her out of his sight again.

Olivia and Dr. Cooke followed. But then she remembered the man and glanced behind them. "Where did he go?" she asked.

"Who?" Dr. Cooke asked.

"Your cousin."

"Warren was out here?"

She shook her head. "No, the other one." She'd been introduced to him a couple of times over the past few months because he was around often. As well as having renovated the hall, he seemed to maintain it, too. She couldn't remember his name, though, but she remembered what he did. "The contractor."

Dr. Cooke tensed. "I didn't even know David was here." He glanced around now. "I don't see him."

"He was with Holly when I found her," Olivia said. "Talking to her . . ." So oddly.

Elijah sighed. "It might not be wise to share that with the sheriff right now."

"Which one of them are you protecting?" she wondered.

"Holly," he said.

She sighed now in begrudging agreement. The girl had been through enough for one day; she didn't need to witness her father arguing with yet another person.

"I have something I need to tell you," Dr. Cooke said. "Something my publicist just made me aware of . . ."

Olivia tensed, knowing she wasn't going to want to hear this.

Deacon had wanted to whisk Holly into his truck and drive her away from the hall. But she'd insisted on going inside and getting her coat and purse. So he stood in the reception area, since he'd moved his vehicle to the front lot, and waited for her and for Olivia.

He wanted to make sure that she was all right. She'd been out in the cold, too, with his daughter—going after his daughter for him. He shouldn't have wanted Olivia near Holly since that proximity alone could put his daughter in danger.

Olivia had a stalker. One who wanted her dead.

He'd asked her for time to investigate, and he'd put those letters and envelopes in his truck before he and Elijah had carried out the blankets for the women who'd run off without jackets. Something tightened in his stomach as he remembered watching Elijah wrapping that blanket around Olivia, wrapping his arms around her. She'd pulled away though—even faster than Holly had pulled away from him.

But where had Olivia gone with Elijah? The minute they'd stepped in the door, they'd disappeared somewhere. He gazed around the reception area, and just as Elijah always seemed to appear from shadows, so did Olivia. It was as if she stepped out of the wall.

Actually she ran, right up to him, and she clutched at the sleeves of his torn jacket. "I need my car," she said, her green eyes wild with fear. "I need to get out of here! Now!"

"What's wrong?" he asked with alarm. What the hell had Elijah done?

"There's a picture in an online tabloid, a picture of me *here*," she said, her voice quavering. "Now he's going to know where to find me."

"I think he already knows," Deacon said. "That's probably who took those shots at you." But how? The bridge had been closed last night. And even if he'd arrived on the island before then, how had he gotten onto the heavily guarded Halcyon Hall property?

"Then you know why I have to leave," she said. "Now!"

Deacon shook his head. "That's why you have to stay," he said. "You have to stay here, where I can protect you."

"Someone's trying to kill you," she reminded him. "You have to worry about yourself. Not me."

"I am worried about you," he said. And he reached out, cupping her cheek in his palm. Her skin was still cold from the time she'd spent outside, going after his daughter, trying to help her, trying to help him. "That's why I think you'll be safer staying here."

"I agree," Elijah said. "I'm going to step up security."

"You're firing Warren?" he asked.

Elijah glared at him. "I'm hiring more guards. They'll walk the grounds. They'll make sure no reporters get onto the property again."

"So you think that's who took the photo?" Deacon asked.

Elijah shrugged. "I can't imagine who else would . . ."

Deacon could. "It could be the stalker," he said. Maybe he'd bribed a guard. Warren? "He's taken all those other photos of you. He's trying to flush you out, to scare you off of Bane Island. That's why you need to stay."

Was that what all those other photos had been intended to do? To scare her into running away? To isolate her from everyone who could help her? Deacon couldn't let that happen again. "You need to let me investigate," he urged her. "You said you would . . ." He still held her face in his palm and stroked his thumb along her cheekbone.

She expelled a shaky sigh and nodded. "Okay, but just a little longer."

"You're staying!" Holly exclaimed.

Deacon jerked his hand away from Olivia's face and stepped back. He hadn't even been aware that his daughter had joined them. How the hell was he going to keep Olivia safe when she so easily distracted him?

He looked over her head to Elijah. "You can get that extra security in right away?"

Cooke nodded. "Yes, I'll increase the shifts of the ones who live on the island, in case the bridge is shut down again."

"Extra security for what?" Holly asked.

"You're not the only one who knows who I am," Olivia told her. "Somebody took a photo of me and sold it to an online tabloid."

Holly tensed and blurted out, "It wasn't me. I swear!"

Her defensiveness startled Deacon. Her mother used to do that—deny doing something before an accusation had even been made. Like the cheating.

Deacon glanced at his daughter, wondering if she would have taken a photo and sold it in the hopes of making enough money to successfully run away from Bane Island and him.

Holly must have sensed his suspicion because she turned toward him and shook her head. "Of course you would think I did it! You always think the worst of me!" Tears shimmered in her eyes, and she turned and ran out the doors Elijah must have opened for her.

Holly's whole life he'd had to chase after her—to make sure she didn't get hurt or hurt herself.

He started after her, but Olivia caught his arm. "Go easy on her," she advised. "She's shaken up . . . a lot."

"She could have been shot," Deacon agreed. That had shaken him, too, to his core.

Olivia smiled at him. "She was shaken over how close she came to losing you."

"Would she have even cared?" he wondered aloud and sighed at his self-pity.

"Of course she would have," Olivia assured him.

Warmth flooded his heart with hope. He appreciated her trying to reassure him. He appreciated her kindness as well as her beauty. "Be careful," he told her.

She nodded. "You, too."

The temptation to lean down, to brush his mouth across hers, overwhelmed him, but he fought it. He had no right to kiss her.

"I can't believe you did that!" Holly yelled at him the minute he joined her in the truck. He'd left it running, when he'd left the stalker evidence in it, so it would be warmed up for his daughter. Now he was surprised she hadn't taken off without him. "I can't believe you . . ."

Kissed a celebrity?

No. She didn't know about that, but she must have seen him touch her. His fingers tingled yet from the contact with Olivia's icy smooth skin.

"You made her think that I betrayed her," Holly said.

"What?"

"You looked at me that way you did this morning . . ." She shuddered. "Like you think I'm a bad person, like I would run you down." Her voice cracked, and her shoulders began to shake with sobs.

He reached across the console to put his arm around her, but she jerked away, plastering herself against the passenger door. He didn't want her to jump out, so he clicked the locks and shifted into Drive. He needed to get her away from the hall. "I know you wouldn't have done anything to hurt me. I'm so sorry for implying that you might."

She glanced over at him then, as if surprised that he would apologize. Her shock made him realize that he hadn't often done that to her or to anyone else. But then he wasn't often as wrong as he'd been that morning.

"I am sorry," he repeated. "I know you're not a bad person." But sometimes good people did bad things. He didn't share that with her, though. He suspected she already knew.

"I wouldn't betray Olivia either," she insisted. "I wouldn't let anyone know she's on the island."

"Good," he said. "She's in danger."

Holly shook her head. "I . . . I don't think somebody meant to shoot at her."

He glanced over at her. "Do you think somebody meant to shoot you?"

She shrugged. "I think it's me . . . that I'm the reason you and Olivia were both hurt."

He reached over to squeeze her arm. "No, honey, this has nothing to do with you. Nobody wants to hurt you."

Tension gripped him with the realization: that might have been why the package had been delivered to his dad's—so that Holly wouldn't accidentally be injured. And while Olivia had been shot at, none of the bullets had come close to Holly. He had a feeling that had been more luck than intent, though.

"Olivia has a stalker," he told her.

Holly gasped. "That's why she's here!"

"Yes," he said. "That's why nobody should have found out she's here."

"Did you know?" she asked. "Did you always know who she is?"

He shook his head, and a smile tugged at the corners of his mouth. "I should have with as much as you play her music."

"I love her," Holly said.

And he didn't think she was talking about just the music now. "You don't know her," he reminded his daughter, and himself.

Maybe her stalker was just some crazed fan who wanted to scare her. Or maybe Olivia had hurt someone so badly that the person wanted revenge.

Maybe she wasn't as sweet and innocent as she seemed. Maybe she had a whole lot of reasons for hiding out on Bane Island and a whole lot of people who wanted her dead.

* * *

"You have a visitor," Evelyn said, sounding as shocked as Edie was that someone had actually requested to see her.

Edie stood up from the dining room table where she'd been working. "Are you sure?" she asked.

Usually people avoided her; they didn't seek her out.

Just like Elijah Cooke kept avoiding her calls and requests for interviews. He'd sicced his publicist on her, who'd made it very clear Edie would never be allowed on the property of Halcyon Hall.

What were they trying to hide?

Olivia Smith? She'd left a message for her, too, but had received no reply. The message probably hadn't even gotten to Olivia or whatever her name really was.

"Who is it?" she asked.

Evelyn shrugged. "I don't know. I didn't know I was your personal secretary. Why don't you go to the parlor and find out yourself?"

Edie smiled at her landlady's *graciousness*. "Thank you. I will."

Evelyn headed toward the kitchen then stopped and turned back. "Do you want tea or coffee or anything?"

Edie's smile widened. Even though Evelyn didn't particularly like her, caring for others was so deeply ingrained in her character that she couldn't help but take care of Edie as well.

"I'll check with my guest," Edie suggested.

Evelyn nodded. "I'll get some cookies ready or some cake. She looks like she could use something to eat."

Even more curious, Edie rushed to the parlor. The pocket doors had been left partially open, and through them Edie could see her guest standing in front of the fire. When Edie pushed them open the rest of the way, their rattling startled the person into whirling around, her eyes wide with fear.

How had Evelyn even been able to tell that Edie's visitor was a woman? A big jacket dwarfed the person's body, and a hood shadowed the face, leaving only the bright eyes visible.

Recognition pulled at Edie; she knew this person from somewhere . . .

"How much did you get paid to do it?" the visitor asked.

And despite the raspiness of the voice, she was definitely female. The voice was nearly as familiar as the face, the mouth . . .

"To do what?" Edie asked. "Nobody's paying me." She mostly freelanced because she liked being her own boss and pursuing only the stories that interested her. She had a feeling that once she got the story ready about Bainesworth Manor, she would have networks and papers fighting over it, though.

The woman snorted. "Yeah, right. I know how much tabloids pay for pictures of me. A lot."

The hood finally slid back, falling away from her face, and the identity registered with Edie. "AKAN. You're that singer."

She snorted again. "Yeah, like you didn't know that. You called the hall this morning and asked for me."

"This morning?" Edie chuckled as finally everything clicked into place. "You're Olivia Smith."

"Stop pretending!" the woman yelled. "You aren't fooling me."

"I don't want to," Edie said. "And while I like your music, I rarely interview celebrities." Politicians. Judges. Activists. She didn't waste her time with singers, actors, or reality stars. There were too many of them and too many other people trying to cover them.

"Then why did you call and ask for me?"

"Because I want to get onto the estate," she admitted. "I want to talk to people about Bainesworth Manor."

"I don't know anything about Bainesworth Manor," Olivia said.

"Then you must not listen to the locals, to what they all say about it . . ."

"I mean, of course I've heard things, but I don't personally know anything."

"I know," Edie said. "I wasn't going to interview you. I just wanted to get through that damn gate."

Olivia pulled a rolled-up sheet of paper from her parka pocket. She unrolled it and showed the printout of some online rag to Edie. There was an article about AKAN being in rehab alongside a grainy photograph of her. "You got on the grounds somehow. There's no way this was taken from the other side of the gate."

Edie studied the picture. "I don't know. Looks like it could have been taken from a distance. But I didn't do it. I don't run around snapping pictures to sell. I'm not a paparazzo. I'm a serious journalist."

She expected the woman to snort again, but something else had drawn her interest. She moved away from the fire and stepped around Edie. Maybe Evelyn had brought the food she'd promised.

Olivia Smith was so tiny that she could understand the older woman wanting to feed her. There was also something quite vulnerable about her, something that made her seem childlike.

But the word that slipped through her lips wasn't one a child would use. It wasn't about the food. She hadn't even glanced at the doorway through which Evelyn would come. She was staring out the window instead.

"I must have been followed," she murmured.

Edie turned toward the window, too, wondering what the other woman saw through the sheer curtain and the darkness. But Edie saw nothing but a faint flash before she was thrown—hard—to the ground.

Chapter Thirteen

"You really don't want your picture taken," the reporter remarked from where she lay on the floor beneath Olivia.

When Olivia had seen that flash, she'd worried that it was a gun, which was why she had thrown Edie and herself to the ground. But the glass didn't shatter like her rear window had. "Do you think it was just someone with a camera?" Olivia asked.

"Isn't that what you think?" the woman asked.

Edie Stone.

That was her name. And as she'd stated, she wasn't a paparazzo; she was a serious journalist. She had a reputation for exposing scandals, but those usually involved politicians and CEOs. Even serious journalists needed to pay their bills, though. That was why Olivia had figured she'd taken the photo. But now Olivia realized, she had not.

"I . . . I . . ." She didn't know what to admit—not to a reporter. That was why she'd always avoided the press as much as possible; she never knew what to say to them because every word was usually twisted into some other context.

"You can talk to me off the record," Edie said. "I'm not

interested in a story about you. I'm focusing on the hall, on what happened when the place was Bainesworth Manor."

A gasp drew their attention to the doorway and the woman who stood there holding a tray. She wasn't alone, and she probably wasn't the one who'd gasped. Another woman stood behind her, as if hiding. Her eyes, a strange cloudy blue, were wide with fear. "It's cursed," she said. "It's cursed." Then she turned and fled.

"What's going on?" the woman with the tray asked.

Olivia jumped to her feet. "I'm sorry. I thought I saw something outside the window and . . ."

"You knocked Edie to the ground to protect her?"

She hadn't wanted the reporter to take a bullet that would have been meant for her. But then she remembered that conversation she'd overheard between Dr. Cooke and his publicist. Maybe the bullet wouldn't have been meant for Olivia this time. But no gun had gone off. She'd over-reacted then, just as she'd probably overreacted to that conversation she'd overheard.

Before Olivia could say anything, the woman continued, "She's going to need a lot more protection than you if she keeps going after Bainesworth Manor."

So the sheriff wasn't the only one who had an issue with Halcyon Hall and the people who ran it. When Olivia had arrived on the island months ago, she'd driven through town without stopping. The only locals to whom she'd spoken had been the ones who worked at the hall. Clearly the sheriff wasn't as paranoid as Dr. Cooke had made him sound.

Edie had gotten up from the floor, too, and she crossed the room to take the tray from the older lady. "I'm perfectly safe, Evelyn."

Rosemary had told her it was Evelyn Pierce who owned

and ran the boarding house. Since Whit had picked up Rosemary from the hall, the shrink had loaned her rental car to Olivia. She'd thought about using it to leave the island, but, as the sheriff kept warning, the bridge had been shut down for the night. Rosemary and Whit had gone into town—such as it was—with Genevieve for dinner.

Olivia's stomach rumbled at the aroma of cinnamon and vanilla drifting from the tray that Edie placed on a coffee table in front of a small, Victorian sofa.

"She is hungry," Evelyn said almost as if in triumph to the reporter.

Edie smiled. "You always think everybody's hungry. Just because you haven't seen someone all day doesn't mean they haven't eaten all day."

"I actually don't think I have . . . ," Olivia murmured. And she suddenly felt so weak that her legs almost buckled beneath her.

Edie must have noticed because she caught her arm and led her to the couch.

"I'll get you something more than cookies then," Evelyn said. "How about soup? Rosemary loves my soup."

Before Olivia could say anything, the older woman bustled off.

"I love your soup, too!" Edie yelled after her.

Olivia thought she heard a chuckle.

"She doesn't love me," the reporter admitted. "She hates that I want to investigate Bainesworth Manor."

"Why are you?" Olivia asked. "Is it because of the body the sheriff found?"

"It's not the only one he's found there," Edie said.

Olivia shuddered. "I know. There was his wife's as well . . ." She couldn't imagine how difficult that must have been for him. No wonder he and his daughter had such a strained relationship; they'd been through so much. "You're not going to exploit that, are you?"

"I was actually talking about the body he found there when he was a kid," Edie said. "But his wife's death certainly makes the place look as cursed as Bonita thinks it is."

Bonita must have been the woman who'd run off.

"He found a body when he was a kid?" Olivia asked, horrified over how hard that must have been for him.

Edie shrugged. "That's the rumor. I haven't talked to him about that yet. And I haven't been able to find out much about that body. Or this most recent one, but there were others."

"With all these deaths, why are you so determined to get on the property?" Olivia asked.

Edie smiled. "Because I want to know the truth about it—about what really happened to those girls who'd been committed there. I want to know everything about Bainesworth Manor and the Bainesworth family." Her voice vibrated with her excitement.

"I can't help you with any of that," Olivia said.

"Will you try?" Edie asked. "If I help you?"

"How can you help me?" Olivia asked. The sheriff had already promised to find her stalker. Not that she trusted he would, not that she trusted anyone.

"I can find out where this photo came from," Edie said as she dropped the paper onto the table next to the tray. "Find out who took it and sold it. I have contacts all over the place."

A ragged sigh of relief slipped through Olivia's lips.

She hadn't expected to find an ally in a reporter. "Thank you."

"It really rattled you," Edie remarked, and she ran her hand over her shoulder, which might have ached from striking the hardwood floor. "I thought I saw a flash, too, but it could have just been the reflection of one of the lights in this room. I don't think anyone's out there. Do you?"

"I didn't think the flash was a camera," Olivia admitted. "I thought it was a gun."

Edie's eyes narrowed as she stared at her. "That's a hell of an assumption to make. Why would you?"

"I have my reasons . . . ," she murmured, and she wasn't sure she wanted to share them with a reporter. A shooting and a stalker might interest a serious journalist. To stall for time, she reached for a cookie. It was soft and warm and when she put it in her mouth, it seemed to melt on her tongue with an explosion of cinnamon and vanilla and nutmeg.

"Don't spoil your dinner," Evelyn admonished as she carried in another tray. This one bore two big crockery bowls with steam rising from them. "Crab and corn chowder," she said as she put it on the table in front of Olivia.

"You didn't need to go to all this trouble."

Evelyn made a tsking noise. "It was already made. Just had to heat it up." She'd heated up a lot and had added a plate of cornbread as well. "There's another bowl," she pointed out to her boarder. "You can have some, too."

Edie smiled. "Thank you for the gracious offer. Should I check for arsenic?"

Evelyn chuckled. "Don't bother. You must have built up a resistance to it by now."

Instead of being offended, the reporter laughed, and Olivia found her own lips curving into a smile. "I think you're wrong," she told Edie once Evelyn left the room again.

"About what?" She leaned forward and sniffed the bowl. "That I should still check for arsenic?"

"That she doesn't love you," Olivia said.

"Oh, I know I'm not that easy to love," Edie admitted.

Olivia could relate; she'd felt that way her entire life. She'd grown up with no love or even kindness. Appreciating the landlady's efforts for her, Olivia dug into the soup and cornbread. Finally, she felt warm and full but not so full that she didn't reach for another cookie after finishing the soup. As she leaned forward, the photo caught her attention again. And she found herself commenting without thinking, "The shooting must have happened just a short while after this was taken . . ."

Because Holly wasn't in the picture yet, but Olivia's guitar case and backpack hung from her fingertips. So this would have been during her second trip to her vehicle.

"What the hell? You were shot at!" Edie exclaimed. "That's why you thought that flash was a gun! Who do you think shot at you?"

She uttered a ragged sigh. "I wish I knew." Who the hell had been stalking her for those six months of her tour? Could it have been . . . ?

Had *he* found her? Had he figured out who she was?

"You didn't see anyone then?" Edie asked.

She hadn't seen anything but Holly and then that exploding glass. Thank God the girl hadn't been hurt, too—because of her. She shook her head. "It all happened so fast. I couldn't even tell where the shots were coming from. Dr. Cooke thinks it was a hunter who accidentally fired in the wrong direction."

"Of course he does," Edie replied, her voice sharp with

indignation. "He wants to believe everything that happens there is an accident."

"It could have been," Olivia said in defense of him. "Or it could have been my stalker."

Edie cursed. "That's why you're here—on the island. You're hiding and not just from the paparazzi."

Olivia hadn't been hiding just from them, though. She had been hiding from what her life had become, from how it had gotten away from her. She had no more control over it now than she'd had when she was a kid. She needed to take back control . . . from everyone.

Including Sheriff Deacon Howell . . .

"Nice of you to come check on your old man after nearly getting him blown up," Sam Howell said from the hospital bed next to the fireplace in his living room.

Except for one boarded-up window, the cottage had withstood the blast amazingly well. Helen, too, had assured him that she was fine when she'd let him in the door seconds ago. Now she squeezed his arm and whispered, "He was scared . . . for you . . ."

Deacon raised a brow in skepticism. His father didn't sound scared at all; he sounded just like his ornery self, which meant he was fine. But Deacon knew he'd needed to check on them, so after bringing Holly home, and making certain the house was safe—he'd come here.

Fortunately, the state police had still been processing the scene, so he'd been able to pass off his bag of evidence of Olivia's stalker for them to process for prints and DNA.

"Sorry it's taken me so long to get back out here," Deacon said. "But I was kind of busy after actually getting blown up."

"If you'd actually been blown up, you wouldn't be here at all," Sam said. "You got lucky."

"So did you," Deacon said. "You wanted me to open that damn box in the cottage. You'd wanted to see what was inside it."

Sam shrugged his bony shoulders. "I've been living on borrowed time for a while now, boy. Wouldn't hurt my feelings if the loan got called in."

Loan . . .

The word struck a strange chord within Deacon, and he moved closer to the bed. "Talking about debts, you still owe anyone anything?"

Sam snorted. "Once I got the diagnosis, I got my affairs in order—before you even deemed to come home. What about you? You got your affairs in order?"

"You think I have a death sentence, too?"

"I think you have a death wish," his dad said. "That's why you keep going after the Bainesworths."

Deacon sighed. "I'm doing my job, Dad. Something you should have done instead of looking the other way."

"You shouldn't be worried about your job," Sam said. "You should be worried about your life."

He was, but he wasn't about to admit that to his father. He didn't know with whom he could share his fears; he didn't have anyone in his life, anyone who cared about him. Unless Olivia was right, unless Holly actually did care more about him than she acted, but he couldn't dump his problems on his daughter. "My job is my life," Deacon admitted—with a pang of sadness about the realization.

"That little girl should be your life," his dad admonished him.

Deacon smiled. "She's not exactly little anymore."

"I wouldn't know," Sam said. "She doesn't come around here."

She didn't want to, and just as Deacon had decided not to force her to quit working at the hall, he'd decided not to force her to visit her grandfather, either.

"She resents you," Deacon admitted.

"Guess that's something you two have in common."

Deacon chuckled. "Guess it is. She resents you as the reason for us moving here." Away from her friends, away from the city she'd loved.

Maybe it wouldn't be such a bad thing if he lost the reelection . . .

Maybe then he could bring Holly back to where she'd once been happy. He hadn't been happy there, though, because Shannon hadn't been happy. She hadn't been happy anywhere. That was why he'd accepted her death as a suicide; it had made sense . . . until he'd found that other body.

"I just called to let you know I didn't have long," Sam said. "I didn't ask you to come back here. I know this place has never been good for you. That you've had this damn obsession about the Bainesworths ever since you were a kid."

"Ever since I found that body," Deacon said.

Sam sighed. "Coroner never determined her cause of death. Could have been an overdose and her drug buddies dropped her body at the manor. Or maybe it was a suicide. It was so long ago. You always tried to make it out to be more, and you're doing the same thing now."

"I'm doing my job now," Deacon maintained, "which is what you should have done when you'd had the position. You should have protected the innocent instead of the Bainesworths."

Sam sighed and leaned back against his pillows. "I was

trying to protect you." He shook his head. "But you just refuse to back off."

"Do you know who left that package for me here?" Deacon asked. "Do you know who tried to kill me?"

Sam shook his head again. "Of course not."

But he could guess; the same way Deacon could guess. His father knew the Bainesworths probably even better than Deacon did.

"I just know they're going to keep trying until they succeed," his father said. "You never should have come back here."

Deacon couldn't argue with him about that. Since returning to Bane Island, he'd lost everything. His wife. His daughter's love. And now someone was trying to take his life.

Holly lay on her back on the living room couch, staring at the ceiling. Listening to the silence . . .

Where is he?

Dad had said he was just going to check in on Grandpa and then he'd be back. She should have gone with him, probably would have gone with him had he asked. But he hadn't asked.

Had he just assumed she'd say no? Or hadn't he wanted her along?

He'd barely said anything to her after they'd talked about Olivia. Did he still think that she might have tried to kill him? That she'd taken that photo of Olivia?

Did Olivia think that, too? Holly was one of the only people who'd actually realized who she was, who would have known that tabloids would buy a photograph of her. But she'd known that Olivia would leave if the press figured out where she was staying, and she didn't want Olivia to leave. Then Holly would go back to being alone. So alone . . .

Usually, when Dad was home, Holly locked herself in her room. But when he was gone, she hung out in the living room, so she could see when his lights hit the front window.

It was dark outside, though.

She got up from the couch and walked into the kitchen. All the lights were on; he'd left them on when he'd searched the place before letting her come inside.

Her dad was in danger.

She knew that he'd probably been in danger before because of his job. Back home, he'd been a detective in a major city, so it would have been more dangerous. But he'd never gotten a scratch on him in Portland.

But here . . .

He had so many scratches and bruises now. Was that why he wasn't back yet? Had somebody tried again to kill him?

She shuddered but shook her head. No. He was probably just at work—like he always was. She glanced at the hooks by the door to the garage. Usually the keys dangled from them, but they were gone. He'd taken her car keys. She shouldn't have been surprised. Maybe he thought she'd go out to the hall and use Warren's vehicle again.

Like that had ever happened.

She wasn't going to be stranded here, held prisoner in her own home. He hadn't grounded her or anything.

She could leave. And she damn well intended to.

This time she grabbed her coat and gloves before she headed out. And this time, she hoped she didn't run into anyone from the hall—not even Olivia. She wouldn't be able to face her now. She didn't want to see that same suspicion in her eyes that she'd seen in her father's.

Holly had to think, and she couldn't do it in the house where she'd lived with her dad and mom, where the echo of so many arguments still hung in the air. She'd thought her dad had driven her mom to kill herself.

But what if her mom had been murdered . . . just like someone was now trying to murder her dad? Did someone have it out for her family? Was that why those shots had been fired this morning—not at Olivia, but at her?

Chapter Fourteen

All the lights were on, illuminating the empty house through the slats in the open blinds. Nobody moved around inside the ranch home despite the sound of the doorbell echoing within it as she held her finger against the button next to the front door. Where were they?

It was late—so late that Olivia wondered if anyone would let her back inside the hall. Not that she really wanted to go back there . . .

But with the bridge shut down, she couldn't leave Bane Island. She'd been offered a room at the boarding house, but she hadn't wanted to stay there—hadn't wanted to put anyone else in danger because of her stalker.

She glanced behind her, peering in the darkness for another flash. Had someone followed her here? She'd driven around the island for a while before coming here, to the address Evelyn Pierce had given her for the sheriff's house. She probably shouldn't have come here either. She didn't want to risk putting Holly in danger again. Or the sheriff . . .

But she didn't glimpse anyone moving around in the darkness. Maybe she had managed to lose whoever had been following her. Or maybe he'd just gotten more careful at not revealing his presence.

Either way, she needed to leave. But as she headed to the vehicle she'd borrowed from Rosemary, light suddenly blinded her. A truck pulled into Deacon's driveway, blocking her borrowed car from leaving. Blocking Olivia from leaving . . .

She could have left on foot; she could have run off in the darkness. But she had a feeling she knew who'd pulled into the driveway . . . because her pulse quickened and her skin tingled from more than the frigid cold.

The lights snapped off, plunging her momentarily into darkness, until the driver's door opened. Light spilled out of the interior onto the driveway, onto the man who slid out from behind the steering wheel. He moved slowly, and a grunt slipped out of his lips as if just standing hurt. And maybe it did—after what he'd been through.

"Are you okay?" she asked.

He nodded. "Yeah, just a little sore." And from how his brow furrowed when he looked at her, he was also confused. "How did you get here? Oh, that's Rosemary's car. Why are you here? You're supposed to be at the hall—where Elijah promised to keep you safe."

Her lips curved into a smile, and she teased him, "You must not be well if you finally believe him."

"I didn't say I believed him," he said. "I just know how hard it is to get inside that place. It wouldn't be easy for your stalker." He glanced around. "As easy as it would be for him to get to you out here . . ."

"I made sure I wasn't followed," she assured him. At least she'd made sure she wasn't followed from the boarding house to his house. When she'd left, Edie had walked outside with her, and they hadn't found any tracks in the snow around the house. She must have imagined that flash. Or maybe the person had just been standing farther away than they'd checked. But it had been so cold and the wind was blowing so hard that they'd kept their search short.

"Has something happened?" he asked. "Has there been another incident, or accident, as Elijah likes to claim?"

She shook her head. If she told him about the incident at the boarding house, he would admonish her for taking the chance she had, and she was done with other people controlling her life. That was why she was here.

But before she could tell him, he asked, "Are you here to check on me? Or on Holly?"

That wasn't her reason, but she had been worried . . . about Holly. About Deacon . . .

"She's not here," Olivia told him.

"Of course she is," Deacon said. He shut the truck door, plunging them into darkness again.

Before her eyes could adjust, a hand closed over her arm, and the sheriff guided her toward the narrow front porch on his house. The light from inside spilled onto that porch and onto them.

"She's not here," Olivia repeated. "I've been ringing the bell and knocking, but nobody came to the door."

"She's probably locked in her room with her music so loud she didn't hear you," he said. His lips curved into a slight grin as he unlocked his front door. "Hell, it's probably your music she's listening to."

Olivia's heart warmed with pride and gratitude that people appreciated her work—her art. Without it, she wouldn't have survived, but because of it, she might not survive either, unless the sheriff made good on his promise to find her stalker and stop him.

Deacon pushed open the front door, but only an eerie

silence greeted them. "Maybe she fell asleep," he murmured, and, with Olivia following him, he rushed across the living room, down a short hall to a closed door. He pushed open that door and cursed.

The room was a mess with clothes and food wrappers all over the floor. The bed was unmade, the sheets tangled. Maybe Holly cleaned so much at the hall that she didn't want to do any cleaning at home. Or maybe she was being a slob as just another way to spite her father, like how she worked at the hall to spite him.

"I told you—she's not here," Olivia said.

Deacon moved faster now, running from room to room, pushing open doors and turning on lights. "Holly!" he yelled.

Olivia caught his arm. "Calm down. If she can hear you, she won't come out."

"You're right," he said.

"About calming down?"

He shook his head, clearly irritated with her. "She's not here. Damn it! She ran away again."

"Again?"

"She's always so angry with me," he said. "She hates me."

"I don't think so," she said.

"Well, she's not here," he said, waving his arm around the empty living room. "She must have found where I hid her damn car keys." He walked through the kitchen and pushed open the door between it and the garage. Then his big body stiffened. "The car's here."

"If she ran away, she probably had a friend pick her up," Olivia said.

"Holly doesn't have any friends," he said. "She refused to try to make any because she doesn't want to be here."

Olivia suspected that she'd deliberately isolated herself. "That makes it easier to run away," she mused, "when the only people you're leaving are the ones who hurt you."

"I haven't hurt my daughter." He groaned and rubbed a hand over his bruised face. "At least not deliberately. But I did hurt her today." His dark eyes shimmered as if tears were rushing to the surface. "No wonder she ran away again . . ."

Olivia didn't want to add to his pain, but her own fears rushed over her. "On foot, in the dark, if you're right and nobody picked her up. We need to look for her." While it had stopped snowing—for the moment—it was still freezing outside.

Deacon was already heading across the garage to the side door. Before he opened it, he grabbed a couple of flashlights from a shelf and handed one to her. Holly must have gone out that door because there were tracks in the snow that had yet to be shoveled away from it.

But unlike last time Olivia had followed her, there were no other tracks obliterating hers. "At least she's alone," she murmured.

"What do you mean?" Deacon asked.

And she remembered that she hadn't told him about the contractor and that Dr. Cooke had recommended she not mention his cousin to the sheriff. Should she tell him now?

With their flashlights shining on the sidewalk, they followed her tracks to the end of the block . . . until they disappeared into the street. They didn't find any on the other side. "She must have had someone pick her up," Olivia said.

"But who?" he asked. "I told you she has no friends."

"Someone from the hall?" she suggested. And she knew

she needed to tell him about David Cooke, but before she could say anything else, his cell rang.

"Is it Holly?" she asked.

He shook his head. "But I should take it . . ."

And when he was through, she would let him know that the last time she'd found Holly, the teenager hadn't been alone. David Cooke had found her first. She hoped the contractor hadn't gotten to her again. He'd acted so strange with the girl, so possessive. At least Holly had seemed as creeped out as Olivia had been, but if she really wanted to spite her father, taking off with one of his enemies would hurt him more than anything else would. He probably wouldn't be the only one who wound up getting hurt, though.

Deacon breathed a sigh of relief. "She's safe," he assured Olivia, his cell phone pressed yet to his ear. "She got a ride."

Olivia tensed. "With whom?"

"Rosemary, Whit, and Genevieve picked her up along this street."

Olivia's breath shuddered out in a sigh of relief that hung, as a white cloud, in the air between them. It was cold and dark, but Olivia had not protested searching for his daughter. She'd willingly participated. She cared. Maybe too much for a stranger to care, but she'd bonded with his daughter—maybe through their mutual love of her music.

Rosemary's voice drew his attention back to the cell phone pressed to his ear. "Deacon?"

"Thank you for picking her up," he said. "I'll come get her."

"Uh, she's very upset," Rosemary said. "She wants to stay here for tonight."

"I can't impose—"

"You were nearly blown up today," Rosemary said. "Maybe it would be best if she stayed here."

"Because being with me puts her in danger," he murmured.

"That's not what I'm saying, Deacon," Rosemary assured him. "I think you've been through a lot, and you can use a break from her teenage angst for the night."

"She's my daughter, my responsibility," Deacon said.

"Then do what's best for her," Rosemary said.

"Stay away from her?" Deacon asked. "Is that what you're telling me to do? You're not like . . ."—he glanced at Olivia—"Ms. Smith. You don't believe that I'm hurting her, do you?" What the hell was his daughter telling people? How much did she hate him?

"I'm not advising you to let her stay here because I'm worried about *you* hurting her," Rosemary said.

Deacon gasped as he realized what his friend was implying. "You don't think she tried to kill me?"

"I think you need a break," she said.

Maybe he needed to listen to the psychologist.

"Just for tonight," he said. With the way his head was pounding, he could do with a night off from slamming doors and loud music. "I'll get her in the morning—for school."

"Okay," Rosemary said. "Now get some rest."

"Thank you," Deacon said, and he clicked off his cell.

"Rosemary?" Olivia asked.

He nodded.

"You like her," she said.

"She's a good person who's been through a lot," Deacon

said. He respected her. At one time he'd even thought
he might be attracted to her, but what he'd felt for the
psychologist didn't compare to what he felt for Olivia
Smith. The celebrity . . .

Like there was a chance of that going anywhere.

Since he hadn't been able to keep his small-town high
school sweetheart happy, he had no chance with a world-
famous woman like Olivia. "I'm sorry," he said.

"About liking Rosemary?"

"About . . ." He lifted his hand and let it drop back to
his side. "About the craziness." He pushed his hand
through his hair, which was getting damp from the snowflakes melting in it. He hadn't even realized it was snowing
again, but then, it was dark but for the beam of the flashlights they'd trained on the ground. His house was just
enough outside of town that it was beyond where the
streetlamps were.

"I'm used to craziness," she murmured with a shiver.

"You must be freezing," he said, and he took her arm,
making sure she didn't slip on the snowy driveway as he
guided her past their vehicles to the house. He pushed
open the front door and led her inside where at least it was
warm—although it couldn't be what she was used to, given
her fame and success.

She probably lived in mansions, and when she wasn't
living in mansions, she stayed in places as opulent as
Halcyon Hall. There was nothing opulent about Deacon's
house. Like his father's cabin, the living room had knotty
pine walls and wide pine floors. A leather couch and chair
filled the space between the exterior wall, the fireplace
above which the TV hung, and the archway into the eat-in
kitchen. Throw rugs, brightly colored curtains, and pillows
softened the coldness of all the wood and leather.

Shannon had hated the unassuming ranch house. She'd hated everything about it—mostly that she'd had to share it with him. And with Holly.

She'd never been the mother Holly deserved. Hell, he'd never been the father she'd needed either.

As if she'd read his mind, Olivia reached out and touched his hand. "She doesn't hate you."

"Then why does she keep running away from me?" he asked. "You don't run away from someone you love."

"Sometimes you do," Olivia said.

He tilted his head and studied her face. "Sounds like you know what you're talking about . . ." And it sounded like she was a runner, just like Holly and Shannon.

She shrugged, and as if to escape his gaze, she walked over to the fireplace. Or maybe she only needed to warm up because she held out her hands toward the fire. Holly must have started one before she'd left.

He suspected that Rosemary Tulle wasn't the only woman he knew who'd had a tough life. Olivia Smith, or whatever her real name was, had had one, too—probably even before her stalker had started threatening her. Maybe even fame and fortune couldn't buy happiness.

She confirmed his suspicion when she said, "Sometimes the people we love treat us the worst."

"I don't treat Holly badly," he said. "I don't know why she led you to believe that I do."

Olivia turned back around then and admitted, "I probably leaped to my own conclusions."

"Why?" he asked. "Experience?"

She shrugged again. "Something like that . . ."

"A person can listen to your songs and figure out that you've been through a lot," he reminded her.

She sighed. "That was a long time ago."

"When you were Holly's age?"

"Younger even," she admitted.

And his heart clenched with the pain she must have felt, must have endured.

"I was younger than she is when I ran away," she said. "Fourteen."

"Why?" he asked. "Is it like your songs—were you being hurt?"

She nodded.

"Oh, God, Olivia . . ." He wanted to embrace her, but she stood before him with her arms wrapped tightly around herself, as if they were the only things holding her together. "I'm so sorry."

She shook her head. "Not your fault . . ."

"Didn't you report the abuse?"

She nodded. "But nobody believed me. I was just a hysterical teenager who cut my arms and had mental problems—"

"Your mother—"

"Backed up his lies," she said. "Maybe because if she didn't, he would have killed her. Maybe he did . . ." She released a shaky breath. "Once I ran away, I never went back."

"How did you live?" he asked. "Where did you go?"

"I grew up in Florida," she said. "So it wasn't too cold to live on the streets. Though, if I got scared, I'd stay in shelters. A few times the police and social workers placed me in foster homes." She shuddered. "I had to run away from those, too."

Obviously, they hadn't been any better than the situation at home from which she'd escaped.

"Could your father have found you now?" he asked. "Could he be your stalker?"

She shuddered. "I've wondered . . ." She shook her head. "But I've been gone so long."

"But you're super successful now," he said. "Isn't that when people from your past show up, wanting something from you. Money. Favors."

She shook her head. "I haven't had people from my past show up, because I've been so careful to conceal my identity—even when I'm performing."

Clearly she didn't want to consider that the monster from her past might be the one threatening her present. He needed to ask her more questions about her father, like his name and where Deacon could find him. Because he intended to find him . . .

But she looked so fragile right now, so ready to break if she had any more problems to deal with. And he kept giving her those problems.

"I'm sorry that you're getting caught in the middle between me and my daughter," he said, knowing that it was probably just something else she would run away from—because it was complicated and messy.

Everything about his life was.

"You shouldn't be here," he told her. "But since you are . . ." He reached out then, wrapped an arm around her and pulled her up against him. Then he lowered his head and kissed her.

How the hell had he failed again? The first time Deacon had moved fast enough that only the mirror had clipped him.

But the bomb . . .

Snippets of wire and a couple of components left over

from another device littered the work bench in front of him. This one would be bigger.

So Deacon wouldn't be able to survive. He would not escape relatively unscathed as he had the previous two times. Those attempts had to have rattled and distracted him.

But was it the attempts on his life that had rattled him? Or was it the woman?

Either way, that distraction was going to prove Deacon Howell's downfall. Because he wouldn't move as quickly; he wouldn't be able to escape again. This time Deacon would die.

Chapter Fifteen

Rosemary stepped through the open pocket doors and back into the parlor where Holly sat on one of the small sofas with Genevieve. "Your father said it's okay for you to stay here tonight," she shared.

"Sure he did," Holly replied. "He will probably feel safer without me in the house."

"What do you mean?" Rosemary asked.

"He thought I tried running him over last night," she said. "He probably thinks I tried blowing him up today."

"Did you?" Genevieve asked.

Her dark eyes wide with horror, Holly turned toward the slightly older teen. "What?"

"Well, all you say is how much you hate him, and you keep running away . . ." Genevieve shrugged. "How can you blame him for thinking you might be trying to get away from him for good?"

Tears shimmered in Holly's eyes, pulling compassion from Rosemary who started to move closer. But Genevieve discreetly waved her back. Obviously, she had a reason for being so rough on the teenager. And maybe as a teenager herself, she knew best how to reach the girl.

"But . . . but . . . I wouldn't do that . . . ," Holly murmured. "I don't want to hurt him."

"Yes, you do," Genevieve said. "Why else do you work at the place he hates?"

A pang jabbed Rosemary's heart, and Genevieve's question reminded her of her own choices. Was her insistence on staying on at the hall, on the island, hurting her daughter?

But as if she sensed the question, Genevieve turned toward Rosemary and shook her head. Then she turned back to Holly and told her, "It's not like you're helping out the guests there."

That pang in Rosemary's heart turned into a flood of warmth. Her daughter understood and appreciated what she did—that she was trying to help people, like she hadn't been able to help herself and her daughter when she'd needed to.

Genevieve obviously didn't appreciate Holly Howell, as she continued, "You're just cleaning up after them. It's not like that's the only place you can work on the island. I just got a job at the bookstore in town."

"It's open?" Rosemary asked. "I thought most of the shops closed for the winter."

"What else is there to do in the winter here?" Genevieve asked. "Besides read?"

Rosemary smiled at the amazing young woman her daughter had become. If only she'd been able to have more to do with her upbringing.

If only she'd been able to claim her as her daughter, but she'd only been sixteen when she'd had her. Holly's age.

"And the diner was hiring, too," Genevieve continued. "You don't need to work at the one place your dad hates.

You just do it to piss him off. Even now, all you're thinking about is yourself."

Holly sucked in a breath.

"He nearly got killed," Genevieve said, her voice shaking now with anger. "He nearly got run down, nearly blown up, and all you're doing is throwing a fit and making his life more difficult. Yeah, no wonder he let you stay here. He needed the break."

Holly turned to Rosemary now, as if expecting her to reprimand her daughter or at least defend Holly. Instead Rosemary's face flushed with embarrassment. Not for Genevieve being so blunt with Holly, but because Rosemary had encouraged Deacon to let his daughter stay with them to give him that badly needed break. Holly must have seen that guilt on her face because the girl jumped up from the couch. Before she could get away, though, Genevieve jumped up, too, and grabbed her arm.

"Oh, no, you're not running off," she told her. "The last thing your dad needs right now is to go out looking for you again. And you're damn lucky that it was us who stopped to pick you up. The next time you run it might be someone else who stops, someone dangerous . . ." She shuddered.

And Rosemary did, too, thinking of the weeks her daughter had spent in captivity with her abductor. The young woman was strong, though. She was doing well, better even than Rosemary had realized.

"I know you're thinking I'm being mean to you," Genevieve said, and her voice was softer now when she spoke to Holly. "Just like you think your dad is being mean. But he's not. He's just trying to protect you. And so am I. I know what can happen if you trust the wrong people. And I know what can happen if you don't appreciate the good ones."

Tears pooled in Holly's eyes. "I . . . I . . ." But she couldn't even say it because maybe she'd finally realized how she'd been treating her father. So badly . . .

"Your father is a good man," Rosemary said. "He helped me find Genevieve. He knew what I was going through as a parent because he loves you so much."

"I . . . I should go home then," Holly murmured.

But Deacon needed that break tonight—after everything he'd been through. "It's late," Rosemary reminded her.

"Let's go up to my room," Genevieve said. "You're sharing with me. I have double beds in mine, and I don't want to put the Pierce sisters to any more trouble."

Tears stung Rosemary's eyes now, with pride in her considerate daughter. Even though she'd been a little rough with Holly, it was because she knew what could happen to the girl if she didn't stop running away. When the girls passed Rosemary in the doorway, she reached out and hugged Genevieve. Her daughter held on for a long moment before pulling away to lead Holly up the stairwell. She waited until she heard their door open and close before she headed up to the room she shared with Whit. "I'm so glad you don't have court tomorrow," she murmured, and she crawled into their bed, into his arms.

"Me, too," he said. "I'm glad I don't have to leave you."

"Because you love me?" she asked. She was still awed that he cared so much about her—after the things she'd once thought of him.

"Mostly because I love you," he said. "But I'm worried . . ."

She was, too, about the sheriff, about Olivia Smith, and about Holly.

They were all in danger, and if the sheriff was right, it had something to do with the hall.

* * *

Olivia reeled under the wave of awareness that crashed over her. She'd always felt things deeply—things that she'd expressed in song. But usually those things had been negative, had been painful. But now . . .

With Deacon's lips pressed to hers, all she felt was pleasure, with the promise of more pleasure to come. But then he jerked his head away from hers and stepped back, panting for breath.

"I'm sorry," he said, like he had in her room. "I had no right to do that. You didn't come here for that."

"You don't know why I came here," she said.

He drew in a deep breath, as if steadying or bracing himself, and asked, "Why did you?"

"To tell you to stop telling me what to do." She smiled. "And what I want and what I don't."

"I'm just trying to keep you safe," he said. "That's the only reason I told you to stay at the hall. But just like Holly, you didn't listen."

"You tell her to leave there," she reminded him with a smile. "And me to stay. Don't you know what you want, Deacon?"

His face flushed, and his dark eyes glittered as he stared down at her. "I know . . ."

"So do I," she said. "That's why I'm here—because I want you."

His brow creased. "But why . . . ?"

Her heart ached as she heard in his voice the same thing she so often felt—like she wasn't good enough, that she wasn't lovable. Not that she loved him . . .

She barely knew him. But that he took his job seriously; he wanted to serve and protect. And he loved his daughter.

And he was brave and smart and strong . . .

Instead of telling him those things, she smiled and reached for the zipper on his torn jacket. She jerked it down and pushed it from his shoulders. "Because you're hot . . ."

He chuckled and rubbed one hand over his bruised and scratched face. "Yeah, a regular male model right now . . ." Then his brow creased again. "That's probably who you usually date. Male models. Other singers. Actors."

She shook her head. "I don't usually date." She was too busy trying to protect herself. "I work. All the time . . ." She sighed. "That's why I came here—not just because of the stalker but because I was burned out."

He touched her then, running his fingertips along the edge of her jaw to tip up her face. He stared at her. "Exhaustion or . . . ?"

So he'd heard the rumors about the spa, that the rich and famous came there for drug rehab. Or maybe he'd heard the rumors about her. There had been articles speculating that she had substance abuse issues. She had tried drugs and alcohol once, a long time ago, to numb the pain. But then she hadn't been able to write, and releasing the pain had felt much better than trying not to feel it at all.

"I hope you don't believe everything you've heard about me," she said.

"Ditto," he said, his lips curving into a slight grin. But then his grin slipped away, and he continued, "Especially the things you might have heard from the Cookes or my dau—"

She pressed her fingers over his lips. "I don't think you killed your wife or that you beat your daughter," she assured him. If she believed either of those things, she wouldn't want him like she did. And she wanted him too much to let the doubts slip in about how little she knew him.

Letting passion push those doubts down, she replaced her fingers with her mouth and kissed him. He kissed her back, but once again he was the one who pulled away first, panting for breath.

"Are you sure?" he asked. "Because pretty soon I'm not going to be able to stop."

"I don't want you to stop," she assured him. Then she linked their fingers and tugged him along with her toward the hallway. They passed the open door to Holly's messy room and came to the closed door at the end of the hall. With her free hand, she reached for the knob, but before she could turn it, his hand covered hers and stopped her. "Is your room a mess, too?" she asked.

He chuckled. "Probably," he admitted. "But that's not why I want to go inside first."

"Why . . . ?" She turned back toward him and saw, despite his chuckle, that his face was tense with concern. "What is it?" she asked. "Dirty underwear all over the room?" Or pictures of his late wife . . .

"I'm worried about something else," he said. "Something explosive . . ."

She gasped. "The bomb . . ."

"I doubt there's another one."

But he wanted to be cautious. She should have been as well. Once he searched his room and returned to where she stood in the open doorway, she should have turned and left. But instead she put her hand in his and let him tug her inside and into his arms.

The door slammed as he kicked it closed. Then he led her toward his bed. The sheets were rumpled, the bedspread hanging from the foot of it, but then they were just going to mess it up anyway . . . just like they were probably going to mess up each other as well. He'd taken off his holster and had dropped that into the drawer of the table next to his bed.

So he wasn't armed anymore with a weapon. But he had his lips and his hands, and he used them to drive her crazy with need. Clothes dropped to the floor along with moans and grunts and groans of pleasure and maybe of pain.

He was bruised and scratched all over, and her head throbbed where the stitches pulled at the skin. Their new wounds weren't their only ones. She bore scars from her past, and so did he. A rigid line of flesh where he must have been stabbed once. Other fainter scars as if from deep scratches. His recent brushes with death hadn't been his first.

But they didn't ask any questions. They didn't speak at all. Their mouths and their hands were too busy. As if to make up for the pain they'd suffered, they worked harder to give each other pleasure.

So much pleasure . . .

What the hell had he done?

Deacon lay back on his mattress, panting for breath, his lungs aching, his heart hammering . . . his body more satiated than he ever remembered feeling. Olivia lay limp in his arms, her head against his heaving chest. Her hair was tangled and damp.

"You really came here to tell me off about bossing you around?" he asked when he regained enough breath to speak.

"That's what I thought," she said. "But I think I really came for this."

"What?" he asked, surprised that someone like her—someone who could have anyone she wanted—had chosen him.

"Well, I intended to tell you that I was taking back control of my life," she said. "And that you couldn't tell me what to do anymore."

"I'm not trying to tell you what to do," he said. "I'm trying to keep you safe." And not doing a very damn good job of it.

He'd been so focused on her that he wouldn't have noticed a bomb going off on the bed. Or maybe one had.

The sheets had been torn from the bed to lie atop their clothes scattered across the floor. And he felt like . . .

He felt like he had after the explosion. Disoriented. Confused.

And so damn fortunate to be alive.

He tightened his arm around her, but she wriggled against him, wriggling out from beneath it. "Where are you going?"

"Back to the hall," she said. "Isn't that where you wanted me to stay so I would be safe?"

"It's late," he said. "They might not even let you back inside the gates."

"Rosemary told me how to get into the employee entrance. If the guard manning the camera doesn't let me in, I can swipe her employee badge and get the gates to open," she said. "I'll get back in."

But when Deacon thought of her driving up there alone . . . walking into the hall . . . in the dark . . . he remembered what he'd once found in the dark in that place. "It's too dangerous . . ."

"Deacon . . ." She trailed off with a sigh that had to be pure frustration. "I can't stay here."

"Why not?" he asked—although he knew.

"We're both in danger," she said. "So being together . . ."

"Doubles the danger," he said. She was right. So he didn't stop her when she put on her clothes. But he wondered if she was just getting dressed to get away or to hide now.

They'd both exposed all their scars. Literally and figuratively. He'd seen the marks on her skin, the signs of old burns and cuts. "You need to tell me your real name," he said.

"AKAN," she murmured.

"Your real name," he said. "I want to check on your family—make sure that your stalker isn't—"

"My father." She shuddered. "Hugh Torrence."

"From Florida?"

She nodded. "Miami."

"And what was your name?" he wondered.

"It doesn't matter," she said. "I'm going by Olivia now."

He'd made love to her, but he didn't really even know who she was. But then, he'd listened to her music so much that he probably knew her better than he realized. He knew she was in danger. He got dressed, too, in clothes that weren't torn and bloody like the ones he'd worn since the explosion.

"What are you doing?" she asked.

"I'm going to follow you back to the hall and make sure you get safely inside," he said.

Her lips curved into a slight smile. "Who knew you're a gentleman?"

"Nobody—because I'm not," he said. "I'm a sheriff."

Her smile slid away. "So you're just concerned about my safety."

"Everything about you concerns me," he said.

"Ditto," she murmured, and for the first time he noticed fear in her eyes. She was scared, and he wasn't certain that it was just because of her stalker. Was she scared of him, too?

She certainly rushed out of his bedroom. He grabbed his weapon from the drawer of the bedside table and hurried after her. He caught her at the front door.

"Let me go first," he said. And he was glad he had—because when he looked through the window, he noticed a shadow standing near his truck. "Someone's out there . . ."

Before he could go, she caught his arm and held him back. "It might just be a reporter," she said. "I noticed someone earlier when I was at the boarding house, but I thought I lost him."

"The only reporter we know for certain is on the island is Edie Stone." And the shadow had looked bigger than the petite blonde.

"It's not her," Olivia said. "I spoke to her earlier. She didn't take that picture of me."

"Good." Despite himself, he was beginning to like Edie.

"She's only interested in the hall—not me," Olivia said.

And that was why he was beginning to like her.

"So she wouldn't have followed you here." But maybe that person wasn't here for her; maybe he was here for him.

"Stay here," he said. "Go into the bathroom that has no window and lock the door. Don't open it for anyone but me."

"Deac—"

He kissed her, to stop her protest and because he wanted to.

"You're not going out there," he told her. "Not until I find out who the hell that is . . ."

"But you're putting yourself in danger," she said.

"That's my job."

That wasn't the only reason he wanted to protect her, though. He cared about her. Hell, he didn't even know her, but he cared. So he waited until she went into the bathroom and he heard the click of the lock.

Then he opened the front door and stepped out, his gun drawn. The shadow was no longer looming near his truck. But he doubted the person was gone; he was out there somewhere, waiting for him.

Or for her?

Chapter Sixteen

A vibration shook Edie awake. Disoriented, she peered around the room. Only a faint light dispelled some of the dark shadows. Where was she?

Oh, yeah, her bedroom at the boarding house—in the attic. Knowing it would have been insensitive, she'd refrained from teasing Evelyn about locking her up where families used to lock up their crazy relatives. That wasn't the case on the island anyway. Here people had locked up their crazy relatives—and their not so crazy ones—at Bainesworth Manor.

The room, tucked into a big dormer, was actually nice, and painted so bright a yellow that she'd joked about not needing to turn on any lights. She had, though, last night when she'd been working. But then she and her laptop had fallen asleep on the bed—along with her phone, which vibrated with an incoming call.

She blinked again and fumbled around in the blankets until she found it. Who the hell was calling her at one in the morning? The number lighting up the screen had a California area code. "There's a difference in time zones," she murmured as she accepted the call.

"There's always a difference in time zones with you," her caller remarked. "Why don't you come out to the West Coast where you could get a real job?"

She snorted. "In entertainment?" Her caller, Arthur Rasche, was managing editor for one of the biggest tabloids in the world. "I have no interest in fluff stuff and fake reality." But if she did, she could cover a major story about AKAN and the stalker who'd driven her to a remote island off the coast of Maine. Temptation tugged at her for the easy money.

But Edie never took the easy route.

"Then why are you asking about that photo of the mystery singer?" Arthur asked.

"AKAN."

"I know," he said. "Also known as nobody. What the hell kind of name is that?"

"Maybe she wants to keep her identity secret." So secret that she used alias upon alias.

"Then she shouldn't have become a fucking pop star," Arthur griped. "That name is just some damn publicity stunt."

Edie might have believed that . . . if she hadn't met Olivia. "If that was what she really wanted, she does a damn good job of avoiding publicity."

"It's what everybody wants—to be famous."

"That's why I won't move to the West Coast," Edie said. "It's how you all think."

Arthur snorted. "And you don't? That's why you want to do your big, important stories, so you'll get your Pulitzer, and everybody will know your name."

Edie flinched at the direct hit. But that was only part of it for her; she also wanted to get to the truth. Always to the truth . . .

"Any story about AKAN would be big news right now," Arthur continued. "That is a rehab place, right, where that photo was taken? Not just some fancy spa?"

He was checking the facts a little late now. In the article that had accompanied that photograph, it had been declared that she must be there for rehab: Since she was so thin, she didn't need the help of the famous personal trainer, Bode James.

"I put out the word to get information," Edie said. "Not give it."

Arthur snorted again. "Figures."

"I don't have any to give," she lied. "But you must, or you wouldn't have called me back."

"I really don't," Arthur said.

"The picture was posted on your website," Edie said. That didn't necessarily mean he'd bought it, though. He could have stolen it from another source. "You pay for it?"

"Yes," he said, as if offended.

"Who did you pay?"

"I don't know," he said.

"Yeah, right."

"I didn't get a name," he said. "Once I received the digital file in an email, I wired the money to some drugstore on Bane Island, Maine. He must have been waiting there for it."

She knew there was only one drugstore in town, but of course, it was already closed for the evening.

"Why are you asking about that photo, Edie?"

"I'm not asking for me," she said. "I'm asking for a friend."

Arthur snorted. "Yeah, right."

Olivia Smith wasn't a friend. Yet . . .

But Edie wouldn't have minded making a friend in her. The way she'd pushed her to the ground . . .

She wasn't some spoiled celebrity looking for someone to take care of her or protect her. She wanted to take care of herself.

But would that be possible now? If she stayed on the island?

Because everybody knew she was here now. Once the bridge opened up, more reporters would arrive.

"Thanks, Arthur," Edie said and disconnected the call before he could ask any more questions.

Then she yawned. Despite falling asleep, she was still tired. But then again, it was late, so late that she needed to use the bathroom and really get ready for bed. Grasping the railing tightly, she walked down the steep stairs to the bathroom on the second floor, since there wasn't one in the attic. The one strange part of living in a boarding house was sharing the bathroom. But usually nobody was up when Edie was, so she was surprised to find the door closed.

She lifted her hand to knock and heard the unmistakable sound of weeping. Was it Bonita?

She'd found her crying before over her lost baby. She probably should get Evelyn to comfort her, though, because all Edie generally did was upset her. But then she heard another noise and noticed a shadow in the hall behind her. She turned and found Bonita peeking out an open door.

"She's crying," Bonita said.

"Who?"

She shrugged. "One of the other girls. They're always crying . . ."

She couldn't be talking about the boarding house. She

must have been talking about the manor. Before Edie could ask, Bonita closed her bedroom door again. And Edie turned back to the bathroom, uncertain what to do . . .

She was such a bitch.

Not Genevieve . . .

Genevieve had only been telling the truth—about everything. Holly was the bitch. She had been such a brat to her dad. All this time she'd treated him like crap. She'd pushed him away and run away and told him over and over again how much she hated him.

What if he hadn't survived those attempts on his life? What if he'd died believing that she actually did hate him?

The tears burning her eyes escaped her throat as gurgling sobs. She tried to smother them with the towel she held to her lips, but they echoed off the old octagon floor tiles and the tall, cracked ceiling of the boarding house bathroom.

She hadn't wanted to cry in the same bedroom with Genevieve. She hadn't wanted to wake up the older girl and prove to her how right she'd been about her. That she thought only of herself.

Because even now that was what she was doing, feeling sorry for herself for how she'd treated her dad. But what about how he felt, how unloved . . .

A light tap rattled the door, and she jumped and nearly slipped off the side of the old clawfoot tub where she'd perched. "Dad?" she asked, her voice cracking.

Had he come for her after all? Had he changed his mind about needing a break from her, like Genevieve and Rosemary had suggested?

Or maybe he needed her?

He was hurt. She shouldn't have left the house. She should have stayed home and waited to make sure he got back safely. She should have taken care of him. Instead she was always forcing him to take care of her. To track her down.

A husky whisper replied, "It's Edie Stone."

Edie Stone?

"I . . . I don't know you," Holly said, but she got up from the tub and opened the door.

"I don't know you," the woman replied. Her short blond hair was standing up and her clothes were wrinkled, like she'd been sleeping in them.

Holly had been, too, or at least she'd been trying to sleep. But every time she'd closed her eyes she'd pictured the explosion that could have killed her father . . .

And she hadn't even been there.

"What . . . are the Pierce sisters taking in runaway teens now?" Edie asked, and she sounded irritated.

Embarrassment sent a wave of heat rushing to Holly's face. "How . . . how do you know that I . . ." Shame kept her from finishing her sentence. Shame that she kept running away from her father, that she kept putting him through so much.

When he'd already lost so much.

"I'm a reporter," the woman replied. "I know everything." But she smiled like she was just teasing.

"You're the reporter my dad's talked about," Holly said.

"What?" the woman asked. "Has he called me a pain in the ass?"

Holly smiled. "He probably calls me that, too."

"Who's your dad?"

"The sheriff."

The blond woman nodded. "Of course, I've heard that you give him a hard time."

Tears stung Holly's eyes. So everyone knew that she was a brat to her dad. How had she not realized how unfair she'd been to him? That she'd been trying to make him as miserable as she was.

She blamed him for that—for moving them to this godforsaken island. That had been his decision. Taking her from their home, from her friends. Anger surged through her again. She'd had a right to be angry with him. He'd turned her life upside down. At least before they'd moved here, she'd had someplace to go to escape from their fights, from her mother . . .

Now her mother was gone forever.

And her dad could have been, too.

"I don't want to be here," Holly admitted.

"The boarding house?" Edie asked.

She shook her head. "On this island. I don't want to be here."

"That's why you keep running away?"

She wasn't sure anymore. She wasn't sure she had friends to go home to; she'd been away so long. And nobody understood what she'd gone through since she'd been here.

Nobody understood . . . but Genevieve. And Genevieve thought she was a brat.

She sighed. "I just don't want to be here."

"I'll bring you home," Edie offered. "If you want . . ."

Holly bit her bottom lip, trying to hold back a sob that moved up the back of her throat. But it slipped out along with more tears. "Rosemary and Genevieve think my dad needs a break . . . from me . . ."

Edie nodded. "They're smart women. They're probably right."

Holly hadn't expected that to hurt so much. She'd always tried to leave her father, but she never considered that he might want her to leave, that he was sick of her. Or sick of how she treated him.

But he had every right to be.

"Did the sisters give you a room for the night?" Edie asked.

Holly shook her head. "I'm rooming with Genevieve. She has two beds in her room."

Edie smiled. "Good. So you have a place to sleep."

Holly doubted that she would sleep, though. She didn't want to close her eyes and imagine that explosion happening again; she didn't want to see how close she'd come to losing her dad.

Would the person keep trying to kill him? Would he keep trying until he succeeded? If he succeeded before she got home, then she would never have the chance to tell her father she didn't really hate him.

She loved him.

She'd come here this evening to tell the sheriff to stop telling her what to do, to stop controlling her. But yet here she was, locked in his bathroom sitting on the edge of his bathtub. She hadn't even turned on a light, he'd rattled her so . . .

He'd seen something outside—someone. Her stalker? A reporter? Had someone followed her here?

She shouldn't have come here. But she had no regrets. Only fears now. She didn't regret what they'd done to each other, with each other . . .

But once her body had recovered from the pleasure, her mind had taken over with all the doubts and fears. She'd taken too big a risk and not just with her life.

The sheriff had taken too big of one, too. With her . . .

And with going outside alone.

He had a gun, but he had no idea how many people might be out there. Even though he'd only seen one, there could have been more. And they weren't necessarily armed only with cameras.

They might not be reporters at all. She had no idea who was after the sheriff. Someone from the hall like he suspected?

Or whoever was responsible for the death of the young woman whose body he'd found?

He was in too much danger to have gone out there alone. He should have called for backup. But he obviously didn't trust his deputy Warren Cooke and probably with good reason.

She didn't trust him either.

And if she called 9-1-1, that was probably who would come . . . if he wasn't already outside, like he'd been when those shots had been fired at her. At least nobody had taken any shots at the sheriff.

The thought had just entered her head when she heard the sharp crack of gunfire.

Somebody was taking a shot at him.

Had they been more successful at hitting him than they had her?

She had to see if he needed help.

Disobeying his order, she unlocked the bathroom door and ran down the hall to the living room. She was just reaching for that door when the knob began to turn.

Oh no . . .

Instead of running back to the bathroom, she looked around for a weapon. And she found a heavy iron poker lying beside the hearth. Arming herself with that behind the door, she waited for it to open.

She wasn't running scared anymore.

She wasn't hiding.

That was why she'd come here tonight. To take back control of her life . . . not to lose it.

Chapter Seventeen

His heart pounding, Deacon rushed back to the house. The person whose shadow he'd noticed near the truck had eluded him; he wasn't sure where the hell the person had gone.

Thinking he'd noticed the shadow nearing the house, Deacon had fired a shot in the air, to force the person away from the house, away from Olivia. But what if he hadn't scared him away? What if he'd gotten inside when Deacon had been distracted by what he'd found in the back of his truck?

Rushing back inside to check on Olivia, Deacon didn't think to call out to her—to warn her—as he didn't want to warn the intruder if he'd gotten inside. And maybe he had, because the moment Deacon stepped inside his front door, something swung toward his head. He ducked, and the hard metal came down on his already bruised shoulder. He grunted and cursed in pain.

And the fireplace poker dropped to the hardwood floor.

"Oh, my God!" Olivia exclaimed. "Are you all right? Did I hurt you?"

"More like impressed," he admitted. "Maybe you don't need anyone protecting you."

"I wouldn't have made it this long if I couldn't protect myself," she said.

She might have survived, but she had scars that proved she hadn't always been able to protect herself. But then she'd been a child—younger than Holly. Now wasn't the time to talk to her about the past, though.

Now was the time to get her the hell away from his present. His nightmare.

"Then get out of here," he told her.

Her brow furrowed. "What happened out there? I heard a gunshot. Did someone fire at you?"

He shook his head.

"So you fired at someone?" she asked. "Did you hit him?"

"I wish," he murmured. "But I didn't have a clear shot. I fired into the air."

"To protect me," she remarked. "Is that why you want me to leave? Is he still out there?"

"No." Since Olivia was okay, the intruder hadn't come into the house. And he wouldn't have risked sticking around after what he'd placed in the bed of Deacon's truck. "But I think he left another bomb for me. So you need to get out of here."

"But . . . you parked behind me," she pointed out.

"Damn it!" He looked out the front door to the driveway. She'd parked on the right of the two-car driveway, which was the side on which he parked in the garage. "You can get out," he said, "with Holly's car."

And he wanted her out. Now. So he tugged her toward the garage. An old refrigerator hummed against one wall. He pulled open the freezer and found the keys he'd stashed in the frost gathered inside it. "Take her car and get out of here."

She didn't reach for the icy keys, so he caught her hand in his and dropped them into her palm. She stared up at him. "I can't leave you here alone . . . ," she murmured.

"I won't be alone for long," he said. "I called the state police." He hadn't. Not yet. "And they might not show up alone. If reporters come with them, they'll find you here. They might recognize you."

Her mouth curved into a slight smile. "Are you ashamed to be seen with me?"

"I don't want you involved in this," he said. "You shouldn't have come here tonight. And you can't come back."

Her smile slipped away.

And a pang of regret struck his heart. He hadn't wanted to hurt her, but he definitely didn't want to keep putting her in danger. He wondered now if those shots fired at the hall hadn't been meant for her. Perhaps someone had been sending a message to him when they'd fired so closely to his daughter?

Was it a threat to stop his investigation?

If so, they didn't know him very well. Threats only made him more determined to find them and make sure they got the punishment they deserved.

"I'm sorry," he said. "But you know we have no future." He probably wouldn't have one at all with all the attempts that were being made on his life.

"I wasn't here looking for a future," she assured him. "You're the one who asked me to stay on the island, or I would have already been gone."

"I was wrong," he said. "I should have let you leave when the bridge was open."

She would probably be safer anywhere else.

She grimaced. "That's why I came here tonight," she said. "To stop you from trying to control me."

"That's not what I'm doing," he insisted. He only wanted to keep her safe—even if that meant staying far away from her. His body ached at the thought, but his heart ached at the thought of her getting hurt again. "But if you find me so damn controlling, you should stay away from me."

She nodded. "I will. Holly can pick up her car from the hall." She unlocked and pulled open the driver's door. And he opened the overhead garage door for her.

At the risk of sounding controlling again, he told her, "Be careful backing out. Don't touch the truck."

He knew how damn sensitive that bomb was. If that was another bomb in the bed of his truck . . .

He hoped like hell that it wasn't, but the box looked the same. Just as innocuous as the one delivered to his dad's. This one had been dropped off the same way—in the middle of the night. It had to be another bomb.

As Olivia steered Holly's old Oldsmobile down the drive, he held his breath—only releasing it when she reached the street. She hesitated a moment, or maybe the car did, before she shifted to drive and headed away from him. And he couldn't help but wonder if he would ever see her again . . .

Despite the cold, Olivia burned with embarrassment and anger and fear. The sheriff sure hadn't been trying to protect her just then—at least not her feelings. But maybe he'd been trying to save her life.

Was there really a bomb in the back of his truck?

If not, he'd gone to extreme measures to get rid of her. What the hell had she been thinking to show up at his house tonight?

After she'd left the boarding house, she should have gone straight back to the hall. But she'd wanted to see him, to talk to him . . .

No. She'd wanted more than that. She'd wanted him.

And now he wanted her to leave. The state police would have to open the bridge in order to get to his house from the mainland. So once she'd returned to the hall for her stuff, she would leave Holly's car there as she'd told Deacon she would. Then she would call a car service.

A blinking red light alerted her to a stop at the intersection with Main Street. If she turned left, she would head toward the hall. If she turned right, she would head toward the bridge. She could wait there until it was open. Once she made it to the mainland, she could always hire someone to pick up her stuff and drop off Holly's car.

An urge burned inside her to escape. To get as far away as she possibly could. But what if the sheriff was right? What if there was another bomb in his truck? What if something happened to him?

She wanted to know. And she wouldn't want Holly to be alone. Her father was all the girl had.

She remained stopped at that intersection for a long moment even though nothing was coming. There were no other vehicles on the road at this hour. Where were the state police he'd called?

Shouldn't the cars be coming across the bridge by now? Or at least the plow truck that would have to make it passable for them? She could see no flashing lights in the distance though. But then, she had no idea where the state police post was and how long it would take them to arrive.

Would they get to his house in time?

She turned at the intersection toward the bridge. But before she reached the wrought iron structure, she stopped in town, at the curb outside the boarding house. Not wanting to wake the ladies who ran the place, she pulled out her cell phone and found the contact she'd entered for Edie Stone. A slight smile curved her lips at the irony of her actually having a reporter's phone number, of her actually wanting to call a reporter.

She punched in the contact and waited a moment before a raspy voice answered—not with a hello—but with, "I already know where the damn picture came from, you don't have to keep calling me . . ."

"You do?" Olivia asked then added, "I haven't called you before."

"Olivia?" the reporter asked.

"Yes."

"It's the middle of the night," she murmured, her voice still all grumbly with sleep and grumpiness. "Why aren't you in bed?"

She had been; it just hadn't been hers. What the hell had she been thinking? Then she realized what the reporter had admitted to her—when she'd obviously thought she was someone else. "Where'd the photo come from?" she asked. "Who took it?"

Edie groaned. "Can we talk about this in the morning?" she asked. "You can put my name on the list at the hall, and I'll meet you there."

Olivia chuckled. "Nice try. I think the only way you'll

get inside is if Dr. Cooke were to put your name on the list."

"And that will only happen when hell freezes over," Edie murmured.

"I didn't go back to the hall anyway," Olivia admitted.

"You left the island?"

She should have. "Not yet. I'm outside the boarding house right now. Can you let me in?"

"I thought you didn't want to stay," Edie said. "That you were worried about putting everybody here in danger."

She had been worried about that and maybe rightfully so. Maybe whoever had been lurking around the sheriff's house had been after her—not him. She glanced around the street on which Holly's car was the only one parked. A Jeep and a Cadillac were parked in the driveway. She looked for the shadow that had spooked the sheriff at his house or for the flash of light that had spooked her earlier. But nothing moved in the darkness but a few snowflakes drifting lazily to the ground.

"I don't want to stay," she said. "But I do want to talk to you." She needed to warn Edie about that conversation she'd overheard. She also didn't want to be alone while she waited to find out if that had been a bomb in the back of the sheriff's truck.

Edie sighed. "I'll come downstairs to let you in."

A light moved through the house now; it must have been from Edie's phone as she descended the stairs. Olivia stepped out of Holly's car and rushed up to the front porch. As she did, she kept glancing over her shoulder—just to be sure she was alone.

She tilted her head and listened, but she couldn't hear sirens yet. Wasn't the island small enough that she would have . . . if the state police were enroute to the sheriff's house?

The front door opened, and Edie gestured her inside. "Hurry, it's freezing out there."

Just now becoming aware of the cold, Olivia shivered and followed the reporter inside.

"Guess I don't have to tell you that, though," Edie added. "If you've been out in it since you left earlier." She glanced out at the street then and turned back to Olivia, her green eyes narrowed with suspicion. "That's not Rosemary's car," she said. "What happened to it?" She reached out and grabbed Olivia's arm. "Did something happen to you?"

A hell of a lot had happened in the short while since she'd seen the reporter last, but Olivia shook her head. "Not to me . . ."

"Good," Edie said, and, still holding her arm, she led her through the open pocket doors into the parlor.

The logs in the fireplace glowed still, drawing Olivia to the hearth for warmth. She was suddenly very cold with fear.

"I wouldn't be surprised if something happened to Rosemary's car," Edie murmured. "She has bad luck with them."

"I don't think anything's happened to it . . ." Just as she hadn't heard sirens, she hadn't heard an explosion either. That was good. That meant the sheriff was safe.

He had to be safe.

Was Olivia? "What did you find out about the photo?" she asked.

"Nothing new really," Edie said. "We already knew that whoever took it is on the island. With as much as the bridge has been closing, they'd have to be. Apparently, they had money wired to them at the drugstore. I'll check with the store when it opens to find out who picked up the money. Then I'll call you if you give me your number. It didn't show up just now." She held out her phone with the screen lit up with the call log. The last one had come in as private.

Olivia smiled at the reporter's obvious ploy to get her contact information. "I'll call you tomorrow."

"Today," Edie corrected her. "It's already today."

Olivia glanced out the window. It was still dark, but maybe not as dark as it had been.

"Is that why you came back? Why you wanted to talk to me?" Edie asked. "About that picture?"

Olivia shook her head. "I wanted to warn you."

Edie's brow furrowed. "I told you—I'm not writing an article about you. My total focus is on Bainesworth Manor right now."

"That's the problem," Olivia said. "Maybe your landladies are right to be concerned about you. I heard the director—"

"Elijah Cooke?" Edie interjected, her voice rising with excitement. "What about him?"

"He was talking to the publicist about getting rid of you," Olivia warned her.

Edie shivered. But that almost seemed to be more with excitement than fear.

"He claimed that they just mean to keep you away from the hall . . ."

"Not kill me?" Edie shrugged. "They're going to have to kill me to keep me away. You're going to help me get inside, right? We have a deal. Once I call you with the identity of the person who sold that photo, you'll get me inside the hall."

"Edie, I don't think that's a good idea," Olivia advised.

"Or maybe I should just call the sheriff instead," Edie said.

"No."

"You told him about the stalker, right?" Edie asked. "He needs to know, so that he can protect you."

"He has his hands full protecting himself right now," Olivia said.

And Edie sucked in a breath. "That's what you meant . . . why you don't have Rosemary's car. Something happened. Just not to you. To the sheriff?"

She glanced out that window again—looking for flashing lights or worse, flames and smoke.

"I don't know," she admitted. "He was fine when I left him, but he just found another package in his truck, like the one that blew up on him earlier."

"Oh, my God! No!" The exclamation came from the doorway where Holly lurked in the shadows of the foyer. Instead of joining them in the parlor, the girl headed toward the front door.

And Edie and Olivia ran after her.

The reporter pulled her back into the house. "Calm down. You can't go running off in the snow without any shoes on."

"But my dad—"

"He has it all under control," Olivia said. "The state police are probably already there, already checking out the package. It's probably nothing anyway."

Holly studied her face for a long moment. "You don't believe that."

Olivia shrugged. "I don't know what to believe anymore."

The girl's face flushed. Her voice sharp with defensiveness, she said, "I . . . I didn't lie to you about my dad."

Olivia sucked in a breath now as shock overwhelmed her. Had she slept with a child abuser? That was something she would never be able to forgive herself for. "So he does hurt you?"

"No," Holly said with even more defensiveness. "And I didn't tell you he did. You just assumed . . ."

Yes, she had. She'd assumed the worst—because that was what most people showed her. Edie met her gaze, and her green eyes held understanding. She probably assumed the worst, too, and maybe for the same reasons Olivia did.

"I shouldn't have made any assumptions about your dad," Olivia admitted. Even now.

She'd assumed he'd wanted to get rid of her, but undoubtedly he'd just been trying to protect her again. Still.

Hopefully he was able to protect himself. For his sake and for his daughter's.

And for hers, because even though he wasn't hers, Olivia didn't want to lose him.

He sat in the dark and quiet of his vehicle. He'd driven away from the sheriff's house but not so far that he wouldn't be able to see what happened.

What *had* to happen . . .

Sheriff Deacon Howell was a survivor. Probably just because of pure dumb luck, though. He wasn't that smart, or he would have figured out the truth before now.

Maybe he had, and just didn't want to face it. He would be spared that, if this package went off like the other one had. There were more explosives in this box.

This bomb would do a hell of a lot more damage than the last one had. That was why he'd driven so fast away from the sheriff's house.

Not because of the gunshot.

The bullet hadn't come anywhere close to him. If Deacon had only meant to scare him away, it hadn't worked. He would come back—if he had to. He would keep coming back until Deacon was dead.

But then the ground shook as the night exploded with the blast of noise and light of a powerful explosion. Too powerful for even Sheriff Deacon Howell to have survived.

Chapter Eighteen

A scream burned Holly's throat, but she couldn't let it out. Instead she clasped a hand over her mouth as she sank to the floor in front of the fireplace. The two women with her tried to hold her up. But she was bigger than both of them. She was built more like her father than her mother—though her mother hadn't been a little woman either.

Tears stung her eyes and slipped through the lids she squeezed shut. She'd heard the explosion. She knew what that meant. The blast had been so big. There was no way her dad had survived this one like he had the last. No way . . .

He had died thinking that she hated him. Her stomach clenched with misery over how she'd made him feel and over how much she was going to miss him. She doubled over from the pain of it, from the pain of losing him. He was gone. He had to be.

She heard the other women talking, wondering what to do. About her dad.

About her.

She barely registered their words, their presence, as isolated as she felt in her pain. Then she heard another voice—the deep rumble of a male voice. The blast had probably wakened Whittaker Lawrence.

But it didn't sound like him talking . . .

That deep voice sounded like her father's. Had she gone as crazy as that old lady Morgana? Was she thinking she could hear dead people now? Because surely her dad had to be dead.

Deacon probably should have let everybody believe that he was dead because the only way to stop the attempts on his life was for his would-be killer to assume he'd succeeded. But Deacon was glad that he'd decided not to when he saw his daughter crumpled on the floor of the boarding house parlor.

His baby . . .

He gathered her up from the floor and clasped her close to his chest where his heart hammered away. The state police had ordered him away from the scene, so he'd come here—to make sure his daughter was safe. He hadn't been that surprised to find her car parked at the curb. Olivia must have been worried about her, too.

When he'd walked in, she'd been leaning over Holly, trying to pull her up. But Olivia was too small to lift his daughter. Holly was tall like him and like her mother. And she was strong . . . physically. Emotionally, he wished she was stronger.

But then, it was no wonder that she wasn't after everything she'd been through already at sixteen years old. "You're dead," she said through sobs. "You have to be dead. That must have been the bomb going off . . ."

He glanced over her shoulder at Olivia, surprised that she'd shared that with his daughter.

"I'm sorry," she said. "I didn't know she was standing in the hall when I was telling Edie."

Edie. She was on a first name basis with the reporter now?

He pushed aside the curious thought and focused on his child. Pushing her back slightly, he cupped her tear-stained face in his hands and stared into her wet eyes. "I'm alive, honey," he assured her. "I'm fine. The state police made me clear out of the area. They got everyone else out from the nearby houses, too."

Had they estimated the danger zone well enough that they'd gotten everybody out, though? Using a state vehicle he'd borrowed from a trooper, he'd been almost at the boarding house when the blast had shaken the big SUV. And what about all the state troopers?

After Olivia had left his house earlier, he'd called the state trooper with whom he'd entrusted Olivia's stalker letters. And the woman had promised her team would arrive at his place with no lights or sirens. He hadn't wanted to alert everyone to the call he'd had to make in case the package wasn't a bomb. There was no doubt now that it had been. Had any of the troopers been injured, or worse? He needed to go back to the scene, but Holly clung to him. And he couldn't remember the last time she'd even touched him or let him touch her.

"I'm so sorry, Dad," she said, her voice thick with sobs. "I'm so sorry I've been so mean to you."

He hugged her closer and assured her, "It's okay, honey. Everything's going to be okay."

She shook her head. "Somebody's trying to kill—" Her voice cracked with fear. "They're not going to stop trying."

"Maybe you should have played dead," Edie Stone suggested.

"I thought about it," he admitted.

"You would have done that?" Holly asked. And she pulled back now. "You would have let me believe—"

Olivia stepped closer, her hand once again going to Holly's shoulder where it had been when he'd walked into the parlor. "He's here," she pointed out. "He didn't let you believe it." She turned her focus from his daughter to him, her gaze intent on his face, her eyes burning with the question: *Would you have let me believe it?*

He wanted to ask if she would have even cared, but he could tell that she would have—that there was something more between them than just sex. But now was not the time for them.

Because like Holly had said, there would be another attempt on his life. He had to find his assailant, had to stop him from trying again.

He turned his attention back to his daughter. "I have to go back to our house—"

"Do you think anything's left of it?" she asked.

He flinched. He hadn't even thought about the house, about her things. He'd thought only of her. And Olivia. "I don't know. I'll go find out."

"I'll go with you."

He shook his head. "No. I don't want you anywhere near me right now."

She stepped back, nearly stumbling over Olivia. Her dark eyes were wide with shock and pain. "Dad—"

"For your safety," he explained. "I don't want you to get hurt." But it was clearly too late for that. The girl had been hurt so much already. He didn't want her hurt anymore.

"He's protecting you," Olivia told her.

He wanted to protect Olivia, too. And to do that, he had to leave—for all their sakes. He had to check on the troopers. But most of all, he needed to stay far away from the people he cared about. And even though he barely knew her, he cared about Olivia Smith.

Maybe too much . . .

Olivia was dead tired. She'd stayed awake all night, sitting up with Holly and Edie and Rosemary at the boarding house until the teenage girl had finally settled down and fallen asleep. Olivia needed sleep, too. But she'd refused the Pierce sisters' offer of a room and had driven Holly's car back to the hall as she'd promised the sheriff she would last night. Or had it already been morning when he'd found that bomb?

She'd stayed awake for the drive back; the falling snow and the slick roads had demanded all her attention. After a guard had let her through the gate, she parked the car in the back lot and, using the ID badge she'd found in the console, she let herself in through the employee entrance.

Maybe nobody would see her. Maybe she'd be able to go right to sleep. Sleep she desperately needed. She felt worse than she had when she'd first checked herself into the hall. Then, she'd been totally exhausted both physically and mentally. Since her first album had struck platinum, she'd been on tour with back-to-back performances until she'd finally burned herself out. She wasn't going back to that—no matter what Bruce—her manager—said. And it wasn't just because she was afraid of her stalker.

Maybe she'd just used him as an excuse to run away. But that excuse no longer applied. If he wasn't the one who'd taken her picture, it didn't matter. Because of that picture, he now knew where she was.

He wasn't the only one. She didn't make it but a few steps down that back hallway before a burly security guard stopped her. "Let me see your employee badge," he demanded.

"This isn't mine," she admitted as she passed him Holly's. "I'm a guest."

"Then you should have come in through the reception area," he said, his eyes narrowed with suspicion. Did he think she was a reporter? Or her own stalker?

"I am a guest," she insisted. "The receptionist will verify that for you." He let her past him then, but he followed closely as she walked to the lobby.

"Ms. Smith," the receptionist called out from behind her polished mahogany desk.

"So she is a guest?" the guard asked.

"Yes, of course," the dark-haired young woman replied.

He left, and Olivia turned toward the stairwell to do the same.

But the receptionist called out to her again. "You have a delivery."

Thinking of the packages that had been sent to the sheriff, Olivia froze with fear. But the receptionist held out an envelope. Not a box.

Not that it still couldn't contain something that might hurt her. But she wasn't nearly as worried as she'd been. While Olivia had told no one where she was, she had set up a mailing system so that important things sent to her previous address were forwarded to the hall. But only important things, things from her manager. Maybe he had sold some of the songs she'd been sending him, and the envelope contained a contract. Or maybe, better yet, he was letting her out of the concert contract.

She took the envelope from the young woman, and her blood chilled at the sight of the blocky handwriting.

Her stalker knew where she was. She didn't even have to open it to verify that she'd been found.

But she thanked the young woman nevertheless and headed up the stairwell to her room. The hand that carried the envelope shook, but she managed to unlock her door with the other and get inside her room.

She forced herself to open the envelope and pulled out the folded slip of paper. A photo fell out along with it. The images in the photo were dark and blurry as they'd been captured at night and through a window, but she recognized herself and Edie Stone standing in the parlor at the boarding house. She unfolded the note and read:

You're going to pay for hiding from me all these months. You're going to pay dearly . . .

The threat was as ugly as all the others she'd received. But what scared her most was when she looked at the envelope. It hadn't been mailed. There was no postmark on it. Someone had dropped it off at the hall.

Her stalker didn't just know she was on Bane Island. He knew exactly where she was and the alias she was using, and he had been following her last night. Just as she'd feared, she had put everyone at the boarding house in danger. Maybe even the sheriff as well. What if her stalker was the one who'd been leaving the packages for him?

Panic rushed over her, weakening her knees so she nearly dropped to the floor like Holly had when she'd heard that blast. When she'd thought her dad was dead . . .

Olivia had nearly dropped to the floor with her she'd been so scared—even more scared than she was now. Then, she'd been scared for the sheriff and for his daughter.

Now she was scared for herself and for Deacon. She pulled her cell phone from her pocket and scrolled through her contacts. She didn't have Deacon's number. She'd slept with him, but she didn't even know how to reach him except through 9-1-1. And she didn't want to dial that. She wasn't in immediate danger.

It wasn't as if the stalker could get past those gates—because Olivia certainly wasn't putting his name on the list of approved visitors. She didn't even know his name.

Maybe Edie did if she'd talked to the drugstore in town.

Olivia called her first.

"I haven't gotten to the drugstore yet," Edie answered. "I had to drop kids at school this morning. Moving into the boarding house has turned me into some damn soccer mom. I'll check into it, though."

Olivia glanced down at the note and felt a flash of concern, not just for herself but for the woman who was actually becoming a friend. "Don't," she said. "We should let the sheriff handle this instead."

"I can call him," Edie said.

"You have his direct number?"

"You don't?"

Olivia choked down a wave of envy and embarrassment. "No." She'd slept with him, but she couldn't even call him.

Edie chuckled. "I guess it's not like you've had the access to Rosemary and Whit's phones that I have."

"You stole the contact?"

Unrepentant, the reporter chuckled again. "I borrowed

it. If you'd give me yours, I would forward his contact to you."

Olivia groaned. "You're unrelenting."

"It's not like I'm going to sell your number to the highest bidder or anything," Edie said. "But I wonder how much I would get . . . ?"

"Damn you . . ."

And the reporter chuckled again. "Send it to me, and I'll send you the sheriff's direct line. Or I can just call him if you'd rather stay private."

"No," Olivia said. "I . . . I have something else I need to share with him." Though he might think she was just calling because of what they'd done.

"What do you have to share?"

"Another threat."

Edie cursed now. "He found you."

"Yes, and you—or at least you're in the picture he took last night."

Edie cursed again. "You were right. There was someone out there."

He was close. Too close. At the boarding house and at the hall.

Maybe, when he'd dropped off that envelope, he'd been caught on camera. She doubted Warren Cooke or even Elijah would show the security footage to her, though. They'd probably even make the sheriff get a warrant for it, like they'd made him get a warrant for everything else he'd wanted at the hall. Like to talk to her . . .

Switching the phone to speaker, she texted Edie her contact information. "I sent it."

A ding from Edie's phone radiated from the speaker of Olivia's. "I'm going to make some bank now," she teased.

Someone else might have considered the reporter's humor inappropriate. But Olivia appreciated it, appreciated the opportunity to ease some of the tension and fear gripping her with a laugh. "I expect a percentage," she said.

And Edie laughed. "Of course." Then her tone turning all serious, she said, "Call the sheriff."

The minute Olivia disconnected from Edie she tried. But it rang several times before going to his voicemail. Was he ignoring her? Or was he unable to answer?

Had someone tried again to kill him?

Chapter Nineteen

Since starting her new position as a psychologist at Halcyon Hall, Rosemary had been careful to help only the guests who asked for her help—dealing with their stress or whatever other issues might have brought them to leave their lives behind and seek out the isolated retreat.

Like ghosts. That was what had called Morgana Drake to Halcyon. The elderly woman professed to be a medium who could speak to the dead. But what had compelled Olivia Smith to check herself into the exclusive spa?

When the young woman walked into the conservatory, she looked as shaky and pale as if she'd seen one of Morgana's ghosts. Or maybe she was just exhausted, which was the reason she'd given on her application to stay at the spa. Halcyon Hall was so exclusive, one had to fill out an application to make a reservation. Unless you knew somebody . . .

Like Rosemary's mother had known one of the other psychiatrists at the hall, Rosemary's old mentor, Dr. Gordon Chase. He'd been scarce lately—since Rosemary's mother had warned her not to trust him. Hopefully, he knew that Rosemary wouldn't believe anything her mother told her. All the woman had ever done was lie to her. Nonetheless, her lies had taught Rosemary not to trust anyone, so she had checked him out. She'd found no proof of her mother's claims, that he'd been fired as a professor over inappropriate relationships with students. He'd once been Rosemary's professor as well as her late father's good friend, and he'd never been anything but sweet and supportive. He was here now, following in behind Olivia. He caught her arm and turned her toward him.

Rosemary couldn't hear their conversation; she could only see Olivia shaking her head and pulling her arm from Gordon's grasp. When she walked away from him, she appeared more shaken.

Rosemary stood up from the table where she'd been sitting in the sunshine and rushed toward the doorway. As she approached, Gordon glanced at her and then quickly looked away before leaving the room. She needed to talk to him, needed to clear the air between them, but at the moment, she was more concerned about Olivia.

"What was that about?" Rosemary asked her.

The blond woman shrugged. "I don't know. For once he wasn't pressuring me to talk about myself. He was asking me about the sheriff."

"What about the sheriff?" Rosemary asked with surprise. She doubted the sheriff and Gordon had had many interactions; at least they hadn't since she'd started working at the hall.

"He asked if I'd heard how he was, if he was hurt." She shivered a little despite the warmth of the morning sun pouring into the conservatory. "I'm not sure why he thought I'd know . . ."

While Rosemary was aware that something was going

on between Deacon and Olivia, she wasn't sure how Gordon would have known. "That's weird," she agreed.

"I thought Deacon might be hurt," Olivia admitted, "since he's not answering his phone."

"But last night he was fine," Rosemary said. Not that she needed to remind Olivia; she'd been there, too. "He came to the boarding house to make sure Holly knew that." But she wondered now if there had been someone else he'd wanted to reassure—Olivia. But then why wouldn't he answer her calls now? "Maybe his phone was damaged in the explosion . . ."

Olivia shrugged again. "I thought that, too, so I called the sheriff's office and spoke with a woman. She said he was fine. That he was in his office and that his phone was working."

"I'm sure he's just busy," Rosemary said.

"I know," Olivia said. "And I wouldn't have called him if it wasn't important."

"What is it?" Rosemary asked with concern. "What's happened?"

"My stalker is here," Olivia said.

Suddenly it all made sense; exhaustion wasn't the only reason Olivia had checked herself into Halcyon Hall. Fear was her other reason. That fear coursed through Rosemary now, too. She glanced around the conservatory. "He's here? At the hall?"

"He left a note for me," Olivia said. "He knows I'm here. He knows what name I'm using."

"You need to tell Warren, so that he'll put the security guards on extra alert."

Olivia snorted again. "Do I dare trust him? I think he's known who I am. He could have taken that photo of me and sold it to that online tabloid."

Rosemary noticed a shadow outside the entrance to the conservatory. Maybe Gordon Chase hadn't gone far, and he was standing yet in the corridor. Or was it Warren's shadow darkening the doorway?

Rosemary didn't trust Halcyon Hall's head of security either. She sighed and admitted, "He could have."

"That's why I need to talk to the sheriff," Olivia said. Then she shook her head. "Screw it. I just need to get the hell out of here. Out of the hall and off this damn island."

"That would be too dangerous," Rosemary cautioned her. "That bridge is hard to drive over even when the weather's good." She knew because she'd nearly been killed on it. "I doubt it's been opened up yet."

"It was open for the state police to get here," Olivia reminded her as she headed toward the door to the hall.

"Don't go!" Rosemary called after her.

Olivia stopped in the doorway and turned back toward her. "You're not my shrink, Rosemary. You can't commit me here like those girls were committed so long ago."

Morgana's girls . . . the ones she claimed she heard.

"Sometimes I think I hear them, too," Olivia admitted. "Maybe I am crazy."

Rosemary hated that word, but she was desperate enough to use it to discourage Olivia from doing anything rash and dangerous. "You are crazy if you leave." Then that stalker would be able to get to her much easier than he could now.

"I'd be crazier to stay," Olivia said, and before Rosemary could reason with her anymore, she rushed out of the conservatory.

Rosemary couldn't help but wonder if she was running from her stalker, though, or from the sheriff and the feelings she was obviously developing for him. Why hadn't he called her back?

Elijah stood before his office windows, staring out at the snow-covered trees and ground. His secretary had buzzed that he had a call waiting for him from the sheriff, but he didn't want to take it. With a heavy sigh, he told her, "Put him through." He knew he didn't have a choice. Since Deacon had become Judge Lawrence's new best friend, he had no problem getting warrants for whatever he wanted. When the call connected, he greeted him, "Sheriff."

Deacon, as usual, dispensed with any greetings. His voice gruff, he said, "I heard back this morning about the DNA."

Elijah whirled around toward the speaker on his desk. "You have the results?" It had taken so damn long he'd almost given up on ever finding out who that woman had been and if the groundskeeper who'd abducted Rosemary's daughter was some offspring of his grandfather, like he'd claimed.

"Well," Elijah prodded him. "Are you going to tell me?"

"In person," Deacon replied. "And you should get everyone together to hear the news."

This was bad. Bad enough that Deacon obviously wanted to see the reactions of those involved, of his suspects.

"I'm on my way," Deacon said, and he disconnected the call.

"Damn it . . . ," Elijah murmured as dread settled heavily in the pit of his stomach, so heavily that he dropped into the chair behind his desk. Then he raised a shaky hand to rub over his face. He wasn't dreading getting the DNA results as much as he was having to admit that, if that groundskeeper really had been related to him, then a member of his family was capable of murder.

But maybe he'd always known that.

He just hadn't wanted to accept it. Hadn't wanted to accept that his family wasn't just cursed; they were criminal. Teddy Bowers had abducted Genevieve Walcott. Surely he was the one responsible for the death of the other woman whose body the sheriff had found.

Deacon hadn't been ignoring the call from Olivia. He'd been on a call with the lab when hers had come in. And given how damn long it had taken to get the DNA results, he hadn't dared risk putting them on hold. Now he knew why it had taken them so long, and it had taken them a while to explain that as well. Fortunately, Olivia had called in to the office and had spoken with Margaret, who had assured him that it wasn't an emergency.

So what was it?

Had she just wanted to talk to him? Check on him? Did she care about him as much as he had begun to care about her?

He would have called her back already, but then the state police had showed up at his office, questioning him like he was a suspect more than a victim. He hadn't set those damn bombs himself.

He wasn't even sure who had the ability to do something like that—though given the Internet tutorials available, probably anyone could have. The trooper had admitted that the devices had been crude; that was why they'd gone off so easily.

Fortunately, not so easily that someone had been seriously hurt. He'd been knocked on his ass from the one at his father's, and a couple of troopers had suffered minor injuries the night before as well. He expelled a sigh of relief, though. It could have been so much worse.

If it had gone off before Olivia had driven away . . .

Or if Holly had been home . . .

Maybe she was smart to run away from him. And maybe that was what Olivia was doing as well—leaving. And she wanted to say good-bye.

He understood her wanting to leave. Now that the paparazzi had found her, her stalker probably would soon, too. If he hadn't already . . . if he hadn't been the one who'd fired those shots at her . . .

Deacon had pressed the state police to rush processing whatever DNA or prints they could find on the threats she'd received. He'd also asked them to track down Hugh Torrence—to make sure that her past abuser wasn't trying to abuse her again. Deacon needed to find and stop her stalker. Even if she left—*especially* if she left—Deacon wanted her to be safe.

And happy.

She would never be happy on the island. Shannon hadn't been and she'd grown up here. She'd never lived the life Olivia had—although she would have loved to. She would have loved anything besides Bane Island and him. Since he hadn't been able to make happy a woman he'd known his whole life, he knew he had no chance of making Olivia happy.

He wasn't even sure he could keep her safe. He was barely able to keep himself safe. Because, as he drove toward the hall, he glanced into his rearview mirror at the big SUV following the Bane Island Police Department sedan he'd borrowed from Margaret. Before getting inside it, he'd checked it for a bomb. Margaret had assured him that it would be fine with her if someone blew it up; she wouldn't mind getting a new vehicle.

Deacon already had one on order to replace his. If he had to add another to the budget, he had no doubt Warren would use it in his campaign to replace him as sheriff. Just as Deacon had accused him of trying to run him down, Warren could have set the bombs. Then he wouldn't have to worry about beating Deacon in the election—if he wasn't alive to run again.

He might need to run now. The vehicle was gaining fast on Margaret's sedan. If it was just heading the same direction he was, and he'd assumed it was because it appeared to be that Halcyon Hall shade of charcoal gray, the driver could have maintained his speed. Why, now that they were outside town, was he accelerating?

Deacon couldn't see the driver—not through the windows that were tinted nearly the same charcoal color of the paint. A woman could have been driving. He'd once considered Holly a candidate for the driver who'd tried running him down.

Guilt flashed through him. She'd been devastated by his not-so-subtle suspicion of her. And she'd been devastated about the blast last night. The way she'd clung to him . . .

It was like she was his little girl again. The one who'd run and jump into his arms the minute he'd walked in the door after work. He loved her so much. And maybe she didn't hate him as much as she'd claimed. So she wasn't driving that SUV—no matter the doubts Warren had tried planting in his head, just as Warren had probably planted doubts in Holly's mind about Deacon.

Warren . . .

It had to be him; he had the easiest access to the hall vehicles and the most motive to get rid of Deacon. But he should have learned by now that wasn't going to be so easy to do.

Deacon pressed his foot on the accelerator, but the sedan hesitated a long moment before lurching forward. Now he understood why Margaret wouldn't mind if it got totaled. It was old and worn out.

The vehicle following him was not worn out because it sped up and easily closed the distance between them. It was taller than the sedan so that its front bumper was higher. Instead of striking the rear bumper of the car, it struck the trunk. Metal crunched and crumpled. If Deacon didn't do something—that was going to be his body next.

Chapter Twenty

Maybe Olivia was crazy. Because she was still here.

Olivia had intended to rush out of the conservatory up to her room, carry her packed bags down to Holly's car, and leave before the bridge was closed again, if it wasn't already. But once she'd been back in the room—with that threat . . .

The idea of leaving had seemed crazy to her.

Sure, the stalker knew where she was, but he wasn't going to find it any easier than Edie Stone was to get inside the gates. Maybe that threat had been meant to flush Olivia out of the hall, just as Deacon had suggested when that photo had been sold. The stalker obviously knew her well enough to know that she was prone to running away. So maybe staying here, even though he knew where she was, was the smartest thing Olivia could do to protect herself.

No, the smartest thing was to figure out who the hell the stalker was and stop his threats once and for all. Could it be her father, as Deacon had suggested? If it was, dear old Dad was going to find that she wasn't the defenseless little girl she'd once been. She could take care of herself.

She left her room, with the packed bags still inside, and headed down the stairwell to the reception desk and the receptionist who'd given her the envelope. The young woman wasn't alone, though.

Dr. Elijah Cooke paced in front of her desk. "You're sure he hasn't called from the gate yet?"

"I'm sure," she replied.

"Maybe the intercom isn't working," Elijah murmured. "Maybe I should send Warren down to make sure it hasn't iced over or something."

"It was working earlier," the woman replied, "when someone buzzed that Ms. Smith had a delivery at the front gate."

"About that delivery," Olivia began.

Elijah tensed and glanced up, his pale eyes widening with surprise. He obviously hadn't realized she'd joined them. Neither had the receptionist who turned toward her, her painted lips parted on a startled gasp.

"Did you let the person inside to bring it up here?" Olivia asked. And could that person possibly still be on the property? She shuddered at the thought—one of the many that had kept her from rushing outside to leave.

"Of course not," Dr. Cooke replied for the receptionist. "Whenever there is any delivery, even the morning mail, a member of the security staff will pick it up from the front gate. No one unauthorized is ever allowed on the property."

Olivia studied the receptionist's flushed face and wondered if the woman would have given her the same answer had her boss not been present. "Which security guard picked up this package?" she asked.

"Warren," the woman replied, so automatically that Olivia believed her.

Dr. Cooke raised a dark brow in skepticism, though.

"Really?" he asked. "He's usually so busy he assigns those tasks to someone else."

"I'd like to speak to him about it," Olivia said. "I want to know what the person looked like, if they said anything . . ."

Cooke groaned. "Damn it! What was it? What was left for you?"

"Another threat," she admitted.

The receptionist gasped again. She was young enough that she'd probably recognized Olivia some time ago. The fans who attended her concerts were mostly teens, though, or younger.

"I'm sorry," Elijah said. "That shouldn't have gotten to you. I'll speak to Warren about it, too. And there's a camera at the front gate." He glanced over the receptionist's desk at her extra monitor that must show the camera footage from the front gate. "What did you see?" he asked her.

She shook her head. "The cameras were down this morning. None of them were working until just a little while ago when one of the security guards got them up and running again."

Olivia tensed with suspicion. That seemed awfully convenient. Had her stalker paid off someone at the hall to help him? Warren? Had he gotten inside the stone wall and gates that guarded the hall?

"Did you recognize the voice?" Elijah asked.

She shook her head again.

"Was it male or female?" he persisted—as if he really cared. Maybe he did.

But Olivia couldn't quite bring herself to trust him or anyone else. Especially not now.

The young woman's brow furrowed as if she struggled to figure it out. "I really can't say. It was muffled. Warren could tell you more. I called him right after the person buzzed into the intercom at the gate, and he said he was just driving onto the property then. So he met the person."

"Where is Warren?" Elijah asked her. "I left him a voice-mail that he was supposed to come to this meeting with the sheriff. And so was Bode." He glanced down at his wristwatch and sighed. "The sheriff should have been here already, too."

"You're waiting for Deacon?" Olivia asked with sur-prise. "Why so anxiously?" With their relationship, she doubted he was looking forward to another visit from the lawman. "Has something else happened?"

He shook his head and sighed again, a long, ragged expulsion of air. Then he replied, "He has the DNA results back."

"On the body," she said. "That's good."

The psychiatrist didn't look as convinced as she was.

"She might have a family that's been missing her," Olivia said. Hers hadn't when she'd disappeared. At least that was what she'd assumed because he hadn't found her. Fortunately, not all families were like hers. It was obvious that Rosemary had a good relationship with her daughter. And despite Holly's complaints about her father, they clearly loved each other.

"She might . . . ," Elijah murmured with an odd expres-sion on his handsome face, one almost of regret. Had he been involved in the woman's death? Her murder . . . ?

He glanced at the receptionist again. "So where is Warren?"

"He left earlier today, shortly after he brought that en-velope to me," she said. "I think he's busy at the sheriff's department. And, oh, Dr. Chase told me that he was leaving a while ago as well. I'm not sure where Bode is."

Elijah sighed. "I guess it doesn't matter since the sheriff's late anyways. He claimed to be on his way when he called. So where the hell is he?"

Fear gripped her, stealing her breath away. Had there been another attempt on the sheriff's life?

"Why are you here?" Grandfather asked, without even turning away from the window in front of which his wheelchair was parked. He must have seen Bode's reflection in the glass, or maybe he'd seen him walking up to the carriage house. The old man had a bird's eye view of the entire estate from his window on the second story of the carriage house.

Bode wasn't sure why he'd come here. It wasn't as if his grandfather had ever given him comfort or even any respect despite all the success he'd found as a personal trainer. Elijah hadn't given him much either, until recently. But would that be about to change now with the discovery of those DNA results?

Bode couldn't force himself to go up to the hall. He couldn't . . .

He didn't want to know.

Instead of answering his grandfather's question, he asked one of his own, "Where's your nurse?"

His grandfather shrugged. "Who knows?"

"You know," Bode said. He suspected the old man knew everything that happened at the hall.

James Bainesworth's thin lips curved into a smug grin. "Maybe I do . . ."

"He shouldn't leave you alone so much," Bode said with real concern. His grandfather was over ninety and confined to that wheelchair.

James chuckled. "Afraid I'm going to run away?"

The cheap shot struck its mark, just as his grandfather had intended. This was why Elijah visited him so rarely. He was too smart to keep subjecting himself to the barbs and arrows his grandfather always threw.

But maybe Erika hadn't run away after all. But where would she have been those months before she died if she hadn't run away? No. He would rather believe that she'd left. Then there would be a possibility that she could return.

"The sheriff got back the DNA results," Bode shared.

"That stubborn son of a bitch," James murmured. "He just can't let it go. Never could . . ."

"The woman's body needed to be identified," Bode said. "He's just doing his job. Investigating a murder."

James snorted. "Ever since he was a kid, he's liked to cry murder."

"The autopsy report cried murder." Deacon had already shared that with Elijah, who'd shared it with Bode. The sheriff wouldn't have been getting all the warrants he had if he hadn't had proof that a crime had happened.

Grandfather sighed and murmured again, "Damn him."

Bode knew there was bad blood between his brother and Deacon Howell. He hadn't realized his grandfather also disliked the sheriff. "I thought you were friends with his father," he said.

James Bainesworth snorted again. "Friends . . ."

Before he'd gotten sick, Sam Howell used to come visit him. But since then, Grandfather had never tried to return the favor, and despite the wheelchair, he was still pretty mobile.

"You don't have to buy friendship," James added.

So the rumors about Sam Howell taking bribes weren't lies. And his grandfather had paid them. Was everything his grandfather had told him—that he'd had nothing to do with those women being harmed—all lies as well? Had Bode gone into partnership—and convinced his brother to join him—with the devil?

A sick feeling rushed over Bode, and he'd already been feeling sick since his brother had called him. A little dizzy, his legs a little shaky, he dropped onto the edge of his grandfather's bed.

"You okay?" James asked. "You're not trying to hide from the truth, are you? Like your brother does?"

Bode was pretty sure Elijah was much more aware of the truth than he was. He'd actually believed the old man's claims of innocence because, surely, if there'd been any evidence to back up those rumors, he would have gone to prison.

His grandfather didn't wait for his answer, just chuckled again. "He won't be able to hide much longer. The sheriff won't give up until he gets to the truth about everything." His pale gaze focused intensely on Bode, and he raised his gray brows.

"Why are you telling me this like you're warning me?" Bode asked. "Can the truth hurt us?"

"The truth always hurts."

Whoever tried to run Deacon off the road hadn't taken the same defensive driving courses Deacon had taken during the police academy. Hell, Deacon had gotten so good at defensive driving that he'd started instructing the courses— before returning to Bane Island. He'd been back long enough that he'd gotten rusty, though. He wasn't as good as he'd been, or he would have managed to catch the person driving the Halcyon Hall SUV.

Or would have at least caught a glimpse of the driver. When Deacon twisted his steering wheel and did a U-turn in front of the SUV, all he'd been able to see through the tinted windshield was a shadow, like the one lurking around his truck the night before. After the U-turn, he'd made a few more defensive maneuvers, until he'd taken over the offense.

But the other vehicle was faster, too fast for him to overtake. So he'd lost the SUV. But he was pretty damn sure he knew where it had gone—to the same place he had. The place where he knew someone was trying to kill him. Who? Elijah?

He rolled down his window and reached for the intercom, but before he could even press the button, the gates began to open. A woman's voice emanated from the speaker, "Sheriff, Dr. Cooke has been waiting for you."

So his old childhood nemesis hadn't been personally behind the wheel. But then Elijah had never done his own dirty work even when they were kids. He'd been too smart for that, so he'd manipulated bigger Bainesworth relatives into doing what he'd wanted.

From the stories Deacon had heard about Dr. James Bainesworth, Elijah was the most like his grandfather. The old man was probably proud. Or maybe he was still pulling the strings.

"Sheriff?" a voice called from the speaker.

He glanced up and noticed the gates standing open. "Thank you," he murmured back through the window. Then he pressed on the accelerator and headed down the long, winding drive. It wasn't long enough, though, because he was at the building too soon. Too soon for his heart to have stopped pounding, for his temper to have calmed enough for him to have any control. He was damn well getting sick of someone trying to kill him just because he was doing his job. Or maybe it was being here—in front of this stone structure that looked more like a prison than a spa—that had his heart pounding so hard.

The minute he turned off the sedan and opened the door, he came under attack again. Elijah Cooke gripped the top of his door.

"Where the hell have you been?" he asked. "What the hell kind of game are you playing?"

Deacon snorted. "I'm playing?"

Ignoring his bruises and aches from the first explosion, he jumped out of the car and shoved Elijah back. The guy's fancy dress shoes slipped on the icy pavement, and he nearly went down.

Instinctively Deacon grabbed his arm and held him up, but he shook him slightly as he asked, "What the hell game are you playing? Do you think killing me is going to stop the murder investigation?"

"How many times do I have to tell you that I have nothing to do with the attempts on your life?" Those pale eyes narrowed. "Was there just another one? Is that why you're late?"

Deacon shook his head. "Like you don't know . . ."

"I don't," Elijah insisted. "I've been waiting for you. I want to know the results."

"You want to know the truth?"

His throat moved as if he was struggling to swallow, but he just nodded.

"You might change your mind once you hear it," Deacon warned him.

"I have to know," Elijah said.

But Deacon suspected that he already did.

Chapter Twenty-One

Elijah stood outside the door of one of the small stone cottages on the estate, his hand lifted to knock, his stomach churning with dread over what he was about to do. Over the horrible, tragic news he had to share . . .

But yet he hesitated while snow swirled around him, falling on his head. It was so cold that it didn't even melt, and when he uttered a ragged sigh, his breath froze, suspended before his face. He was going to freeze if he stood out here any longer. So he forced his fist to strike the door, but it was several long moments before Bode finally opened it to him.

"What took you so long?" Elijah grumbled, as his body began to shake with the cold. "And where have you been?"

When Bode hadn't turned up for the meeting with the sheriff, Elijah had called his house and talked to the nanny who said he wasn't there either. Could he have been the one the sheriff claimed had tried forcing him off the road?

No. Elijah didn't want to think that, but the doubts kept creeping in.

"I was here," Bode said.

"That's not what your nanny said when I called here," Elijah said, calling him on the lie.

Bode shrugged. "I stepped out for a bit, for a walk." Then he stepped back so Elijah could pass him before he closed the door behind him. The cottage was warm—a fire burned in the hearth. Stockings hung from the mantel and a small tree stood in the corner, decorated with twinkling lights. Elijah had nearly forgotten it was almost Christmas. Clearly his brother had not.

There were a few of these small stone cottages on the estate. Elijah would have liked to live in one, too, but as the director, he'd felt he needed to always be available, so he stayed in the main hall in a private suite of rooms. But then, Bode had his reason for staying here.

Adelaide wriggled in her father's arms, gurgling and smiling. Then she held out her little pudgy arms toward Elijah, and something squeezed his heart hard. He'd been studying up on babies lately, and at her age, almost four months, she wasn't supposed to be able to reach out like that. But then, she was a Cooke, so of course she would be smart. And strong . . .

"Do you want to go to Uncle Eli?" Bode asked her. "Do you want to cheer up the grump?"

Elijah glared at him, but almost of their own volition, his arms reached out for his niece. Over the past few weeks that he'd finally brought himself to acknowledge her, he'd gotten a little less awkward with holding her. For some odd reason she seemed to like him. He wasn't sure why. Whenever he'd dated a woman with a child, the kid had always hated him. "I'm not a grump," Elijah said. Not usually.

But with everything happening around the hall lately . . . and with his doubts . . .

"You don't look too damn happy right now," Bode said.

"But then you never are after a run-in with Deacon Howell. The two of you ever going to grow up and put your school-kid rivalry behind you?"

"It's more than that and you know it," Elijah said.

Bode sighed. "I know. I know he blames you for his wife dying."

He wasn't the only one. Elijah blamed himself. How had he not realized how troubled Shannon was? Or hadn't it been the suicide everyone had thought? Because there had been another murder on the property, another life senselessly lost.

He tightened his arms around Adelaide, whose eyes, that were beginning to lighten from dark blue to light blue, widened with surprise. Her bottom lip began to tremble, as if she already knew what he was going to say. He loosened his grip and jiggled her against him, and a little laugh gurgled out of her.

Bode's chuckle echoed his daughter's.

Elijah was tempted to hand Adelaide back to him and leave. Leave them like this, laughing and smiling. But he heard the hollow ring to Bode's laugh and knew that he knew.

"You haven't asked me what Deacon said about the DNA," he pointed out to his brother.

"So, do we have more family?" Bode asked. "Was that crazy groundskeeper one of Grandfather's spawn?"

Elijah shook his head. "That DNA hasn't come back yet." According to Deacon there had been a problem at the lab, and the results had been accidentally destroyed. Was that the truth? Had it actually been an accident or was Grandfather still paying to cover up his past sins?

Elijah wouldn't put it past him. How far would he go to cover them up, though? Murder? Was he orchestrating all those attempts on Deacon's life?

"The DNA you should be most concerned about has come back, though," Elijah said.

Bode shrugged. "Doesn't concern me."

"It damn well should."

"Why?" he asked with defiance in his voice. He sounded like he had when they were kids, when he was trying to act as old and tough as Elijah and their cousins. "I know it's not her."

"Jamie . . ." His old name slipped out of Elijah's lips, maybe because his brother was acting like a child now.

He shook his head. "It can't be her." He reached for his daughter now, but Elijah stepped back and held his niece closely. Despite Bode's denials, he saw the tears pooling in his brother's eyes. "It can't be her . . . ," he murmured again, his voice gruff with emotion. "It can't be Erika . . ."

"It is," Elijah said. "It was . . ."

There hadn't been much of her left after the coyotes had dug up her body, though. Just enough for the coroner to determine she'd been murdered.

Bode shook his head again, and the tears spilled over, streaking down his face. "No . . ."

"I'm so sorry," Elijah said. For his brother and for his niece. Adelaide would never know her mother. Unfortunately, Elijah really hadn't known her either. Like Bode, Erika Korlinsky had been a personal trainer, so on the body side of the business at the hall, whereas Elijah focused on the mind. Until he'd nearly lost Bode a few weeks ago, after the groundskeeper had struck him and left him for dead, Elijah hadn't really had much of a relationship with his brother either.

"But she left the island," Bode persisted. "She left that note, too. You've seen it. She couldn't handle having a baby, the seclusion of the island . . . none of it was what she wanted. I wasn't what she wanted."

Elijah flinched. The sheriff had said that Bode had probably killed the woman when she rejected him. That the personal trainer's enormous ego hadn't been able to handle the rejection. So he'd stopped her from leaving him by killing the mother of his child.

Bode didn't miss his reaction. "He suspects me, doesn't he?"

He nodded.

"Do you?"

"I told the sheriff he was being ridiculous as usual," Elijah said. "That he's so determined to think the worst of everyone associated with the Bainesworth family that he's blind to the truth—"

"But *do you* suspect me?" Bode asked again, his pale gaze hard on his older brother's face.

He couldn't believe that, as much as Bode loved his daughter, he would take her mother from her. He couldn't.

But yet those damn doubts niggled at him. Who else would have had a motive? Nobody had been as close to Erika as Bode had. And Bode was a Bainesworth . . .

In fact he'd been named after the old man or, as some claimed, the devil himself. Bode's real name was James, just like Grandfather. Sick of being called Jamie, he'd renamed himself Bode and launched his career as a fitness guru on the West Coast.

With all the years between them, they hadn't really grown up together. And then Jamie had moved away. So Elijah barely knew his brother anymore.

"Elijah, do you suspect me?" Bode persisted.

Making him realize that he hadn't answered, that he couldn't . . . not honestly. So he forced a smile and a shrug.

Bode shook his head again. "You son of a bitch . . ."

"We both are," Elijah reminded him. From what he remembered of her though, their mother hadn't really been a bitch, just self-involved and messed up. She'd run off when Jamie was a baby, just like he'd believed Erika had. "I want to believe that you had nothing to do with it. And most of me does."

Finally, Bode nodded. "Okay. I get that. There's a part of me that still doubts you, too." This time he didn't just reach for his daughter, he took her, plucking her almost protectively from Elijah's arms.

Bode's words struck him like a blow. "Me? What have I done? I didn't even know Erika. She worked for you."

"She worked for you," Bode said. "You're the director. We all work for you. You're in charge of everything, Elijah. So how do people keep dying on your watch?"

Deacon had asked him that, too, along with some real pointed questions about Shannon's death. Had that been a murder as well?

"I don't know," Elijah answered honestly, helplessly. He felt so damn helpless over everything that had been happening at the hall. He could have blamed his head of security like Deacon had earlier. After all, the security of the hall was Warren's responsibility. But like his brother had pointed out, Elijah was the one in charge of everything. So it was all his responsibility.

Deacon thought someone was out to get him, and after the explosions, there was no doubt that someone was. But maybe he wasn't the only one with someone out to get him. If Elijah gave in to the paranoia creeping up on him, he might consider that someone was actually after him, to discredit and destroy him.

"I don't know . . . ," he repeated in a murmur.

Who could hate him that much?

His own brother—because Bode added insult to injury when he said, "Maybe you're the one who should have been named after the old man."

Elijah nearly doubled over from that blow, as pain pierced his heart and stole his breath away. He was glad that Bode had taken his daughter away from him—because if his little brother wasn't holding the child, Elijah would have hit him.

As it was, he needed to get the hell away from him before he said or did something he would regret—like he hoped his brother regretted what he'd just said. He turned and pulled open the door and stepped into the cold, but despite the snow blowing around on a frigid wind, he felt warmer than he had with his family.

Hell, anything was warmer than his family.

"Elijah!" Bode called after him. His shout must have startled the child because she let out a wail.

Or maybe she, too, was trying to stop Elijah from leaving.

But he didn't stop. He just pulled the door closed and walked away. He'd been made a fool of long enough; it was damn time that he found out who was raising all the hell around the hall.

Past time that he found that person and permanently stopped him.

Deacon paced the marble floor of the foyer, his gaze going again and again to the bottom of the stairwell—to where he'd found that body so long ago. The manor had been so dilapidated then, the stone walls crumbling, the windows broken out, holes in the roof . . .

Why would anyone have been inside it—besides a little boy too proud to resist a dare?

Had that woman actually committed suicide, like his father had claimed? Or been dumped here after an overdose? He needed to look at that old file and find out if the woman had ever been identified and exactly how she'd died.

Had Shannon's death really been a suicide?

He'd asked Elijah a couple questions about it, but the director had been too distracted over the DNA news to say much. That was why Deacon had chosen to address his concerns then; he'd figured Elijah might slip up. But even distracted, the man was too damn smart to incriminate himself or his brother. He'd vouched that Bode had nothing to do with the death of his baby's mother.

Just like nobody at the hall had had anything to do with Shannon's death or Genevieve Walcott's disappearance or the mysterious body that Deacon had found so long ago in the ruins of the manor.

Bainesworths never took responsibility for anything. That was about to stop. Deacon was going to stop it. But first he needed a warrant to check the vehicles, so he could find the one that had tried running him down in the street and off the road just a short while ago.

"There you are!" Rosemary exclaimed as she emerged from the shadows of the hall into the gloomy light of the foyer.

Deacon's impatience eased. "Did Whit call you? Did he get the warrant for me?" he asked.

Her brow furrowed. "No, I don't know what warrant you're talking about."

Deacon wasn't about to explain in case Whit didn't

want her involved. He didn't particularly want her involved himself, and he wasn't in love with her like the judge was. He shook his head. "I shouldn't have asked. I'm sure he'll call me directly." Or have it emailed to him like he had in the past.

"Is the warrant about the stalker?" Rosemary asked. "Are you working on it?"

"I am." But he didn't need a warrant to have the state police lab process the threats and check on Olivia's father's whereabouts.

Rosemary expelled a shaky breath of relief. "That's good. I know she is very scared that he found her here."

"What?" Deacon asked, fear gripping his heart in a tight fist. "She knows for certain that the stalker is here?"

"So you haven't talked to her?" Rosemary asked. "She said you hadn't picked up when she called, but I figured you would have returned her message by now."

He would have—had he not been trying to save his own damn life first. "Where is she?" he asked. He needed to make sure that she was safe.

Rosemary shrugged. "I think she went back to her room."

He turned toward the stairwell, running up the steps to the second story and her suite. He stopped at the door, winded and not just from his jaunt up the stairs but from the fear pounding in his heart. What if she was already gone?

He fisted a slightly shaking hand and raised it to knock. For an interminably long moment, there was no answer. So he knocked again and again.

And he worried that he was already too late. That Olivia

had already left and, in doing so, might have walked right into the clutches of her stalker.

Olivia had gone back to her room once the receptionist had told Elijah that the sheriff was at the gate. She hadn't rushed outside to meet him, like the hall director had. She wasn't sure, with the stalker here, that she was safe anywhere but locked in her suite.

She must have felt safe enough to succumb to the sleep she'd given up the night before, because knocking at her door startled her awake. She pressed her hand over her mouth to hold in the cry that had risen up the back of her throat. Was he here? Had he gotten inside?

But would her stalker just come up and knock on her door? Wouldn't he be afraid of someone seeing him? Hearing him?

A voice called out, "Olivia!"

She jumped up from the bed and hurried over to the door, jerking it open. "Deacon!"

She'd already known he was all right. But she couldn't contain the relief that surged through her again. Almost of their own volition, her arms reached for him.

His arms closed around her, and his big body shuddered with either the same relief she was feeling, or with pain. Maybe it was because of the bruises he'd received yesterday in the explosion. Or maybe he had new bruises.

She pulled back and stared up into his face. "Are you all right?"

His head jerked in a sharp nod. "Yes. Are you? I'm sorry I didn't answer your call." He looked away then, and his skin flushed.

"I wasn't calling because I'm falling for you or anything,"

she said, although she had a sick feeling that she was. Just touching him affected her, being close to him, so she stepped back even farther until feet separated them now. "I'm not some lovesick woman hung up on you because we had sex one time."

He flinched as if she'd slapped him. "I know. Rosemary told me that the stalker was here. What happened?"

She walked over to where she'd left the envelope, the photo, and the note on the bed. When she reached for them, he caught her wrist.

"Don't handle them anymore," he said. "I need to send it all to the state lab, so they can process it with the others." He gasped when he looked at the photo. "That's you and Edie at the boarding house last night." He looked at the envelope then. "There's no postmark."

"It was dropped at the gate," she said.

"Nobody saw who dropped it?"

She shrugged. "You'd have to ask Warren. He was the one who brought it up to the receptionist. Supposedly the cameras were down then, so there is no security footage of the person who dropped it off or of Warren picking it up from him."

"Warren," he murmured, his voice husky with bitterness.

"He left the hall shortly afterward," she said. "So I haven't been able to talk to him."

"Of course he's gone," he said. "I'll track him down." He leaned over her shoulder, too close again, as he studied the note. "Are you sure it's from the same person?"

His comment unsettled her, made her look more closely at the handwriting she'd thought she'd recognized. Was it the same? She didn't have those other notes to compare it to now.

"Do you think I picked up another stalker here on the island?" she asked. "Nobody here even knows who I really am."

"I think more people know than you realize," he said.

She expelled a shaky breath and nodded in reluctant agreement. "Edie said that the person who took the first picture had the tabloid wire money to the drugstore here on the island."

"Did Edie ask who picked up that money?"

"She was going to find out and call you. Did she?" Olivia asked.

His face flushed again. "I saw a missed call from her, too. But I've been busy."

She nodded. "Of course, I know that, with the bomb last night." Her voice cracked as she thought of how close he'd come—over and over again—to dying. She turned away, so that he wouldn't see the tears filling her eyes. Then he would know that she'd lied, that he meant more to her than she was willing to admit.

He slid his arms around her and turned her toward him. "When you and Edie called earlier, I was on the phone with the lab. They were explaining the DNA results to me as they faxed them over. Well, they were excusing their screw up."

"Screw up?"

He shook his head. "Not about the body. I know who she is. Erika Korlinsky. Did you know her? She was a personal trainer here. She supposedly disappeared months before her death, though."

She shook her head. "No. Even if she'd been here, I've stayed away from the personal trainers." She'd tried to stay away from everyone—to isolate herself. But Rosemary, and her concern for her daughter, had affected her. And Holly had eventually gotten to her as well.

"That's so sad and scary that someone was murdered here," she said, her heart filling with sympathy for that woman even as panic began to press on her lungs. Maybe this place was as dangerous as the sheriff and the Pierce sisters and Edie Stone claimed. "I thought I would be safe here. But now I really need to leave."

"You can't keep running from him," he said. "We need to find out who he is."

"You're too busy," she said. "You're too busy for me, with this body and with someone trying to stop you from investigating her murder." She winced at the trace of self-pity that had slipped into her voice. Even though she'd wanted him the night before, this wasn't what she wanted. She didn't want to need someone, to depend on someone, because she'd learned long ago that kind of dependence only led to pain and disappointment.

Deacon reached out then, trailing his fingers along her jaw. "I'm sorry," he said. "I'm sorry that someone's been threatening you. I'm sorry that person found you. And I'm sorry I didn't answer when you called."

Tears stung her eyes. She blinked them back. "That's—"

A loud ring emanated from his pocket, jarring her. He pulled it out and glanced at the screen before dropping it back in his pocket.

"Take it," she told him. "I know you have a lot going—"

"I'm worried about you," he said.

"I'm not your responsibility," she said. And it was true. "You have more than enough of those already—to your daughter, to this island, to yourself. You need to focus on staying safe."

"I want to keep you safe."

"They're just threats," she said. "Just written warnings. In the six months that I was receiving these on tour, nobody has actually tried to hurt me." So maybe she'd just used them as an excuse to leave, to drop out of the public eye.

"You probably had security for the tour," he said. "With as much as you prize your privacy."

She nodded.

"And somebody shot at you," he said, his voice gruff with anger. "That was a damn dangerous warning."

"But I wasn't hit," she said.

He touched the stitches on her forehead. "You were hurt."

"I'm going to get hurt a lot worse if I stay here," she said, and she sighed. "Maybe everybody's right, and this place is cursed." And now so was she because she'd come here.

No. She'd been cursed since the day she was born.

"I don't want you to go," he said.

"Because you want to catch my stalker?"

"Because I want you . . ." Then he lowered his head and brushed his mouth across hers.

The tears stung her eyes again, as passion and the need that scared her so much, rushed over her. This wasn't just desire for her; this was love.

How had she been so stupid?

How had she fallen so hard for a man she barely knew? A man even his own daughter blamed for his wife's death?

He pulled her closer, but as he did, his phone began to ring again and vibrate between them.

She wriggled free of his arms and stepped back. "You need to take that. You need to deal with everything else going on. I can take care of my own problems. I've been doing that for years."

"You've not been dealing," he said as he continued to ignore his cell. "You've been running away, just like Shannon and Holly."

She couldn't deny that she had spent most of her life running and hiding. "You know that I had to . . ." She'd told him all about her difficult childhood. He hadn't told her much about himself—except that his father had been an alcoholic. "Why did Shannon run away?"

"She was never happy," he said. "I could never make her happy. She would leave me and Holly even before we moved here. She would need time and space, and after a couple of weeks, she would come back to us. And for a while, it would seem like things would be better. Then she'd leave again."

"Sounds like she had depression." So maybe she had killed herself.

He shrugged. "I don't know. Elijah probably does. She came here so that he could help her. And she wound up dead."

So would Olivia, she feared, if she stayed here. But she didn't want to leave. She didn't want to leave Deacon and Holly like Shannon had. They were beginning to mean too much to her. Too much for her to run away . . .

But could she risk staying? Could she risk death?

Chapter Twenty-Two

Staring at her as intently as he was, Deacon noticed the panic enter Olivia's beautiful eyes. She raised a hand to her throat, as if she was struggling to breathe.

"What's wrong?" he asked, her panic pressing on his lungs now. "What happened?"

"I . . . I just need a minute," she murmured, and she stepped back, nearly stumbling as she retreated farther into her suite.

Had he overwhelmed her with talking about Shannon? Was she starting to believe like some others did, that he'd pushed his wife?

"I won't hurt you," he promised. "I won't ever hurt you."

"I'm not scared of you," she assured him. "I'm just scared. I need a minute."

That was all he intended to give her. They needed to talk—needed to figure out how to keep her safe from her stalker. How the hell had the person even made it onto the island with as often as the bridge had been shut down over the bad weather?

None of that mattered, though. Nothing mattered but

keeping her safe. And maybe it was better that her stalker was here—because then Deacon could catch him and make sure that he could never carry out all those threats.

He stepped out of her room and drew the door shut behind him. He might not be able to give her enough to convince her to stay on Bane Island with him forever—but he could give her the moment to herself that she'd asked for.

Once in the hallway, he pulled his cell from his pocket to see all the calls he'd missed while he'd refused to answer it when he'd been talking to her. As he scrolled through the call log, he saw that the first one had been from Whit, followed by another call from Edie. And then there was one from the state trooper who'd been assigned to investigate the bombs. He didn't care so much about that now—about himself—but he'd also given her the stalker threats and had followed up with her earlier to check into Hugh Torrence.

He played her message first. "Sheriff Howell, I'm aware you reached out to Judge Lawrence for a warrant to inspect the Halcyon Hall vehicles."

That must have been why Whit had called.

She continued, "That warrant was granted, but we are to carry out the search. Not you."

He wasn't surprised. They'd made it clear to him in his office earlier that he wasn't allowed to investigate the attempts on his own life. And they didn't even know about the latest one. He hadn't reported it. But since they were going to be checking for damage on those vehicles, he had better let them know they would find more now. On the front bumper.

So he called back the direct number from which she'd called him.

"Trooper Montgomery," she answered.

"This is Sheriff Howell," he said. He quickly filled her in on what had happened what felt like ages ago but had actually been less than a couple of hours.

"Sheriff, let us assign you a protection detail until we can catch whoever's been making these attempts on your life," she said.

He glanced over his shoulder at the door behind him, the door to Olivia's suite. She was the one who needed protection. Was she okay now? Nobody could get through him to her, but what about the panic he'd seen in her eyes?

Would she do something to herself?

"I can take care of myself," he said. "I'm more concerned about Olivia Smith."

"Olivia Smith?" she asked, and her voice had an odd pitch to it.

"You know. The woman I told you is being stalked. She's actually that singer—AKAN. I gave you the notes and asked for you to check into her father, Hugh Torrence."

"Hugh Torrence is in prison for assault," Trooper Montgomery replied. "Or he was. I will check to see if he got paroled yet, but I don't think that's necessary."

"Why not?" he asked. If the son of a bitch had been released, he might have decided to track down his daughter for some money or for some even more terrible reason.

"The notes were processed for prints, and there were only two sets on them," she replied. "Or maybe it was one. Their report isn't really clear."

Deacon groaned, wondering if there'd been another "mix-up." "What does the report say?"

"A report came back with two Olivias. One, Olivia Torrence, aged 34, with a prior record for shop lifting and vagrancy. The other, Olivia Smith, aged 34, with a record for drug possession and assault."

"I don't understand . . . ," he murmured.

"I don't either," she admitted. "I don't know if the lab found one set of prints belonging to one woman with two identities or if they found two sets of prints for two separate women. I'll check into that and let you know. But as of right now, the woman you call Olivia Smith may only be a threat to herself."

And to him . . .

He'd believed her. He'd worried about her. He'd begun to fall for her and what had it all been?

A publicity stunt? A mental health issue? Was that why she was here? Had he been about to fall for a woman exactly like his late wife?

For once he understood Holly and Shannon and Olivia's penchant for running away from their problems. He was tempted to do the same. To run away . . .

But instead he clicked off the call with the trooper, and he reached for the doorknob to Olivia's room.

Olivia Torrence.

Olivia Smith.

Was she one in the same?

She wanted to stay. And not just on the island. Olivia wanted to stay with Deacon and Holly. The risk was high—to her heart and to her life. Dare she take it? The thought of it had had her panicking, struggling for a few long moments to breathe.

But once the door had closed behind Deacon, she'd wanted him back—had wanted to be back in his arms. And not just because she was scared. Then, as if he'd known that she needed him, the door opened, and he stepped back into the suite with her.

But instead of crossing the room to where she stood at the windows, he leaned back against the door as if he was too weary to come any farther. And maybe he was . . .

He'd been through so much. But yet here he was, making sure that she was okay. That she was safe.

Dare she trust the promise he'd made to her? Dare she believe that he would never hurt her?

She started toward him then, but when she noticed the look in his dark eyes and the rigid tension in his jaw, she stopped. "Deacon?"

"Who are you?" he asked, and his voice vibrated with fury.

She froze as his tone brought her back to her past.

Who the hell do you think you are?

You're nobody!

You're nothing!

I wish you were never born!

Tears stung her eyes, but she blinked them back. "What do you mean? You know who I am."

"Who are you really?" he asked. "Your real name."

"It's Olivia," she admitted.

"Olivia Torrence or Olivia Smith?" he asked. "Because fingerprints came back for both those women—women with criminal records—from those threats your stalker sent."

She gasped with sudden realization. Olivia Smith.

"Surprised I figured it out?" he asked. "What was all this, Olivia? Just some publicity stunt? You were going to use your stalker story to get the press interested in you again after you spent months in this place? Or was it a cover in case anybody found out why you were really here?"

She furrowed her brow with confusion. "What are you talking about? You're not making any sense. I'm not really Olivia Smith."

He snorted. "You're not making any sense. You think I'm going to believe that you randomly picked an alias of a person whose prints showed up on those threats?"

She shook her head. "Olivia Smith is a real person. She's one of the backup singers that was on the concert tour with me. As well as sharing the same first name, we also look enough alike that she gave me her driver's license, so that I could fly out of LA without being recognized or tracked down."

"So she's in on this with you?" he asked.

She shook her head again. She hadn't told Olivia why she'd needed to leave. She hadn't showed her the threats or the photos. So the only way her prints could be on them was if she'd sent them, if she'd taken the pictures . . .

She'd certainly had access and opportunity. But what was her reason?

Was there nobody she could trust?

She couldn't trust Deacon—not after how quickly he'd broken that promise he'd just made to her, that promise not to hurt her. Instead he'd leaped to wild conclusions about her. He wanted to believe the worst about her. She understood that; she tended to do the same herself. But she'd thought—she'd hoped—he was beginning to trust her like she'd been beginning to trust him.

"Somebody's working with you," he persisted. "You couldn't take those pictures of yourself. Or take those shots at you. Who is it? Who came to the island with you?"

"Nobody," she said.

"That person could have hit my daughter," he said, his voice gruff with that fury that burned in his dark eyes. "Your damn stunt could have gotten Holly killed!"

"*I* would never hurt Holly!" she yelled back at him, wanting to hurt him like he was hurting her. From the way he flinched, it was clear that she had, and she felt a pang of regret.

"You don't think this is going to hurt her?" he asked. "To find out her hero is a big fraud?"

He'd struck a nerve, too. Ever since she'd started getting successful, she'd felt like a fraud. Like she wasn't good enough.

Like she didn't deserve it.

But she was sick of feeling that way. And she was sick of his accusations. "It wasn't a stunt. Olivia Smith must have taken those photos, must have sent those letters to me."

"Why?" he asked.

She shook her head. "I don't know." Even though she hadn't become friends with any of them, she'd always treated the backup singers and dancers with respect. "Maybe she was jealous or . . ."

But of what? AKAN's success? Olivia hadn't wanted it, hadn't wanted any of it. But she refused to believe any longer that she hadn't deserved it. Those songs had been her pain—her past. And her triumph over having survived all that.

"So you think she's jealous enough to hunt you down on this island and take those shots at you?" he asked, the skepticism in the arch of his dark brows.

She shrugged. "I don't know. I don't even know how she would have gotten on the island or onto the grounds of the hall. You're the sheriff. You figure it out." She was done. Done with the stalker.

And done with Deacon Howell.

She stalked around him then and jerked open the door to her suite. "Get out!"

"Having another panic attack?" he asked, but he stepped out of the room and into the hall. "Worried I'm going to press charges for your filing a false police report?"

She snorted. "You were the one who took the threats, who investigated them."

"That's why you didn't file a report before," he said. "You knew you weren't really in danger."

"I knew I really couldn't trust anyone," she said. "And you just proved I was right. You made a promise to me and then turned around and broke it just moments later."

The promise wasn't all he'd broken, though. She felt something else breaking, aching inside her chest. Too proud to let him see the pain he'd caused her, she slammed the door shut in his face. She never wanted to see him again.

Had Deacon seen him? With the way the sheriff had been driving, with how he'd turned that car around, he could have spotted him easily through the windshield. Was it tinted dark enough that he hadn't been able to recognize him?

He peered through it now as he waited outside the stone wall. As he waited for Deacon to leave.

For sure the sheriff had recognized the vehicle, but that was all right. There were so many people at Halcyon Hall who wanted the sheriff to go away. Forever.

But nobody wanted that more than he did. At least nobody with enough balls to make sure it finally happened.

No matter what it took.

Why the hell was it taking so much to kill him, though? Had Deacon lived with the curse so damn long that he was indestructible? At least physically . . .

Emotionally—mentally—he had to be getting close to losing it. And if he wasn't yet, he would be . . . when he lost what mattered most to him.

Chapter Twenty-Three

A burning sensation emanated from between Edie's shoulder blades down her spine, and it wasn't just from all the hours she'd spent leaning over her laptop at the dining room table. Someone was watching her. Expecting to catch Bonita, as she had a few times previously, she peeked over her shoulder, but then she jumped when she noticed it was Evelyn standing in the doorway. And she was not alone.

"For someone who doesn't know anybody on the island, you sure have been getting a lot of visitors lately," the landlady remarked with her usual disapproving tone where Edie was concerned.

But Edie noticed the twinkle in Evelyn's eye. She enjoyed their banter as much as Edie did. "Don't be jealous," she teased the older woman.

Evelyn's lips twitched as if she was trying not to smile or laugh. "You don't need to worry about that with me. Bonita's the one who has her eye on the sheriff."

Edie knew that Bonita wasn't the only one; a certain celebrity liked him, too, maybe too much. She emitted a heavy sigh and said, "So she's been poisoning my food, too."

"I'm not about to confess to anything in front of the sheriff," she said, that twinkle getting brighter. "I wouldn't want to share a cell with you in case he's here to arrest you." She turned toward the sheriff who'd been watching their exchange with his eyebrows raised. "Sheriff, you look like you're half-frozen. Would you like some tea, coffee, or cocoa?"

He looked like hell—and that was something for a guy as good looking as he was. Dark circles rimmed his eyes, competing with all the other bruises on his scraped and battered face. As if it took all his energy, he slowly nodded. "Anything hot would be appreciated."

Evelyn headed toward the kitchen. But she stopped before pushing through the swinging door and turned back toward Edie. "Anything for you?" she asked begrudgingly.

Edie nodded. "Yes, anything without arsenic this time."

Evelyn sighed. "If you insist . . ."

Deacon Howell chuckled as the door swung shut behind Evelyn, but then he tensed, as if he'd surprised himself with the sound. "You're making friends on the island."

"She's just playing," Edie said. "Or at least I hope she is . . ."

"That's why I'm here," he said. "I want to talk about getting played."

She narrowed her eyes. "Whoever's been trying to blow you up isn't just playing, Sheriff."

"No, that person isn't," he agreed. "Which is why you need to be careful going after the hall."

She shrugged off his warning, just as she'd shrugged off everyone else's. It didn't matter to her if Elijah Cooke wanted to get rid of her. She wasn't going anywhere until she got her story—the full story. "So what person are you talking about playing you?" she asked.

"Olivia Smith."

Edie snorted. "It's not that hard to figure out that's an alias." They both knew who she really was. Unfortunately, for Olivia and her safety, many more people knew that now, too. One in particular.

Deacon pulled out a chair at the table where she sat in that little bay window area of the dining room. He dropped heavily into the chair, as if he was completely exhausted. "Is it?" he asked. "Or is that really who she is?"

Before Edie could even address his odd question, Evelyn joined them. She carried a tray with steaming mugs and a plate of cookies. "Those aren't for you," she told Edie as she settled the tray onto the table next to her laptop. "You'll just spoil your dinner."

Edie smiled. "Yes, Mom . . ."

Evelyn glared at her, but despite the glare, her lips curved up at the corners. She pressed a hand over her chest. "God forbid . . ." Then she turned toward the sheriff. "Have you heard yet . . . about that groundskeeper?"

Deacon shook his head. "Not yet. I don't know if he was—"

Bonita's grandson. That was what he'd claimed just before Bonita had killed him in this house. That was another story Edie wasn't going to tell, though. She had more than enough to cover about Bainesworth Manor without exploiting those whose lives were ruined because of the damn place.

She waited until the kitchen door swung shut yet again

behind Evelyn before asking, "Isn't that taking a long time?"

"There was a snafu at the lab," he said, his voice gruff with bitterness.

She arched a brow in skepticism. "Snafu?"

"Yeah, I know . . ." He sighed. "I'm not sure who the hell to trust anymore."

"So you've come to me?" she asked.

He chuckled. "Not because I trust you."

"But you want information," she surmised. She pointed to her open laptop. "I've been doing a lot of research on the manor."

"I'm not concerned about the past," he said. "I'm concerned about the present."

"And Olivia Smith?"

He nodded.

"So that's not an alias?" she asked. "That's AKAN's real name?"

"I don't know . . . ," he murmured. "I don't know what to believe . . ."

"You think she's lying?"

He flinched and closed his eyes, as if he was in a lot of pain.

"Sheriff? Are you all right?" She glanced toward the doorway, wondering if she should have Evelyn call the doctor.

He shook his head. "I think I made a terrible mistake. I think I broke a promise that . . ."

"What?" she prodded when he trailed off. "You can trust me. I'm not going to report anything about Olivia. In fact, I'm going to try to kill the story that got out about her."

He opened his eyes then, but only narrowly as he studied her face. "Why?"

"I'm going to tell her that it's because of the deal we struck."

"You struck a deal with Olivia?"

She nodded. "If I found out who took that photo of her, she'd find a way to get me into the hall."

Another chuckle slipped out of him. "Of course."

"I also like her," Edie admitted. "She's pretty damn impressive. It's clear to see she's been through a hell of a lot, and she's still standing."

"How do you know that?" he asked. "Did she tell you about her childhood?"

"She's told everyone about it," Edie said. "In every song she's sung."

He groaned then. He was definitely in pain.

She stood up. "Let me get Evelyn to call the doc—"

But he reached out and grabbed her arm, stopping her. "You left a message that you found out who picked up that money from the drugstore. Who was it? Do you know?"

She nodded now. "You know him, too. He's your deputy. Warren took that photo. He sold her out for ten thousand dollars and the promise of more if he got more pictures of her." She'd just learned that a short while ago. "When the lady at the drugstore told me Warren's name was on the wire, I called my contact back at the tabloid and blasted him for holding out on me. He admitted he was buying Warren time to get more photos of her. It had to be him who took that one last night of her and me."

"That bastard!" he exclaimed, and he vaulted up from the chair.

Edie chuckled. "He actually seems the least harmless of that family."

"I'm not so sure about that," Deacon said. "But you need to be careful, Edie. They're all dangerous."

She shivered then, thinking of the threat Olivia had warned her about. About Elijah Cooke wanting to get rid of her . . .

"Have you told Olivia yet, what you found out? That it was Warren?"

Heat rushed to her face. She'd intended to tell her at the hall—once Olivia let her inside the place. They'd had a deal. "Not yet."

"Don't," he said. "I don't want her confronting Warren or tipping off anyone else at the hall about what he did. Hell, I don't want her talking to any of them."

"You really think one of them has been trying to kill you?" she asked.

"Probably Warren," he said.

"Then you need to be careful," she warned the sheriff, because she had no doubt that was where he was heading as he rushed out of the boarding house and headed toward the battered police cruiser he'd parked at the curb.

Because if Warren was trying to kill the sheriff, Deacon was just about to make it easier for him.

Olivia stared out the patio doors of the conservatory, watching the state troopers as they inspected the vehicles in the lot. Looking for damage . . .

Looking for the person trying to kill Deacon.

Nobody was trying to kill Olivia. She knew that now. The minute Deacon had left her suite, she'd refused to give into the sobs that threatened to rush up the back of her throat. She'd pushed them down with some deep breaths, and she'd called her manager.

Bruce had been furious that she'd stopped taking his calls, furious because he'd known what had happened, but he hadn't known where to find her to tell her. Olivia Smith had admitted to one of the dancers what she'd done, how she'd tried to get them all out of their contract to tour with AKAN. Apparently, Olivia Smith had been offered a recording contract of her own, but only if she had no other contractual obligations.

So she'd sent those pictures and threats with the hopes of getting AKAN to quit touring, to go into hiding. Apparently she'd known—from listening to all her damn songs— how vulnerable she was to threats, to fear . . .

Olivia Torrence—AKAN—had spent the past couple of years telling the whole entire world how to manipulate her, just as her father had. That son-of-a-bitch had caused her so much pain, but he wasn't the only man who'd hurt her.

Deacon had—despite his promise. His accusations and mistrust had hurt her so much. She knew now that she had no reason to stay on the island, especially if she had picked up another stalker here. Because Olivia Smith had had no reason to send her that last threat . . .

Bruce had released her from her contract and reported her threats to the police and to the record label that had offered her the deal. He didn't know that was the same reason that AKAN was coming back to LA—to void her contract with the touring company. So he was thrilled she was coming home—although it didn't feel like home to her. It never had. He was sending a car to bring her to the airport. The snow had finally stopped, so the bridge was open. Unfortunately, the only flight he'd been able to find to LA didn't leave until morning, but she would stay on the mainland until then. She couldn't stay here anymore.

After making the call to her manager, she'd felt compelled to make another. She'd gotten the number from the receptionist and put it in her phone. And now, in the conservatory, she placed the call from her cell.

"Hello?" Holly Howell asked, probably suspicious of the number that had showed up on the ID.

"I'm leaving," she told the teenager.

"Wait!" Holly exclaimed. "You can't go. It's too dangerous!"

It would be more dangerous for her to stay and keep getting her heart broken. "My stalker has been caught."

"My dad found him?"

"Her. In a way, he did," Olivia acknowledged. "But she was apprehended back in LA." She didn't know what had happened to her since—if she'd been released on bail or what charges would even be pressed against her. But she really didn't care; she didn't believe the woman had been a serious threat. Not like Deacon was.

"Then you don't have any reason to leave," Holly persisted.

"I've already stayed too long." Long enough to fall for a man who couldn't return her love or her trust. Was that because of his wife? Because of how Shannon had died or how much he still loved the dead woman?

"Please," Holly implored her. "Let me at least say good-bye. I'll have Genevieve bring me to the hall." From somewhere in the background a groan emanated. Clearly Genevieve wasn't thrilled about coming to the hall. But then how could she be—after what had happened to her here?

Deacon had been right to be concerned that his daughter

worked at this place. It wasn't safe for her, except maybe now that the state troopers were here today.

"You can just drop me off and leave. My car is there, so I can drive myself back," Holly told the other girl who must have been with her. But then Holly wasn't home—because her home had been damaged in the explosion. She was staying at the boarding house. Where was the sheriff going to stay?

Olivia shook her head, shaking the thought of him from her mind. He wasn't her concern any more than she was his. He'd promised not to hurt her.

"Please," Holly implored her with tears in her voice. "Will you wait for me? I'll be there in just a little while."

Olivia held in the sigh burning the back of her throat. "Yes, I will wait for you." But her heart ached at the thought of having to tell the girl good-bye. The teenager was attached to her, probably just because of her music, but Olivia was getting attached to her, too. She felt a protectiveness toward her that she'd never let herself get close enough to feel for anyone else. She'd already been playing around with lyrics about the girl and her father . . . about a relationship strained but full of love.

It would be a big departure from the other songs she'd written. But Olivia had never known love before.

Holly clicked off her cell without a good-bye, as if she didn't dare waste a moment before getting here. That was good, though. She would arrive before the state police left. Hopefully . . .

There were just a few troopers walking around now as the faint light in the gloomy sky began to slip away.

"I hear her," a female voice remarked.

Startled, Olivia jumped and whirled around. Had Morgana been here the entire time, or had she just crept into the room recently? She was so flamboyant with her bright red hair, heavy makeup, and loud-patterned clothes that it was unlikely Olivia had missed her. But then she'd been preoccupied.

"Her?" Olivia asked. Had she eavesdropped on her conversation with Holly? But then the self-proclaimed medium rarely spoke about the living. "Erika?" Wasn't that the name of the dead woman?

Morgana shook her head, and her corkscrew curls bounced around her face. "No . . ."

"I'm pretty sure her name was Erika," Olivia said. That was what Deacon had told her. Olivia had never met the fitness trainer. Morgana might have, though. She'd been a guest longer.

"Shannon . . . ," Morgana murmured, and she closed her eyes. "Her name is Shannon . . ."

Goose bumps rose on Olivia's skin despite the bulky oversized sweater she wore, and a chill chased down her spine. "Shannon . . ."

Morgana tilted her head as if the woman's ghost was speaking in her ear. "Yes, yes, I know . . ."

What? What? The question burned the back of Olivia's throat, but she held it inside. Morgana was just a goofy old lady; she couldn't actually communicate with the dead.

"I'm sorry . . . ," Morgana murmured, her voice cracking on the words. But it almost didn't sound like her voice at all. It was breathier, younger sounding than however the hell old Morgana was beneath all that makeup and hair dye. "I'm sorry . . ."

Olivia shivered. She was sorry, too. Sorry she hadn't left sooner. This place was too damn creepy. She wasn't going to miss Halcyon Hall, but she was going to miss Holly and, even though he'd broken his promise, Deacon, too.

* * *

He was a goddamn fool.

Warren was just an opportunist. Deacon had always known that, but now he had proof over his selling that picture. His house was also proof. It was even closer to the manor than Deacon's dad's house; it might have even been built on part of the grounds. The house was one of the nicer ones on the island. Deacon had always figured that was just because his brother was a contractor and because the man had two jobs. Until now . . .

Now he realized the man would do anything for a buck.

Through the windshield of the battered sedan, Deacon studied the two-story brick house from where he'd parked in front of the four-stall garage. No lights shone inside the big house's many windows, and it was dark enough outside that they should have been on . . . had anyone been home.

Where was Warren?

Trying to get more photos of Olivia? Olivia Torrence.

That was who she was. Not Olivia Smith.

As he'd been leaving the boarding house, Trooper Montgomery had called him back to confirm that Olivia Torrence and Olivia Smith were two very different women. He wished she would have taken the time to do that before he'd talked to his Olivia.

His . . .

She wasn't his, and whatever chance he might have had with her, he'd blown when he'd broken that promise, when he'd hurt her as so many other people had. No wonder she didn't trust anyone to help her. No one ever had. Least of all him . . .

The shooting—it must have been a threat against Holly, meant for him, to scare him into backing off from his investigation. Olivia Torrence—AKAN—wasn't in any danger as long as she stayed away from him. Olivia Smith had already been reported for the stalking. Olivia Torrence's father had been released early, but supposedly his parole officer was keeping very close tabs on him, so he wouldn't attack his ex-wife—his second wife—and their children again.

Olivia had siblings. Would she want to know? Would she even want to talk to Deacon again? Maybe it would be better if he had Rosemary or Edie or even Holly share that information with her. He doubted she wanted to see him ever again.

And he didn't blame her.

No. He blamed Warren . . . for so many things. Where the hell was the sneaky little bastard? Hiding in the dark in his house? Waiting for Deacon to step out of the police cruiser so that he could try to run him over again?

He had to risk it. He had to find him. But first he clicked on the radio and called in his location to dispatch.

"That's Warren's address," Margaret said. "You shouldn't be there. That Trooper Montgomery has been very clear that you're not to investigate the attempts on your life."

"I'm here on another matter," Deacon said. And that was probably what had brought him out here—the picture Warren had taken and emailed to the tabloid. He had to have taken the last one, too, and sent that threat.

You will pay dearly . . .

Had that been his attempt to extort money out of her?

"We both know it's gotta be Warren," Margaret said.

Even though he thought so, too, he snorted. "You think Warren is smart enough to build those bombs?"

"No," Margaret agreed. "He had to be working with someone else."

Or for someone else . . .

"That's what I'm going to find out," Deacon said. He was going to check the garage for Warren's company vehicle and for some bomb-making materials.

"You're outnumbered, Sheriff. Wait until the state police arrive. I'm calling them right now."

He wasn't going to wait for them to arrive. There was no point anyway. He doubted anyone was even home. But just in case, he left the radio on. Then he pulled his gun from his holster before he pushed open the driver's door.

In the quiet of the cold night, he could hear an engine running—one that was louder and more powerful than the cruiser. Was Warren out there in that damn SUV again?

Deacon glanced at the garage; light leaked out beneath the overhead doors. How hadn't he noticed that before? Something was inside. Deacon began to move closer, but just as he did, a shot rang out.

Warren wasn't trying to run him over; he was trying to shoot him dead. Deacon ducked back behind the open driver's door just as bullets struck the sedan, pinging off the metal. And the shots continued to ring out.

Deacon couldn't even raise his head, couldn't see from where the shots were coming.

He just knew the bullets were getting closer and closer, driving holes through his vehicle, breaking glass . . . and soon one was going to hit him.

Chapter Twenty-Four

Since it was dark outside the conservatory, all the glass reflected back their images. Holly was so much bigger than Olivia was. She turned away from the windows to look down at the woman through the tears that filled her eyes. "Are you sure you can't stay?"

Holly had started out as an avid fan, but now she was so much more. Olivia was so much more to her than just the singer who had seemed to give voice to her doubts and fears.

"You know that I can't," Olivia said. "My life isn't here."

"But you've stayed so long already . . ."

Olivia sighed. "Too long according to my manager. He swears that I'm probably irrelevant now."

"Never!" Holly gasped. "You could never . . ."

"I wouldn't mind if I was," Olivia murmured almost wistfully. Clearly she didn't want to be famous anymore. She just wanted to be left alone.

"Then stay here," Holly urged her. "Stay here with me . . . and with my dad."

Olivia liked him; Holly was sure of it. And Dad liked

her, too. She'd seen the way they looked at each other, the same way that Judge Lawrence looked at Rosemary Tulle.

But Olivia shook her head and her voice cracked when she replied, "I can't." Were there tears in her voice? In her eyes?

"Is it because of my dad?" Holly asked. "Was he mean to you?"

"No," Olivia replied, almost too quickly.

"If he was, I'm sure he didn't mean it. It was just because he's so stressed out about everything." And he had much more reason to be stressed than her mother ever had. "I thought you liked him."

"I think he's a good man . . . if a little too suspicious," Olivia murmured, and there was a heaviness to her husky voice.

"What did he do?" Holly asked. "Did he accuse you of something, too?"

"Let's just say we had a misunderstanding."

"Then clear it up," Holly replied. "You can do that if you stay. Things would be better for all of us if you stay."

There were definitely tears in Olivia's eyes; they nearly brimmed over now until she furiously blinked them back. "I can't help you . . . either of you. I'll only be in the way with everything else going on."

"Dad will figure out who's trying to kill him." Holly was certain of it. Back home, he'd been a decorated detective; he'd solved major crimes, much bigger ones than the ones that happened here. But since the murder and the kidnapping, maybe the island wasn't all that different from back home. Heck, maybe it was even more dangerous. It certainly seemed that way for her father. And maybe it had been for her mother, too, if someone had murdered her.

Holly wasn't sure if that would make her death better

or worse. But maybe it would hurt less if she hadn't killed herself, if she hadn't hated her life and her family so much that she'd chosen to leave them. Although it had felt like that to Holly, that she'd hated them. That was why she'd kept leaving them. And now Olivia was leaving too.

The pain in Holly's chest was nearly unbearable. She felt like doubling over with it. "And if Dad can't figure it out, the state troopers are here to help him. Genevieve and I saw them leaving by the visitor gate when we were driving up to the employee one. Were they checking to see which of the vehicles had damage from trying to hurt my dad?" She flinched with concern that it might be Warren's that had the damage; apparently, he'd already tried throwing her under the bus for it.

"They could have been here about Erika Korlinsky," Olivia said. "That's whose body your dad found."

Holly remembered her. She hadn't liked her, though, because the woman had constantly suggested diets and exercises for her to do. She'd criticized and wanted to change her just like her mother always had. Olivia had never wanted to change her; she'd only wanted to make sure she was safe, just like her dad had been trying to do all this time.

"Is that why you're leaving?" Holly asked. "Because you're worried about all the reporters showing up now for the murder investigation or because that stupid picture got posted online?"

Olivia sighed. "I just need to return to my real life."

Tears stung Holly's eyes. "That's all I've wanted since Dad forced us to move here . . ." She never heard from her old friends anymore. Her real life was gone, and this was it. At least she'd had Olivia though.

"And I will need to do some damage control over that picture," she said. "I don't want people thinking I was here for rehab. I have too many really young, impressionable fans."

"Didn't your stalker take the picture?"

Olivia shook her head. "She had already been caught and punished for sending the other pictures, and nobody in LA even knew that I was here."

Panic pressed on Holly's chest now. "Do you still think it was me? That I would have done that? That I would have sold you out."

"Of course not," Olivia replied.

But had she answered too quickly?

Then she followed up, "I'm sorry." And she slid her arm around Holly's shoulders. "But I need to leave. I've already made arrangements to go back. The car should be here soon to take me to the mainland. And I'll fly out in the morning."

"I didn't do it," Holly told her, the tears burning her eyes again. "I don't want you to leave. That's the last thing I want!" She sounded like a brat again, just like she did with her dad. He loved her despite it because he was Dad. But her mom hadn't loved her . . . even when she'd been good.

How could Olivia love her? Why would she even want to put up with her?

She sucked up the tears and blinked her eyes clear. "I . . . I get it," she said. "There's nothing for you here. I know you have to leave." Then she forced herself to let Olivia go . . . just as she'd had to let Mom go. For some reason it had been easier to let her mother go, though. In some ways it had been a relief.

There hadn't been all the drama and screaming and pain . . .

Until she'd taken over for her mom and started treating her dad that way. Her shame deepened until she felt as if she couldn't hold up her head. She certainly couldn't look Olivia in the eyes anymore.

"I'm sorry that I'm being selfish," Holly said. "Of course you have a life. And you have to protect that. I knew you weren't going to stay here." Holly couldn't stay either. Instead of risking another scene, she hurried out of the conservatory.

She needed to leave the hall and to never come back. Just as her father had warned her so many times, the place was cursed.

"Holly!" Olivia called after her. "Holly! Please, don't be upset. I know—"

"Ms. Smith, there's someone at the gate for you." Holly heard the receptionist stop Olivia in the hall outside the conservatory.

Holly kept going down the hall to the outside door that opened onto the employee lot. Her car was there, parked in the glow of the exterior lights on the building. She started toward it, but before she could reach it, someone grabbed her arm.

Had Olivia come after her? Had she changed her mind about leaving?

A smile of relief on her face, she turned toward the person holding her. And that relief froze like the wind that blew snow across the lot. What the hell was he doing here now?

"What . . . what do you want?" she asked.

"I want you," the man replied.

Holly tugged her arm, trying to pull free of his grasp, but his grip tightened so painfully that she cried out.

"I don't want to hurt you," he said, as if trying to reassure her even as he dragged her away from the light of the building, away from her car. "So just come along quietly—"

But she had already opened her mouth to scream. His hand covered it, clasping so tightly over her mouth and nose that she could barely breathe. He was big. And strong . . .

She was too stunned to fight, to scream even when he moved his hand from her mouth to shove her toward the open passenger's door. She was dead weight now, though, numb, and he struggled to lift her.

"Come on, Holly. You have to come with me. You belong with me," he said, his voice all creepy.

She shivered and shook her head. "No, no, I don't . . ."

"You're mine," he said. "You belong to me. Your mother told me that. She told me you're mine." His bushy brows lowered, and a dark scowl crossed his face. "Then she tried taking it back when I wanted to claim you as my daughter. She swore up and down that you were Deacon's, but I know you're mine. She kept lying though. Lying and lying . . . that's why I had to . . ."

Her already chilled flesh froze. He had killed her mother.

Even though he stopped short of confessing, she knew it. Her mother hadn't jumped off that cliff; she'd been pushed by the man trying to claim that he was Holly's father.

But he wasn't . . .

He couldn't be.

She looked exactly like her dad—her real dad. Deacon

Howell was her father. And he had been right about David
Cooke—maybe about all the Cookes.

And about this place. He'd been so damn right about
this place. It was cursed. And so was she . . .

Olivia couldn't leave. Not like this.

Not with Holly so heartbroken.

She cared about the girl, and she hated seeing her so
hurt—because of her. Because of what she'd said.

That there was nothing here for her. Just as her father
had so many times, Olivia had made Holly feel like nothing. And her heart ached at the thought.

"Tell the car to come back in the morning," she told the
receptionist, although she might cancel again.

Seeing Holly run away from her had made her realize
that Deacon was right. Olivia kept running, too, and not
just from her problems. She ran from her chance at happiness as well.

Deacon and Holly, as difficult as their situations cur-
rently were, were also her chance at happiness, at having
the family she'd always wanted. But taking a chance to find
her happiness scared her nearly as much as her stalker did.
Maybe that was why she hadn't tried harder to explain the
situation to Deacon, to make him understand that she'd
been honest with him. Maybe it was why she'd pushed him
away the minute he'd doubted her, hurt her . . .

She was used to fear and disappointment and pain. She
wasn't used to the pleasure Deacon had given her, the love
that Holly showed her. She'd always thought, because it
had been drummed so hard into her head, that she didn't
deserve it, that she wasn't worthy of it. But she was.

And Deacon and Holly were worth taking that risk.

She ran—this time not away, but toward what she wanted. She ran down the hall the way Holly had gone and pushed open the back door to the employee lot where she had parked the teenager's car. The lights on the back of the building illuminated the lot and the girl's car. She hadn't left yet.

But she wasn't in her vehicle either. Where had she gone?

Had she run off somewhere on the property—like her mother had run off the day she'd thrown herself over a cliff? Olivia shivered against the cold. She'd come out wearing only her sweater. At least Holly had a coat; she wouldn't freeze right away. But Olivia needed to find her before she did something stupid, before she hurt herself.

"Holly!" she yelled. "Holly!"

As she started across the lot, her foot slipped on the snow-covered pavement. She steadied herself, then glanced down, and she noticed the marks in the snow. The big boot prints and the other marks, of something or someone being dragged.

Holly hadn't run off on her own.

"Holly!"

A scream answered her, drawing her attention to an SUV parked far from the building, so far that it was outside the light. All she could see were two shadows struggling.

And she heard another scream and a slap.

"Stop!" she yelled as she raced toward them. "Stop! Don't hurt her!"

The bigger shadow whirled toward her, and even in the darkness, she saw the glint of the gun barrel pointed at her. She sucked in a breath of cold and fear.

"Don't shoot!" Holly screamed. "Don't shoot her. I'll

go with you! I won't fight you anymore! Just please don't hurt her!"

Tears stung Olivia's eyes at the sacrifice the girl was willing to make for her, to keep her safe. "No. You're not going with him," she said. "You're not going anywhere."

"You're not stopping me," David Cooke said. "You're not taking my daughter away from me."

"She's not your daughter!" It would kill Deacon to hear another man claiming his child. It killed Olivia to hear it.

"Yes, she is. Her mother admitted it to me before she started lying about it," he said. "She was a liar and a cheat. That's why she had to die."

He'd killed Deacon's wife. Holly's mother.

He wouldn't hesitate to kill Olivia, too. But she had to stall, she had to buy time to get Holly away from him. "You're who shot at me that day," she said.

"I was just warning you to stay away from her," he said. "I didn't want to hurt you then. But you didn't listen. You didn't back off."

"Is that why you took that picture?" she asked. "Did you sell it to the tabloid in the hopes that the scandal would get me to leave the island?"

He snorted. "Don't flatter yourself, lady. I don't give a shit who you are. My idiot brother took that picture and sold it to make a buck. Then he figured he could make some more by taking another picture and threatening you with it."

You'll pay dearly . . .

It hadn't been a threat against her life but a request for money. Warren hadn't followed up on it, though.

"What happened to your brother?" she asked.

"The same thing that happened to Deacon Howell," he said. "The same thing that's going to happen to you. You're going to pay all right, for getting in my way. You're going to pay with your life—just like they did."

Holly screamed again. Olivia couldn't utter a sound. She couldn't move. She was frozen with shock and horror and unimaginable grief.

Deacon could not be dead. He could not be gone for so many reasons. One that she loved him, and Holly loved him. And without him, they had no chance of escaping this madman. David Cooke was right. She was going to wind up just like Deacon.

Dead.

She only hoped that she could find a way to save Holly before she died.

Chapter Twenty-Five

"Deacon? Deacon?" Margaret's voice crackled out of the radio. "Are you okay?"

Deacon wasn't sure. He was so damn cold from lying on the ground that his body was numb. He was sure whoever had fired those shots would have walked up—would have put one in his head to make sure he was dead—if not for the warning scream of sirens. The state police must have been close when Margaret called them.

Deacon hadn't been lying there much longer when Trooper Montgomery ran up. "Sheriff Howell? Sheriff Howell? Are you hit?" She reached out toward him, but instead of touching him, she took his weapon. Or she tried.

Deacon's hand had locked around it, and he had to pry his frozen fingers from the metal. Once she'd taken his gun, he pressed his hands against the ground and tried to push himself up. His jacket zipper was stuck to the icy snow that covered the driveway, so stuck that it began to tear as he continued to push.

"Don't move. Wait for the ambulance," she said. "Let them assess your wounds."

But Deacon knew now, as anger pumped his blood hotly

through his veins, that he wasn't injured. "I haven't been hit," he said.

"How . . . ?" the trooper asked, with skepticism and maybe even suspicion in her voice.

"There's another victim!" someone called out from the darkness.

But it wasn't really dark anymore. Lights flashed, reflecting off the snow and the glass of Warren's big house.

Using the open car door, Deacon pulled himself up from the ground. And he saw that the garage doors were open now. Vehicle exhaust surged out in a cloud. But the cold air quickly cleared it, and he could see the victim.

Warren Cooke sat stiffly behind the wheel of his Halcyon Hall vehicle. The front bumper was crumpled; the mirror dangled off the side of the driver's door. Through the open driver's side window, it was easy to see how red Warren's skin was, how bugged out his eyes were. Like he was surprised . . .

He wasn't the only one.

"If he's the one who was trying to kill you, who fired the shots?" Trooper Montgomery wondered aloud as she held out Deacon's weapon to him. "It hasn't been fired recently."

He shook his head. "I didn't have a chance to get off a shot," he admitted. "I was looking at the garage, and the shots came at me from the street."

"There are shell casings there," another trooper confirmed.

"You should have accepted that protection detail," Montgomery admonished him. "You could have been killed."

"Like Warren . . . ," Deacon murmured.

"This looks like suicide," the blond trooper remarked.

He shook his head. "I don't care what it looks like. It was murder." Just like Shannon's death.

He knew for certain now that whoever had killed her had just killed his accomplice. That was probably why Warren looked so surprised. Whoever had turned on him had once been close to him. As close as brothers?

Or cousins?

"It's late," Elijah said. Too late for visitors now. But he suspected the sheriff wasn't here just to visit; he probably had another damn search warrant. So when Deacon had buzzed the gate, Elijah had personally let him into the foyer.

Deacon's eyes widened with surprise when he saw him. "Wow, I don't remember ever seeing you without a tie."

"I was getting ready for bed," he said, although he doubted he would have been able to sleep—not with all the thoughts and doubts swirling through his mind.

"Yeah, but I figured you even slept in a tie," Deacon persisted.

The tie had felt like a noose earlier, tightening around his throat so much that he'd struggled to breathe. "Did you just come here to harass me again? Or do you have an actual reason for being here? If it's to see Ms. Smith, she might not even be here. A car came for her earlier this evening."

But she'd sent it away. Or so the receptionist had told him. However, he hadn't seen Olivia since then. Had she changed her mind and left tonight after all?

The color drained from Deacon's face. "She's gone?" he asked, his voice gruff. He sounded devastated, almost as much as he'd been when he'd learned Shannon had died.

"She's not dead," Elijah told him. "She just left. I think. She might have changed her mind." That look on Deacon's face got to him, enough that he turned toward the stairs and offered, "I'll check."

But Deacon reached out and grasped his arm. "No, don't. Even if she's here, I doubt she wants to see me."

He sounded so damn miserable that Elijah shared, "She saw your daughter earlier. That's why she turned the car away. She was still talking to Holly when it came for her."

A muscle twitched along Deacon's clenched jaw. "I'm glad Holly got to see her before she left."

"You screwed up," Elijah guessed.

Instead of getting defensive as he usually would, the sheriff just nodded. Elijah had never seen him so defeated. "If you're not here to see Ms. Smith, why are you here?"

"Warren's dead," he said.

Elijah gasped. "Did you kill him?"

Deacon shook his head and sighed. "I might have been tempted, but he was already dead."

"How?"

"An autopsy needs to be done. But it looks like carbon monoxide poisoning from sitting in his damaged Halcyon Hall vehicle in his garage with the motor running."

Shock elicited another gasp out of Elijah, and he shook his head. "No. Not Warren."

"I don't believe it either," Deacon said. "Any more than I believe that Shannon killed herself."

Elijah asked, "Did you notify David?"

"I tried," Deacon said. "I haven't been able to find him."

Had something happened to that cousin as well? Or . . .

He closed his eyes, trying to block out the traitorous thoughts. David had been his best friend. His protector.

No. He couldn't even bring himself to think it.

But Deacon obviously could. "You're worried he has something to do with his own brother's death?"

Elijah shook his head. "No. He wouldn't have hurt Warren. I would have believed he'd have tried to kill you before his brother."

"It is him, isn't it?" Deacon asked the question, but he sounded like he already knew, like he was certain. "Not Warren. He might have been helping, but he was too stupid to plan it. David's the one who's been trying to kill me. Every contractor on the island has access to explosives. They need them because of all the rocks. And he hates me more than anyone does."

Elijah couldn't argue with that. David had hated Deacon ever since they were kids. And when Deacon had stolen Shannon from him in high school . . .

"Where would he be?" Deacon persisted. "He's not at his house. So where the hell would he be?"

Where the hell were they? Holly peered around in the faint light coming from David's phone. This cold, dark cabin was somewhere on the grounds of the hall. He hadn't driven far from the main building before stopping and making her trudge through the snow to this falling-down structure.

Why had she agreed to leave with him? With the man who'd killed her mother?

And her father?

She shook her head. No . . .

Sobs choked her, and tears streaked from her eyes. Dad couldn't be dead.

He couldn't.

No matter what this psycho claimed. He was saying that

he was her father, and that was a lie. So he had to be lying about . . .

He had to be lying about Dad. But if he was lying about that, he'd probably been lying when he'd agreed not to kill Olivia if Holly left willingly with him. But he hadn't left Olivia at the hall. He'd insisted on bringing her along with them.

Holly wasn't stupid. She knew why. He hadn't wanted Olivia to be able to get help for her. Then he'd even put a condition on letting Olivia live; before they'd even left the parking lot, Holly had had to tie her up and put duct tape over her mouth. She'd been careful, though, so she wouldn't hurt her. But she'd wrapped the tape so tightly around her ankles that David had had to carry Olivia through the snow.

Then he'd dumped her hard on the floor of the cabin, so hard that tears had sprung to Olivia's eyes. And Holly had cried out for her—in pain and fear. She didn't know what to do—how to save them. Because she had a horrible suspicion that David was going to break that promise. He was going to kill Olivia.

He was such a psycho that he would probably kill Holly, too, and maybe even himself.

The nightmare that had haunted Olivia for so many years had come to life. No. It wasn't a nightmare that had haunted her. It was the past. Her past.

Being helpless and hurt and unable to call for help.

But even when she'd called, no one had come to her aid. No one had helped her then, so she'd had to help herself. She needed to do that now. This man was a killer. He'd killed Deacon. Deacon was dead. Sobs rushed up her throat, but with the tape over her mouth, they couldn't escape. And she began to choke.

With no air, her head lightened.

"She can't breathe," Holly said. "She's going to pass out. Let me take the tape off. Nobody's going to hear us make a sound out here, wherever the hell you've taken us."

Olivia fought to open her eyes, to stay conscious. She had to worry less about helping herself than about helping Holly. The poor girl.

She drew a deep, calming breath through her nose. Her nerves settled. She had to focus . . . on saving Holly and herself. Holly had to calm down, too. She had to treat this man with more respect than she treated her real father, or he might pull the trigger on the gun he held. He might shoot her as well as Olivia.

Olivia had no doubt that he intended to kill her. He'd only brought her along, so that she couldn't get help. And if he'd shot her that close to the main building of the hall, someone would have heard the gunfire. Maybe she should have pushed him then, should have made him fire a shot, but she'd been so afraid of Holly being alone with him.

That was going to happen, though, if she didn't do something quick.

"I'm taking the tape off," Holly said, but she paused with her fingers on the corner of the tape, as if waiting for him to protest.

But he said nothing. They must have been far from anyone who could hear them, who could help them. He hadn't driven far, but deep into the trees so thick that there had only been a narrow path between them.

Holly began to pull the tape away, bringing Olivia's skin with it. Tears springing to her eyes, she grimaced, but she held in her cry of pain even once the tape was gone. She didn't want to upset the man.

He was anxious, pacing back and forth in front of the door of the small, cold cabin. Not that it was much of a cabin; the place was really rundown with cracked windows and a decaying roof.

Had he not thought this out?

When Holly reached for the tape around Olivia's wrists, he shook his head. "No. Don't untie her."

That was what he was worried about—one of them trying to get out the door. They needed to get out of here.

"You look cold," Olivia said quietly to Holly, with a pointed glance at the man with the gun. In order to bring in wood for the rusted woodstove, he would have to put down the gun.

Holly's eyes widened, and she nodded and shivered. "Yes, it's freezing in here. Can we start a fire?"

David glanced from one of them to the other and shook his head. "Then you need to get the wood for it. I cut some and piled it outside the door."

Olivia raised her duct-taped-together hands. "I would like to help."

"I bet you would," he said. He pointed his gun barrel at Holly, and both of the women gasped. "You go, and if you don't come back, I put a bullet in her brain."

Tears welled in Holly's eyes, but she blinked them back and nodded. "Okay. I'll get it."

Olivia silently urged the girl to run, but as if Holly had read her mind, she promised, "I'll be right back."

"That foils your plan, huh?" David asked when the teenager stepped outside the door.

"I don't have a plan," Olivia said, but she wished like hell that she did, that she could come up with one. All she had to work with was the very thing she'd hated most: her celebrity. "Do you know who I am?"

David snorted. "My goofball brother was all impressed with you, but I'm not. You're nothing to me."

Neither was Holly, but that apparently wasn't what he believed. Holly looked exactly like her dad—her real dad—Deacon Howell.

Just hours ago, Olivia had thought that she never wanted to see him again. But now she would give anything if that was possible.

She blinked against the tears that threatened to overwhelm her. She had to do anything possible now to keep Holly alive.

"I'm something to Holly," Olivia told him. "And you care about her."

"I love her," he said. "And I've been denied a relationship with her for too long."

"I understand that," she said.

"No, you don't. You know nothing, and you're nobody."

She flinched at the phrase she'd heard so often when she'd been growing up—the one her parents had told her over and over again until she'd had no choice but to believe them.

"I know that you're not going to be able to live your life the way you used to. You're in hiding, so you won't be able to work. How are you going to support her?" she asked. "You can't stay here forever. The state police will find you here." Hopefully they would see the smoke from the fire, but with it being dark now, they wouldn't be able to until dawn.

"They'll find *you* here," David said, as he trained the gun barrel on her face. "Not us. We'll be off the island before morning."

So he'd only brought Olivia here to kill her.

She swallowed down the lump of fear that rose in the back of her throat; she couldn't give in to it now. "Let me live," she said. "And I'll give you the money you need to start a new life for yourself"—she nearly choked, but she had to finish—"and your daughter."

He tilted his head; he was listening. Unfortunately, he wasn't the only one.

Holly pushed open the door and walked in, tears streaming down her face. She carried in a load of wood, her arms shaking from the effort and from her reaction to what she'd heard.

She probably thought Olivia was sacrificing Holly to save herself—when she was trying to figure out a way to save them both. She wasn't buying her freedom; she was trying to buy them some time.

But was anybody even looking for them? Did anybody realize they were gone?

Chapter Twenty-Six

Was Elijah telling Deacon the truth? Did he really have no idea where his cousin was? "The state police blocked the bridge when Margaret reported shots fired. He couldn't have gotten off the island." Thank God Deacon had left the radio on.

"If he's not at his house . . ."

"Then he has to be here," Deacon said, and he stomped across the marble foyer to head down the hall toward the security room.

Elijah hurried after him. "What are you doing? Where are you looking?"

"Let's check the security footage," Deacon said as he stopped outside the room. "See if any of the cameras caught him going through the gates. I assume he has an employee badge and is able to come and go as he pleases."

Elijah's face flushed, and he nodded. "He handles the facilities maintenance," he replied as he opened the door.

The guard on duty jumped and turned toward them, trying to blink the sleep from his eyes.

"So much for your increased security . . . ," Deacon murmured.

"Get out of here," Elijah told the man who quickly jumped up from his chair. The doctor sat down, but before he could touch any of the equipment, Deacon reached over his shoulder and pressed the buttons that rewound the footage.

He knew when the bastard had fired those shots at him. And he knew about how long it would have taken him to get to the hall from Warren's nearby house. And there he was . . . on the security monitor . . . driving his truck in through the employee gate.

"Speed ahead," Elijah said. "See if he left . . ."

But other monitors were showing footage from other cameras at that same time. And on one of them, Deacon recognized another person. Holly.

His heart stopped beating for a second before it resumed—pounding so hard with fear that his chest ached. Holly had been here when David was here, right after David had tried to kill him.

He watched as she pushed open the employee door and ran into the lot. But she didn't get far before a dark shadow grabbed her and dragged her away from the building, away from the cameras. But he knew who had abducted his daughter. He would have recognized the brawny giant of a man anywhere.

"That son of a bitch!" Deacon said, as anger and fear overwhelmed him. "David grabbed her. Why the hell would he take her? What does he want with her? What the hell?" Deacon didn't have any money to give him, but maybe he intended to use Holly to make Deacon destroy evidence or drop charges. He refused to consider anything else, refused to consider that he might hurt her . . . or Deacon wouldn't be able to focus at all. And he needed to focus; he needed to find her.

"Oh, God," Elijah murmured.

"What?" Clearly he knew something about his cousin that Deacon didn't know.

Elijah gasped again and pointed toward the screen. They watched the recording as the employee door swung open again and a petite blonde woman walked into the lot, and then she started running . . .

And for the second time within seconds, Deacon's heart stopped beating, before again resuming that frantic pace. Without a single thought to her own safety, Olivia had rushed to save his daughter. Tears stung his eyes, and a wave of emotion overwhelmed him. And he realized he had fallen hard for this woman. So damn hard . . .

He couldn't lose her or his daughter.

On the monitor, lights flashed in the dark lot, swinging in a circle, as David drove off with the only two people Deacon loved.

"Where is he going? Where would he take them?" The direction of the headlights didn't point toward the street but into the trees. Was he driving directly into them, purposely crashing his SUV?

Deacon ran out of the security room, down the hall, toward that door both women had crashed through, but before he could push open the door, a strong hand closed around his arm. "Slow down. He has a gun," Elijah said.

"Oh, God." Elijah was right. David Cooke had a gun and the women Deacon loved. "Where . . . where is he going with them?" he asked.

Elijah drew in a deep breath. "I think I know."

Deacon pulled open the door now. "Let's go!"

"Me," Elijah said. "You can't go with me. I have to go alone."

"That's not going to fucking happen," Deacon said.

"He'll kill them if he sees you," Elijah said. "Or you'll . . ."

"I'll kill him?" Deacon asked. "That's what you're really worried about. He's abducted a woman and a teenage girl at gunpoint, and you're worried about him?"

"I'm worried about you," Elijah said. "You're not going to save anyone if you can't keep it together."

With the way Deacon's heart was hammering, he couldn't argue with his old nemesis that he was calm. He wasn't. He was losing his mind . . . because he was afraid that he'd already lost Holly and Olivia. "I'll call the state police," he said.

Elijah sighed. "Call them but tell them to come in with no lights or sirens." Elijah pushed open the door now and headed into the lot. He clicked a key fob and lights blinked on a Halcyon Hall SUV.

Deacon would call the trooper in a moment, but he wasn't going to lose Elijah. He followed him to that SUV and pulled open the passenger door. "I'm going with you," he said.

"Just stay down, so he doesn't see you," Elijah said as he climbed into the driver's side. "And let me talk to him first. You know I have the best chance of getting through to David."

"Damn it . . ." Deacon murmured. Because he knew Elijah was right. If anyone could get this situation to end peacefully, it was Elijah Cooke. If that was what the psychiatrist wanted . . .

He narrowed his eyes and, in the light from the dashboard, studied the face of his old nemesis. Deep circles rimmed those pale eyes of Elijah's; he looked tired and scared.

"You could always manipulate David into doing what you wanted," Deacon agreed.

"You better hope that I still can," Elijah said. "I don't want anyone else to die, including my cousin."

Deacon couldn't make any promises. If they were too late to save Olivia and Holly, he wasn't sure how he would react.

From the nervous way Elijah kept glancing at him, it was clear he was aware that Deacon was barely in control. And if either of the women he loved had been harmed . . .

Nothing was going as he'd planned. He shouldn't have taken the woman with them. He should have killed her in the parking lot and been rid of her. Because now she was messing with his head . . .

And with Holly's.

The girl wept uncontrollably, and his heart ached that she was so upset. That wasn't what was supposed to have happened. She was supposed to be so happy that he was rescuing her from that man she'd professed so many times to hate. Like David hated him.

But Deacon was dead. With all those shots he'd fired at him, he had to be.

"You want this," he told Holly. "You kept running away from Deacon Howell—just like your mother did. You always knew you didn't belong with him. You belong with me."

Holly opened her mouth, but if she'd been about to argue with him, the woman shook her head and stopped her. And Holly's eyes widened.

"Yeah," he said. "She's trying to play me. She thinks if she offers me money, I'll drive her to town, and she can get help. She doesn't realize that I'm too smart to fall for her trick. And that there is no help coming."

But as he said it, lights shone on the front of the cottage, momentarily blinding him through the grimy, cracked windows. "Damn it!"

"Run!" Olivia told Holly.

But he grabbed the girl before she could get anywhere close to the door. "You're not going anywhere!" She damn well wasn't going to run away from him like she had Deacon. She belonged with him. "And you . . ." He swung his gun barrel toward the blonde. "You better shut the hell up!"

It was too late to extinguish the fire, so they couldn't hide. Someone knew the cabin was occupied. But who the hell knew it was here?

Except . . .

"David," Elijah called through the door. "I know you're in there. And I know you're not alone."

Damn Elijah. Everybody thought he was such a damn genius, that he always knew everything. But there was so much he didn't know . . .

Like that David was smarter than him, that he'd always known more than him, and Deacon Howell. "Are you alone?" he asked his cousin.

"Of course, I'm alone," he replied, as if David was an idiot. "If Deacon was with me, he would have already kicked the door in to get to his daughter."

"My daughter!" David shouted, and inadvertently tightened his grasp so much on Holly's arm that she cried out in pain. "You know she's mine!"

"Then don't hurt her," Olivia said. "Don't hurt her!"

"Is that Ms. Smith?" Elijah asked as he pushed open the door. "You took two hostages?" He shook his head as if David was a child he was disappointed in.

"I didn't want her," David said. "She tried to stop me." He turned his gun toward his cousin. "That's why you're here, isn't it? You're going to try to stop me too."

Elijah nodded. "Yes, I told you that I don't believe Holly is your daughter."

"But Shannon said . . ."

"She told you once that she was, but then she told you later that she only said that to get back at Deacon. That he's really Holly's father."

David shook his head. "She was lying then, and not the first time . . ."

Elijah glanced at Holly, almost apologetically. "She was always lying, David. You know that. You and Deacon think I manipulated you, but she's the one—she manipulated you both."

David shook his head again. "No, she loved me. She did. She wanted to be with me. But Deacon wouldn't let her go."

Holly sniffled and said, her voice quavering, "I think he would have been happy to let her go. He would have been happier without her. I would have been happier, too."

David shook the girl. "Don't talk about your mother that way. She loved you."

"Then why did she hit me?" Holly asked. "Why was she so mean to me?"

"Because of Deacon," David said. "Because he made her so unhappy, just like he makes you. That's why you always run away from him. Now we can run away together." He swung his gun back on his cousin. "And you're not going to stop me."

Elijah raised his hands. "You know I'm not armed, and you know that you've always been bigger and stronger than I am—"

"And smarter," David said. "I've been smarter, too. You just don't want to admit it."

"I know," Elijah said. "You're right. I didn't want to admit it."

"Don't patronize me," David said.

"I'm not," Elijah said. "I'm here for her . . ." He pointed toward the blond woman on the floor. "She's the reason I'm here."

"Why?" David's brow furrowed.

"I care about her," Elijah said. "I can't let you hurt her. I just want to get her out of here, and I'll leave you alone."

David narrowed his eyes. Damn Elijah . . .

The shrink was trying to work some angle on him. "You're not involved with her. You're not like your brother. You don't fraternize with coworkers or guests. What are you really up to?"

"Saving you from a murder charge," Elijah said. "You haven't hurt anyone yet. And I know you won't hurt . . ." His throat moved as if he was struggling to swallow. "I know you won't hurt your daughter. And if you don't hurt Olivia, you won't get in trouble. You'll be fine."

"But I . . ."

"Shh," Elijah said, shaking his head. "You haven't done anything that can be proved. You're fine. You're going to be fine. Just put down the gun." He moved closer now, toward the woman on the floor. "Let me get her out of here."

Olivia shook her head now. "No. I won't leave her alone with him. I won't."

David snorted. "So much for your bullshit earlier." He

swung the gun back toward his cousin. "And so much for yours. I'm not listening to any more of your head games. I killed my own brother because he got in my way. He was threatening to tell you that I killed Shannon. I killed the woman I loved more than life itself, Elijah. You think I would hesitate over killing you?" He swung the barrel of his gun toward the woman on the floor. "Or her?" He moved his finger toward the trigger and squeezed.

The gunshot reverberated throughout the night, the sound so loud that snow fell from the trees surrounding the cabin. It fell onto Deacon's head and slipped between his collar and the back of his neck. But his blood was pumping too fast and furiously for him to feel the cold.

He shouldn't have let Elijah go in alone, shouldn't have trusted him to handle his deranged cousin.

And the man was deranged.

Clasping his gun tightly in his hand, Deacon kicked open the door and burst into the dilapidated cabin. More gunfire rang out, but Deacon ducked low. Wood splintered on the doorjamb near him. Something stung his shoulder. He flinched but then ignored the pain—ignored everything but the scene. David held his weapon in one hand while his other wrapped tightly around the arm of a struggling Holly.

Was she hurt? Tears ran down her face, and screams emanated from her open mouth. She was in pain, but it might not have been physical. He'd heard what that crazy bastard had been saying, that he'd been trying to claim Deacon's daughter as his. That was why Elijah had looked so odd back at the hall. He'd known exactly why David had taken Holly.

That son of a bitch . . .

Elijah lay on the floor near Olivia, who struggled with the bindings around her ankles and wrists. Blood spattered her face and hair. Her blood or his?

She was strong enough that she kicked out with both legs and knocked David to the floor, which shook from the weight of his body striking the brittle floorboards. More shots rang out as David, dragging Holly with him, went down firing. And Deacon couldn't duck any lower to avoid getting hit.

Chapter Twenty-Seven

James Bainesworth stared out the window, watching the headlights move through the trees. Again. There had been other headlights earlier. First one set. Then another.

Now a few rows of them followed one another like a small army of ants moving through the trees.

"Why did you call me over here at this hour?"

James turned toward the doorway where his grandson stood, holding a baby in his arms. The child stared at him with eyes bleary with sleep—the pale silvery blue of the Bainesworth. Pride flashed through him that the Bainesworth bloodline would carry on; of course, it would have been better had she been a boy. But James had had only daughters himself; now he had grandsons.

"Are you all right?" Jamie, or Bode as he preferred to be called now, asked.

No. He wasn't all right because—for once—he didn't know what the hell was going on.

"And where is Theo?" Bode asked. "He's supposed to be here twenty-four seven with you."

James had sent him to find out what the hell was going on. When he'd called Jamie, it had been clear from his grandson's gruff and grumpy voice that he'd been sleeping. He clearly had no idea about what was happening on the estate. Yes, it was good that even though it had been his idea to renovate and reopen the manor, he wasn't running it.

"Where's your brother?" James asked. "I called you both, but he didn't pick up his damn phone." And James had tried over and over again to reach him. "It just went to his voicemail." And for once James had left him a message. Had he received it?

Bode shrugged. "I don't know. It's late. He's probably asleep."

James shook his head and pointed out the window. "No. He's in the middle of that . . ." He would be because Elijah was the most like him; he didn't just live in his environment, he tried to control it. James could guess who else was in the middle of that—Deacon Howell.

Bode joined him at the window. "What the hell . . . ?" he murmured.

The little girl wriggled in his arms, reaching out for James. He lifted his hands toward her, but Bode stepped back, as if he didn't want him touching his child.

A twinge of hurt struck his chest, but he ignored it. He had bigger things to worry about now. Like the manor . . .

Like Elijah . . .

"What's out there?" Bode asked.

Of course he wouldn't know. "An old cabin," James replied. "Not many people know it's even there, it's so deep in the woods."

"Who does know?" Bode asked.

"Probably your brother," James replied. "I think he knows this property nearly as well as I do." He almost laughed at the thought of that. There was plenty that Elijah didn't know—so damn much.

Had that ignorance gotten him killed?

There was someone else that James should have called, someone who knew nearly as much as he did. Had he started up again? Had Elijah stumbled upon it?

That twinge struck his chest again, and he gasped at the intensity of it.

Bode moved one hand from his daughter to James's shoulder. "Grandfather? Are you all right?"

He rubbed a hand over his chest but nodded. "Yes, yes, I'm fine. I just want to know . . ."

Heavy footsteps pounded up the steps, and he breathed a little easier with relief. Elijah must have gotten his message; he'd showed up after all—just in his own damn sweet time like he usually did. But it wasn't Elijah, with his thick black hair and the palest silver eyes, who showed up in the bedroom doorway. Theo had returned, and the expression on his face was even grimmer than when James had wakened him and ordered him out into the cold to investigate.

"What is it?" James demanded. "What happened out there?"

Theo shook his head. "They wouldn't let me close to the cabin."

"Who is they?" James asked.

"The state police."

"Police?" James asked, skeptical. "There were no flashing lights. No sirens." He hadn't heard any, and his hearing was good—so good that he was convinced he'd heard gunshots. And maybe even a girl screaming . . .

But that could have been a memory.

So many memories involved girls screaming.

He shook his head, shaking off the past to focus on the present. On his grandson.

"What about Elijah?" he asked. "Did you see him?"

Theo shook his head.

Damn it. Frustration churned inside James like acid. He should have gone himself—would have if not for the damn wheelchair. "Did you even ask to see him?"

"I told you the troopers wouldn't let me close to the cabin. They were already struggling to get the ambulances down that narrow trail to the place."

"Ambulances?" Bode asked the question now, his voice deep with dread and concern. He glanced at the window again, which reflected back flashing lights moving through the trees now. "So people were hurt? Wounded?" His voice cracked. "And you didn't see Elijah?"

Theo shook his head again—even though Bode was no longer looking at him. James was studying his nurse's face, though. He knew the man well—even better than he knew his own kin. "Tell me," he ordered him. "Tell me what you're holding back."

It was clear that he was keeping something from them. "You know more than you're saying," James prodded him.

Bode looked at the nurse again, his eyes narrowed. "What the hell is it?"

Theo drew in a deep breath. "I did see them carry someone out . . . in a body bag."

So there hadn't just been people injured; there had been at least one casualty. Elijah?

Bode must have thought so because he shook his head and whispered, "No, no, no . . ."

And his child, as if feeling his stress, began to cry.

James didn't reach out for either of them. He couldn't comfort them—not when he needed comfort himself. He could have handled losing Bode before Elijah.

Elijah was the only hope for the hall to stay in operation. If it got shut down, then James would be forced to leave the manor again. And he'd intended to die here.

He hadn't intended for his grandson to die first.

"I'm so, so sorry," Holly said, her voice hoarse from all the screaming she'd done. She felt like such a fool . . . such a damn fool . . . about everything.

Olivia reached up from the hospital bed and grasped Holly's hand in her much smaller one. "I'm fine."

Holly released her shaky breath. "Dad is, too," she said. He was alive.

David Cooke had lied about that, just as he'd lied about everything else. Or maybe just some of it.

She believed he'd killed her mother and even his brother.

"I still feel like it's my fault."

Olivia squeezed Holly's hand a little harder now. "No, it's not. None of this is your fault!"

But Holly shook her head, and her tangled hair swirled around her face. "It is. It is . . ." Her hoarse voice cracked with emotion. "My dad was right about everything. About how sick and twisted the Cookes are, about that place . . ." She shuddered. "I should have stayed away from it. I should have stayed away from them."

"They're not all bad," Olivia said. "Elijah saved me."

Holly nodded in agreement and relief.

The doctor had leaped between Olivia and the bullet his cousin had fired. Unfortunately, they'd both still been hit. It could have been worse though. The bullet had just grazed them both. But then David had struck his cousin's head with the butt of the gun, knocking him out. He'd turned the barrel back toward Olivia, had been about to squeeze the trigger when Dad had kicked open the door.

Tears poured out of her eyes at the memory. At the relief she'd felt, and the awe. Her dad was amazing. A hero . . .

She needed to tell him that. She needed to go back to him. She'd been running between his room and Olivia's since they'd arrived at the hospital, guilt churning in her stomach. She hadn't said anything to him yet; she hadn't been able to speak through the tears overwhelming her.

Holly patted Olivia's hand and pulled the blankets up over her. "I'm sorry," she said again. "They told me you should rest. That you're probably in shock—"

"And so are you," Olivia said. "You should be in a room, too. Has anyone checked you out yet?"

Her concern overwhelmed Holly again, and she started shaking.

"What?" Olivia asked. "What's wrong?"

"You care so much," Holly said. "How can you care after all the trouble I've caused?"

"You are not to blame for any of this," Olivia assured her. "And I care because I love you."

"I don't deserve your love," she said. "And I don't deserve my dad's. I've been so mean to him, and all he's ever done is try to protect me. I've been such a brat."

"You've been a teenager," Olivia said with a smile.

Holly shook her head again. It had been so much worse than that. She'd been so much worse than that. "I've been an idiot. If only I would have listened to my dad . . ."

"I agree," a deep voice chimed in, and Holly whirled to find Dad standing in the open door to Olivia's private room. He stepped inside and closed it behind himself. He wore his jeans beneath a hospital gown, and he looked worn out and roughed up and in pain despite him and the doctors assuring her that he was fine.

Holly froze for a moment before running to him and throwing her arms around him. "Dad, Daddy . . . ," she cried.

He tensed and Holly pulled back, worried that she'd hurt him. A bullet had grazed him. But like Olivia, he hadn't needed many stitches.

"I'm sorry," she said. "I'm so very sorry, Daddy!"

Her dad pulled her close again. "My baby. No matter what that sick bastard said to you, you're mine. I know that for a fact. You're my daughter."

The tension that had been left in her eased, and she hugged him even closer. "I know," she said. "I know he was lying. I know I'm yours." She tried to suck up her sobs; she was getting the hospital gown he wore all wet.

He cleared his voice and said, "We do need to have a doctor examine you," he said. "You must have hit your head or something or you wouldn't be hugging me like this."

Holly drew back and opened her mouth. But instead of arguing with him like she would have in the past or taking offense, she laughed. She was so damn happy, happier than she could ever remember being. "You're funny, Dad."

"Yeah, you definitely hit your head," he replied with a chuckle. But then he cupped her face in his hands and held her. "Are you okay? Really? So much happened tonight . . ."

She shuddered as all of it rushed over her again. "I know. But we're okay. You, me and Olivia . . ." She glanced back at the bed where Olivia lay, but her eyes were closed. She wasn't sleeping though because tears streaked from beneath her lids to trail down her face. Wanting to reassure

Olivia and herself, she continued, "That's all that matters. And he's dead. He can't hurt anyone else like he did Mom. He killed Mom." Her voice cracked. "He admitted it. He admitted to killing her and his own brother . . ."

"He can't hurt anyone else," her dad reminded her. "We're safe."

She nodded. "I know."

"Let's get you checked out, though," he said. And he opened the door to Olivia's room and stepped into the hall.

Holly felt a flash of panic as the door closed behind them; she hated the thought of Olivia being alone, like she'd sung of so often. "Stay with her," she urged her dad. "Don't let her leave!"

"But Holly . . ."

"Please, Dad," she implored him. "I know she cares about us—a lot. She was willing to die for me . . ." Her voice cracked again with the enormity of that. "You can't let her go. You have to stop her."

He shook his head. "How?"

And he sounded like he really wanted to know, like he had no idea . . .

Holly smiled at him. "You tell her how you feel."

His mouth dropped open, but no words came out.

"I know that's not easy for you," she acknowledged. It wasn't easy for her either. "But you have to . . ."

Then she turned to walk away, to find that ER doctor who'd been bugging her to get checked out. But she didn't get far . . .

Deacon stopped her. He stopped Holly with a hand on her arm. Then he turned her around and pulled her into his arms again. "I love you!" he told her. God, the thought of losing her . . . like he nearly had . . .

She was right. It wasn't easy for him to express his feelings, but from now on he would. "And I promise I'm going to be patient with you. I won't be as hard on you as I—"

Holly pulled back and said, "Don't apologize. Everything you ever said or did was for my own good. I know that now. I can't promise that I won't ever be a brat again, but I will never run away again. I will never leave you." Tears streamed down her face.

Deacon pulled her into his arms and held her tight. She shuddered against him. He held her for a long moment before he pulled back and smiled down at her. "You can leave me a little bit," he said. "To have a doctor check you out and so I can talk to Olivia without an audience."

"Remember, Dad, tell her how you feel," she said.

Sorry.

He felt so damn sorry. While Holly didn't think he owed her an apology, he sure as hell owed one to Olivia. But would it be enough?

Would it get her to take a chance on him?

He wouldn't know unless he asked. So once Holly walked away, he pushed open the door to Olivia's room and startled her so badly that she nearly fell over from where she'd been pulling on her jeans next to the bed. Deacon caught her and swung her up in his arms.

"Don't," she protested. "You're going to hurt yourself."

"Not by lifting you," he said. "You're light." His arms tightened around her, not because of her slight weight but because he didn't want to let her go. Ever.

"You should be with Holly," she said. "Make sure she gets checked out."

"She didn't want me to leave you," he said. "As a runner herself, she must have realized that was what you were about to do."

Her face flushed, but she shook her head. "I'm not running. I have no reason to stay."

"You have two reasons," he replied. "Me and Holly."

Her mouth opened with shock. "What do you mean?"

His face flushed with embarrassment, and he placed her on the bed then sat on the edge of it. "I'm sorry," he said. "I know that's a crazy idea. Why would you want to stay here? I have nothing to offer you . . . but . . ."

Olivia audibly sucked in a breath but didn't release it. It was like she was holding it in anticipation of what he had to say.

"An apology," he said. "I'm so sorry about earlier . . . about jumping to conclusions. I was such a damn fool. I know you had nothing to do with those threats."

She released her breath in a ragged sigh. "Olivia . . . ," she murmured.

"I'm so sorry I accused you of pulling a stunt. I know you don't like publicity. And that you were just here to get away from it all, not for any other reason." Definitely not rehab, like he'd accused her. "God, I said such terrible things . . ." Tears filled his eyes with the guilt and anguish he felt over what he'd done.

Olivia was crying, too, tears streaking down her face.

"I'm so sorry for those things I said," he continued. "But I'm most sorry about breaking my promise. The last thing I ever want to do is hurt you. You're the most amazing woman I've ever met. So damn talented and loving and . . ." A tear slipped out of one of his eyes now. "And loved."

Olivia reached out, and she brushed that tear from his bruised cheek and murmured, "I don't understand . . ."

This was it.

His chance.

He had to share his feelings—just like Holly had told him. "I love you," he said. "I've fallen for you." Hard. So damn hard that if she left him, he wasn't sure how he would survive.

It would kill him more effectively than David's bombs or those attempts to run him down had.

Chapter Twenty-Eight

Shocked, all Olivia could do was stare at Deacon. But she couldn't doubt his sincerity. He was the strongest man she'd ever met, but yet he'd wept over his apology to her and over his profession.

Of love?

Could he really love her?

Now he was talking about his daughter's feelings for her. "And Holly has always loved you," he said. "From every song of yours she's played, she's gotten to know you. She's gotten to count on you. And if you left . . ."

Olivia had already been crying. She'd been crying since the minute David Cooke had claimed he'd killed Deacon. And she wasn't sure she'd ever stopped. But the thought of leaving Holly . . . and knowing how much the girl had already gone through . . .

Her heart wrenched at the thought. "I can't stay just for her." Even as much as she loved her.

"I know that's too much to ask," Deacon said, and he sucked up his tears now. "There's nothing for you on this island. I know that I don't have anything to offer you."

"Are you trying to convince me to stay or to leave?" she asked.

His face flushed, and his voice was gruff when he replied, "To stay."

"Then why do you keep telling me that you have nothing to offer me?" she asked. Hadn't he meant what he said . . . when he'd mentioned love? She had to know. "Is this about Shannon? Are you still in love with her?"

"I don't think I ever was. Infatuated, yeah. But if I couldn't make her happy, how the hell would I make you happy?" He jumped up from her bed then and stepped closer to the door. "I'm sorry. I shouldn't have even mentioned my feelings for you . . . since I have nothing to offer you."

"Stop saying that," she admonished him. And she moved from the bed to come to him, to cup his face in her hands, so that he would meet her gaze. "You have everything to offer me. The thing I've always wanted but never had."

"What?" he asked.

"Love," she replied. "If you really have fallen for me . . ."

His breath shuddered out in a ragged sigh. "I sure have. I love you, Olivia."

Tears filled her eyes. "And I love you. And I love Holly. And I would love, for the first time in my life, to be part of a loving family."

Deacon closed his arms around her and hugged her tightly. But then he pulled back and told her, "You have more family, you know."

She shuddered at the thought of her parents.

"Not just your dad and mom," he said. "Trooper Montgomery tracked down your father. He had been in jail for abusing his second wife and their kids. You have siblings, Olivia."

A twinge of pain struck her heart now, dimming her happiness. "Oh, God. And he's hurt them?" Like he'd hurt her . . .

"A parole officer has him on a tether," Deacon said. "They're not letting him near them. He won't hurt them anymore."

She released a breath and nodded. "No, he won't. I'll make sure of that. I'll protect them somehow." She could use her money for that.

"Just like you protected Holly tonight," he said. "Like you risked your life for hers . . ." His big body shook. "I was so worried that I was going to lose you both."

"I'm not going anywhere," she assured him. "Everything I want is right here on Bane Island. You make me happier than I've ever been."

"I want to drop to my knees right now," he said. "I want to propose, but I can't rush things too much. I want to make sure Holly's really okay after everything she's been through. I want to make sure that you're really okay."

"You are the most amazing man, Deacon Howell," she said.

He always put himself and his needs last and his daughter and everyone else's first. She'd never known anyone as selfless.

"I don't need a proposal," she assured him. "I don't need a ring. I just need you."

"What about me?" whispered a hoarse voice as Holly pushed open the door to Olivia's room.

She held out her arms for the girl. "And you, of course, you're my family, too." Which was all she'd ever wanted.

* * *

The sensation of someone staring at him pulled Elijah from his state of oblivion. He forced his eyes open then squinted and grimaced at the glare of the overhead lights. Blessedly a shadow fell over him, partially blocking the light. Was it a blessing, though, or another damn curse?

He peered up . . . into the face of an angel. Her features were so delicate, her eyes so big . . . her hair so bright and blonde. He must have died. But how the hell had a Bainesworth made it to heaven?

"Good, you're awake," a husky female voice remarked.

And he realized his angel was the devil. "How the hell did you get in here?" he murmured.

Edie Stone chuckled. "Security at this podunk hospital isn't like what you have at the hall. Though I hear that's not all it's cracked up to be."

He flinched and not just because of the pain reverberating inside his skull. Had David crushed it with the butt of that gun?

"Is everyone okay?" he asked. "Holly? Olivia? Deacon?" He couldn't ask about David, not after what he'd done.

She chuckled again. "I'm the reporter. I'm the one who's supposed to ask the questions."

"Right now you have more answers than I do." He had no idea what had happened after David had struck him.

"Your cousin is dead," she told him.

"And the others?"

"They're all right. Better than you, actually." And she reached out, her fingertips skimming along his jaw before she jerked her hand back.

His skin tingled from that brief contact. Maybe he was just getting his feeling back from being frozen. How long had they been out there before help had arrived? But help had arrived; that was all that mattered. A ragged sigh of relief slipped out through his lips.

"I answered your questions," Edie said. "Now you owe me some."

He shook his head and grimaced at the pain shooting through his skull. "No."

"What are you doing in here?" a familiar voice asked.

"Checking on your brother, of course," Edie replied. "I've been so concerned about him."

Bode snorted. "Yeah, right. Get the hell out of here before I call security on you."

She laughed, and the sound quickened Elijah's pulse. "What? You're not strong enough to get rid of me on your own?" she teased the personal trainer.

And a smile twitched at Elijah's lips.

"Out!" Bode told her.

And Elijah flinched.

"Careful," she said. "You're going to hurt your brother's head. He has a concussion, you know."

"How do you know? You're not next of kin. Nobody better have told you anything."

"Why?" she asked. "Worried that I'm going to learn all your family secrets?" She walked toward the door then, but she stopped before she opened it and turned back to flash a cocky smile. "You should be worried . . ."

"Out," Bode said. But it was much softer now. And probably not just in deference to Elijah's concussion, but because he was worried.

Elijah was, too. Edie Stone wasn't going anywhere even though she finally stepped out of the room and closed the door.

His brother's breath shuddered out with relief.

"Don't be too relieved. She'll be back," Elijah warned him.

"I'm relieved that you're alive," Bode said.

He lifted a hand to his pounding head. "Am I?"

His brother chuckled. "I feel your pain. Or I felt it myself not that long ago. Lucky for us we were born with thick skulls."

Elijah chuckled, too. "Yeah, lucky . . ." That was something he rarely considered himself, but he had survived. "Is David really dead?" Not that he doubted Edie. She had no reason to lie to him.

"He's dead," Bode confirmed. "Even though I know you guys were close, I'm not sorry—not after what he did."

Panic gripped Elijah's heart. "Are Olivia and Holly really all right?"

"Yes," Bode assured him.

"And Deacon?"

A smile curved Bode's lips. "Since he got to kill the bastard who's made his life miserable, he's probably better than he's ever been."

Elijah wasn't so sure about that. Deacon wasn't like David; taking a life would affect him. How hadn't it affected David that he'd killed his own brother and the woman he'd loved? How had he done that and continued on as if nothing had happened? What was wrong with him? What was missing?

He jerked, startled when he realized what else was missing. Or rather who else . . .

"Where's Adelaide?" he asked with alarm. He knew her nanny only worked during the day. "You didn't leave her with Grandfather and his nurse?"

"No wonder they want to keep you overnight for that concussion," his brother mused. "You must have been hit

really damn hard to think that I would leave my daughter
with Dr. Frankenstein and Igor."

Another chuckle slipped out of Elijah's lips and reverberated inside his cracked skull. He winced. "So where did
you leave her?"

"Boarding house," Bode replied. "With Rosemary and
Genevieve. Of course, then I had to tell them what had
happened. That reporter must have overheard and beat me
to you."

"Damn it."

Bode sighed. "She won't be the only reporter covering
this. Maybe we should get ahead of it, do some damage
control."

"Let Amanda Plasky handle it," Elijah advised. It was
better that someone without Bainesworth or Cooke blood
in their veins handle the press. "And focus on Adelaide."

"I will," Bode assured him. "It's a tragedy that her
mother is gone, that she'll never get to know her." Tears
filled his eyes. "She won't get to help pick out her prom
dress or wedding gown . . ." He sucked in a shaky breath.
"But at least it's over now, right? David must have killed
Erika, too."

Remembering his cousin's last words, his last confes-
sion, Elijah shook his head. Then he had to close his eyes
for a moment until the room stopped spinning on him.
"No, he didn't . . ."

"What do you mean?" Bode asked. "Of course he did.
He was obviously batshit crazy."

Elijah winced again. He hated that word, hated more
that it could be applied to so many of his family members.
"He admitted to Warren's death and Shannon Howell's."

Would Deacon ever forgive Elijah for that, for suspecting him instead? At least the sheriff knew the truth now

and so would the rest of the island soon enough; Elijah would make certain of that. He owed his old nemesis that much and more. Deacon had saved his life and Olivia Smith's for certain. There had been no way for him to save David, no way for anyone to save David. He'd been too far gone.

How had Elijah missed it all these years? How had he missed how unstable his cousin had been?

And what else had he missed?

"So?" Bode persisted. "Just because he didn't confess to it doesn't mean that he didn't kill her. Or maybe that kid that kidnapped the Walcott girl, maybe he did it. Either way, it's over, Elijah. We don't have to worry about anyone else getting hurt. It's over."

Elijah wanted to believe that almost as desperately as his brother did. But he had a feeling that it was far from over . . . and that there would be more bodies.

But he kept his fear to himself. He didn't know who to trust anymore. David had been more than his cousin; he'd been his best friend.

And a killer . . .

How many other secret killers did Elijah know. And would one of them kill again?

Prologue

She had to get away. She knew that if she didn't escape, she would wind up like the others.

Dead.

Or worse.

But, in order to escape, she had to fight the elements, too.

A bitter wind swirled around the rocky bluffs, blowing spray from the sea onto the rocks, leaving them slick and icy. The wind hurled shards of ice from the dark sky. The sleet stung as it struck her face and arms. She flinched, but she forced herself to keep moving up from the bluffs and the water, up the steep slope. She grabbed at the trunks of pine trees, bark biting into the palms of her hands while the dusting of snow already on the ground seared the bottom of her feet. That burning sensation spread up her legs, which were bare but for the damp hospital gown clinging to her thighs.

The higher she climbed the louder the howling grew— not of the wind but of the coyotes. They yelped and then released high-pitched howls that sounded like screams of pain or terror.

She held in the scream of terror and pain that clawed at

the back of her throat. She didn't want to reveal her location. The tracks in the snow would do that, though—would lead them right to her. She had to keep moving—had to run. But her legs were so heavy and the ground was so uneven and slick. And the sleet kept lashing down at her, blinding her even more than the darkness, stinging like needles.

The needles . . .

She'd fought those. If she hadn't . . .

If they'd drugged her . . .

She wouldn't have made it out of that dungeon of horrors. But she wasn't safe yet—from them or from the coyotes. The animals called out to one another, their howls echoing in the woods around her, echoing off the bluffs and the rocks. They were getting closer and closer.

The wind wasn't the only thing rustling the trees and brush. Something or someone was following her and drawing nearer with each slip of her sole against the snow. She cleared the top of the bluff only to find the slope on the other side steeper and more treacherous. As she started down it, her frozen feet slipped from beneath her. She fell hard to the ground and a cry escaped her lips.

She wanted to lie there in the snow, wanted to close her eyes. But they were too close. So close that they could probably hear her panting for breath and the mad pounding of her heart.

Fear propelled her to move again, and she pushed herself up from the ground. Her legs, numb now, buckled beneath her, and she fell again. But she couldn't stay down.

If they found her, she would never be seen again.

Chapter One

The long bridge shuddered in the wind, creaking and groaning as the car traveled along it. The car shook as well, and Rosemary grasped the steering wheel in tight fists, fighting to keep the tires straight, fighting to keep the vehicle from blowing right off the bridge into the icy water below. The wrought iron railings were low and too spindly to provide any real protection for a car or a person.

If someone had tried to walk across this bridge . . .

She glanced across the passenger's seat and over that railing to the icy water far below that swirled and frothed around huge outcroppings of jagged rocks. She didn't want to think about what would happen to something or someone that fell from the bridge.

But because of the rocky shore, the bridge was one of the only ways on and off Bane Island, which was located three miles off the coast of Maine. Helicopters could land on the island, too, but it was too rocky and uneven for planes. And ferries only braved the distance from the mainland in the summer when the waves weren't quite as high and the water as icy. At least that was what Rosemary had discovered when she'd tried to make travel arrangements to Bane Island—to her sister.

If only she'd gotten the message sooner . . .

Her cell was tucked into the console of the rental car, charging. The weak reception drained the battery here just like it had when she'd been in New Zealand the past week. That was why she hadn't played the message sooner—because she hadn't even heard the call. Since the phone had been dead, it had gone directly to voicemail.

Even if she had dared to take one hand from the wheel, she didn't need to play the message now to remember what it said. It played over and over again in her mind, haunting her:

Rosemary . . .

Help me . . .

Mom and Dad sent me away to this horrible place, and I'm scared. So scared . . .

She hadn't had to say it. Rosemary could hear the fear painfully in her voice, making it shaky and high-pitched. Nearly hysterical . . .

And even though she was a teenager, Genevieve was never hysterical. She wasn't overly dramatic or emotional. Growing up in the same house as Rosemary had, it wouldn't have been allowed.

Because Rosemary had once been sent away, too, and it hadn't been within the same state like the place where Genevieve was. Bane was just a few hours north of Portland where Rosemary's family still lived. Rosemary did not.

She shuddered just as the bridge did when the car traveled along the last few yards of the three miles of flimsy metal and finally struck solid ground. Rock-solid ground. The tires skidded over the slick asphalt, and she clenched the steering wheel even tighter. But she didn't jerk it; she just gripped it and rode out the skid as the car careened dangerously close to the WELCOME TO BANE ISLAND sign. When the car straightened, she expelled a ragged breath.

She wasn't going to be able to help her sister if she crashed before she even found her. She knew where she was, though.

They sent me to this treatment center called Halcyon Hall. More like House of Horrors . . .

Then her voice had cracked with sobs as she'd pleaded with Rosemary.

Please come get me!

The minute Rosemary had played the message she'd tried calling her back, but then Genevieve's phone had gone directly to voicemail. Seeing the remoteness of this place, Rosemary could understand why. It was a miracle that Genevieve had been able to make the call at all.

"I'm here," she whispered into the cold interior of the car. "I'm here . . ."

Genevieve wouldn't be able to hear her, but would she sense it? Although Rosemary was so much older than her sister that they hadn't grown up together, they were close. Despite not living together, they shared a special bond.

So why hadn't Rosemary known Genevieve was in trouble? What had the girl gotten into that Mother had thought it necessary to send her for treatment? Or had she just done that to get her out of the way for the holidays? Rosemary had chosen to go away on a trip, too, because she hadn't wanted to come home to Portland for Thanksgiving—for the awkwardness that ensued whenever she was around her mom and stepfather.

They had taken a trip for the holiday, too, leaving on

a European cruise once they had shipped off Genevieve to what she'd called the House of Horrors. From what Rosemary had found when she'd googled the place, she didn't think her sister was being overly dramatic now either.

The history of Halcyon Hall, formerly known as Bainesworth Manor, sounded like the plot of a horror movie complete with a curse and the ghosts of the cursed. The place had once been a psychiatric hospital for young women whose families had committed them for treatment. Treatments that, even if she wasn't a psychologist, Rosemary would have considered atrocious and inhumane. According to the articles she'd read, many of the patients had not survived those treatments, and legend claimed that for decades their ghosts had roamed the ruins of Bainesworth Manor. Even though the buildings and grounds had recently been renovated and advertised as a new age treatment center, its history and maybe its ghosts continued to haunt the property.

She shuddered again in revulsion and because of the chill that permeated her sweater and the tights she wore beneath a long skirt. The rental car's heater wasn't overly generous, or maybe it just couldn't keep out all the cold of this remote place with its miles of rocky shore, bluffs, mountains, and pine trees. But as she continued driving down the road from the bridge, she came upon a collection of buildings and houses and more streets intersecting the main one.

Halcyon Hall wasn't the only thing on the island. There was a town. She even passed a hotel as she continued down the street. Not that she was going to stay there or anywhere else on Bane Island. She intended to collect her sister and leave as soon as possible.

First, she had to find the damn place, though. Since it was on an island, it shouldn't have been that hard. According to the directions she'd downloaded before her phone died, the hall was on the main street that started at the bridge and ended at a pier that extended from the rocky shore to the water.

She reached the pier without finding it, though, and when the tires skidded on the icy pavement, she nearly wound up driving onto the pier. Instead of riding out the skid, she twisted the wheel and swerved as she braked. The car slid toward the rocky bluff and the waves crashing against it. With a sudden jerk, it finally stopped, and Rosemary's breath whooshed out with relief. Her hand trembling, she pulled her cell from the console. Even though the phone showed fully charged, nothing came up on the screen. There were no bars. No reception.

She drew in a breath now and turned the wheel again, steering away from the pier to head back toward town. Someone there would be able to tell her how to find the hall. To reach town, though, she had to travel back along that long stretch of empty road with only pine trees lining it. The road didn't remain empty for long, though. Before she reached town, lights flashed onto her rearview window and a siren pealed out, breaking the eerie silence.

She hadn't noticed the police SUV behind her or anywhere else along the road. It had appeared out of nowhere. And why was it now pulling her over? She'd done nothing wrong. This time . . .

But she dutifully pulled to the shoulder of the road, which was just a thin strip of gravel between the asphalt and the trunks of the pine trees. The police SUV didn't pull over as far, nearly blocking the lane behind her. Then the door opened, and an officer stepped from the vehicle. He was tall, clad in a dark uniform and, despite the overcast sky, dark sunglasses as well. As he approached her side of the car, she fumbled with the unfamiliar controls to lower the window.

"I'm sorry, Officer," she said. "This is a rental, so I don't know where everything is." In the car or on Bane Island. Maybe he could help her.

However, he stared at her with no expression on his face, his lips pressed in a tight line and his square jaw rigid. Finally he spoke. "Sheriff. I'm the sheriff."

Then why was he wasting his time making traffic stops? Not that there was any traffic on the road. Just her car.

"I'm sorry, Sheriff," she corrected herself. "I don't understand what I've done wrong."

"You were driving carelessly," he said. "You nearly went over the edge back by the pier."

"I slid," she said.

"You were driving too fast for conditions."

"I didn't realize how icy the roads are," she admitted. She shouldn't have been surprised, though, since it was late November. Michigan, where she lived now, got snow and ice storms before winter officially started, too.

"The roads are always icy this time of year."

Was he always icy? There was nothing welcoming about his demeanor, and he had to have guessed that she was not from Bane Island. He probably knew everybody on the island, and maybe that was the real reason he'd pulled her over—to find out who she was.

Because his next comment was, "License and registration, please."

She reached inside her purse and pulled out her wallet. After taking out her driver's license, she reached across the console for the glove box. "I don't know if the registration is in here or not."

"This is fine, Ms. Tulle," he said. And with her license in his big, gloved hand, he turned and walked back toward his SUV.

The cold was blasting through her open window, but she hesitated to raise it. She didn't want to piss him off any more than he appeared to be. She drew in a breath of air so cold that it burned her lungs. Even though it had proven ineffectual, she reached over and cranked up the heater. The fan rattled as the air blasted from the vents. But the air wasn't hot. It was barely warm.

A cough startled her. She jerked against her seat belt before turning back toward her open window. "I didn't hear you come back," she murmured. And she hadn't expected him so quickly. She held out her hand for her license and whatever citation he was going to give her.

But he passed back her license alone. "What is your business here, Ms. Tulle?"

"Halcyon Hall."

Behind those dark glasses, he studied her face for a moment before nodding. "Of course."

"I'm here for my sister," she said. "To pick her up from the treatment center." She doubted Genevieve needed treatment for anything but Mother's overprotectiveness.

He shrugged, as if he didn't care or didn't believe her.

"Can you tell me where it is?"

"Here," he said.

"I know it's on the island but . . ."

He jerked his thumb behind him. "It's here," he said. "Behind those trees and the stone wall."

She peered around him. And now, stopped, she was able to study the trees and catch glimpses of rocks behind the trunks and pine boughs. "Oh, how do I get inside?"

"Are you sure you really want to?" he asked.

"I'm here for my sister," she reminded him.

He jerked his thumb farther down the road. "You'll find the gate if you drive slowly enough."

"I—I will," she assured him, and she waited for that ticket, which he must have realized.

"I'm letting you off with a warning this time," he said. "You need to proceed with more caution, Ms. Tulle. Much more caution."

Did his warning actually pertain to her driving or to something else? He didn't clarify, though, just turned and headed back toward his SUV.

Before she could raise the window, another noise startled her. This wasn't a cough but a cry—a high-pitched, forlorn cry.

Was it human?

"What was that?" she called back to the sheriff.

He stopped next to his vehicle and listened. Then his mouth moved, curving into a slight smile. "Coyote."

Shivering, she raised the window to shut out the cold and the cry. The sheriff got into his SUV but then just sat in it, as if waiting for her to pull away. So she did, slowly, just inching along the road until she found the wrought iron gate in the middle of the rock wall. Pine boughs stretched almost across the drive, obscuring the gate.

Didn't they want anyone to be able to find the place?

The gate was closed, but an intercom system was mounted onto the stone wall next to the gate. She could have lowered the window again, but she wouldn't have been able to reach the controls. So she opened her door instead and stepped out of the car.

And that cry echoed around her, that forlorn cry. Her finger trembled as she punched the button on the intercom panel.

"Halcyon Hall, how may we help you?" a melodic voice greeted her. The woman sounded upbeat and welcoming, completely opposite of everything that had greeted Rosemary since her arrival on Bane Island.

She breathed a sigh of relief. "I'm here to pick up my sister, Genevieve Walcott."

"Your name?"

"Rosemary Tulle," she replied.

A long silence followed, so long that she pressed the button again. "Hello? Are you still there?" she asked. The wind kicked up, blasting icy bits of snow at her face as her long skirt swirled around her legs and her long hair whipped around her shoulders. She pulled a black strand from where it had tangled in her eyelashes and peered through the gate—at where a narrow driveway wound between more trees and rocks. "Hello?"

The speaker cracked, and the voice sounded nearly as cold as the wind when it replied, "Ms. Tulle, you are not on the list."

"List?"

"You are not on the visitor list."

"Genevieve called me," she said. "She asked me to come get her." Pleaded was more like it, desperately pleaded.

"You are not on the list." A click emanated from the speaker now as the intercom was shut off.

Rosemary repeatedly jabbed the button and called out, "Hello? Hello? Open the damn gates! Open them now!"

But the gates didn't open, and nobody replied to her. Nobody answered her but the coyote that cried out again—so forlornly. Rosemary stepped closer to the gates and peered through the wrought iron. A shadow fell across the driveway on the other side. It could have been from one of the trees or the boulders. But the shape of it looked more human than that—like someone stood there, watching her. . . .

The frozen ground crunched beneath the soles of his shoes as he walked across the grounds of the manor. Except that it wasn't the manor anymore. It was a hall now. A treatment center to help instead of harm.

But no matter how much renovation and remodeling had been done to the stone mansion and the other buildings on the property, the place would never fully escape the past. And no person would ever fully escape from Bainesworth Manor.

He hadn't.

Where was the cop—the *sheriff*—now when she needed him? As she traveled back to town, Rosemary didn't catch so much as a glimpse of another vehicle. But then she hadn't seen the sheriff either until his light had flashed in her rearview mirror.

Instead of looking for him, she should have just dialed

9-1-1 while standing at that gate. But the shadow falling across the driveway on the other side had unnerved her, and she'd rushed back to the rental vehicle. That must have been how Genevieve had felt when she'd left that voicemail—desperate to escape.

It wasn't just the treatment center property that was creepy, though. The entire island with its rocky landscape was cold and forbidding with gray clouds hanging low, casting shadows over everything and everyone. Maybe that was all Rosemary had seen—just the shadow of a cloud.

She doubted it, though. She'd *felt* someone's presence . . . until she'd jumped back into the rental and locked the doors. Ever since then she'd felt alone, as if she was the only one left on the island. No cars passed her; no people walked along the road.

Then she drew closer to town, and a few cars drove along the streets intersecting the main one. She was not alone. She wasn't sure if that was reassuring or not, though—not here—on this godforsaken island.

Despite the brightly painted clapboard exteriors of the old buildings lining the streets, the town didn't appear any more welcoming than the rocky coast had as Rosemary had driven across that rickety bridge. Many of the awnings had been rolled back with closed-for-the-season signs posted on the front windows. She wasn't looking for a place to buy souvenirs or fudge, though. She was looking for the police department.

If the firehouse, a two-story brick building with a turret and fancy garage doors, hadn't drawn her attention, Rosemary might have missed it. The flat-roofed one-story building was squeezed in between the firehouse and a two-story Victorian house with a diner sign dangling from the gingerbread trim of the front porch. Light shining from the windows of the diner cast a glow on the front door of the short building and on the sign, in the shape of a badge, that adorned the tall steel door: BANE SHERIFF'S OFFICE.

A breath of relief slipped out of her lips and hung, like one of those gloomy clouds casting shadows over the island, inside the car. Maybe the heater had stopped working entirely. She didn't reach for the controls, though. Instead she gripped the steering wheel and turned the car into the lot on the other side of the diner. Ignoring the DINER-ONLY PARKING signs, she pulled into a space. Her heart beating fast with fear for her sister, she pushed open the door and rushed toward the police department. As she passed the diner, the smell of roasting chicken wafted across the porch; her stomach rumbled, reminding her it was empty.

She hadn't eaten that day. She'd barely eaten since she'd played that message. Maybe once she got Genevieve out of Halcyon Hall, they would stop here before they left Bane Island. Or maybe Genevieve would just want to go home.

Home . . .

Rosemary's stomach churned, but it wasn't with hunger now. It was with dread. She didn't want to bring Genevieve home any more than she wanted to leave her here. Determination surging through her, she pushed open the door to the sheriff's office and stepped inside the building. Not that she felt like she was inside when faced with another wall—with another door and window in it. She gripped the knob of that door, but it didn't turn no matter how hard she twisted. So she stepped over to the window. A desk sat behind it—an empty desk.

She tapped on the glass and called out, "Hello!" Urgency rushing through her, she pounded harder. "Hello! Hello!"

A door behind the desk opened, and a man in the same blue uniform the sheriff had worn stepped through it. He wasn't the sheriff, though. He wasn't as tall or as broad, or maybe the sheriff had only seemed that way because she'd been sitting in the car. The officer pressed a button on the desk, and his voice echoed throughout the small reception area. "How may I help you?" he asked.

"You can help me get into Halcyon Hall."

He gestured at the window with his index finger, making a pointing motion. She glanced around and noticed a speaker and button next to the glass—which must have been sound-proof and probably bulletproof. The security was nearly the same as at the hall. Pressing the button, she repeated her request.

The man's mouth curved into a slight grin. "You and everyone else . . ." he murmured. "The hall is a private facility. We have no jurisdiction there no matter how much . . ." He trailed off again, leaving her to wonder what he left unsaid.

"My sister is at the treatment center," Rosemary explained. "But they won't let me in to see her."

"You're not on the list."

She tensed. "How do you know that?"

"You don't get inside unless you're on the list," he replied matter-of-factly.

She narrowed her eyes and studied the officer on the other side of that glass. He was younger than she was, probably still in his twenties, or maybe he looked that young from the fullness of his face. He wasn't broad like the sheriff, but he was stocky, his belly straining the buttons of his uniform. "You know a lot about the hall despite having no jurisdiction there."

He shrugged and remarked, "Bane isn't that big an island."

Not big enough to justify bulletproof glass in the police department . . . unless it was a more dangerous place than it appeared, which increased Rosemary's sense of urgency. "My sister called me to pick her up," she said.

He shrugged again. "Then she should have put your name on the list."

"I—I'm sure she did," she insisted.

He shook his head. "Then you would have been on it."

"They must be lying," she said.

"They?"

"The hall—whoever picked up when I pressed the intercom button." Like the button she pressed now—to speak to the officer. "They're lying."

"Why?"

"I don't know," she said. "That's why I'm here. They're holding my sister hostage in that creepy place."

"People pay a hell of a lot of money to go there. They don't need to hold anybody against their will."

"They're holding my sister," she said. "I have a voice-mail from her to prove it." But when she reached for her phone, she remembered she'd left it in the rental car—charging. She'd been so anxious to get help. She suspected the officer wasn't interested in helping her, though. Maybe once he heard the voicemail . . .

"I'll go get my phone," she said. "You'll hear it in her voice—the fear. She wants out of that place."

"Why doesn't she just check herself out then?" he asked. "Or better yet, why did she check herself in there?"

"She didn't," Rosemary said. "Our parents put her in there." So they could go on their vacation without worrying that she'd get in trouble . . . like Rosemary had.

His brow furrowed. "Your parents? How old is your sister?"

"Seventeen," she said.

His lips curved again into another slight smile. This one felt patronizing. "Oh . . ."

"She's being held prisoner," she insisted. "She was put in there against her will." Just like the girls she'd read about, the ones who'd been committed to the manor all those years ago. "You need to help me get her out of there."

He shook his head.

"Why won't you help?"

"Because it's not a police matter, Miss," he said. "It's a family matter. You need to talk to your family."

"I tried," she said. "The damn hall won't let me through the gates."

"Your parents," he said. "You need to talk to them. They must have a reason for admitting her for treatment and a reason for not putting you on the visitor list."

That dread churned in her stomach again. "I tried talking to them," she admitted. She'd left voicemails for them like Genevieve had left for her. But they hadn't returned her calls.

He shrugged. "This is a family matter."

The door behind her creaked open, and a woman stepped into the small reception area with her. She also wore a navy-blue uniform. How many officers did this small island have? Just how the hell dangerous was it?

"Can you help me?" she asked the older woman. Her

face was softer and kinder than the male officer's and certainly more so than the sheriff's.

Before the woman would answer, that voice emanated from the speaker again. "I've got this, Margaret. She's here about the hall."

The woman's soft expression hardened then. She juggled containers in her hands as she reached for the door Rosemary had tried opening just moments ago. The knob turned easily for the woman, and she pushed open the door to step inside what appeared to be an even narrower foyer than the reception area. Rosemary considered following her, but she doubted it would matter what she said to these officers. She wouldn't be able to convince them to help her.

Not unless . . .

But she wasn't ready to share her secrets with strangers; she hadn't even shared them yet with a friend. Most of the time she wouldn't admit them to herself.

The door closed behind the woman, locking Rosemary out again. She pressed that button again and asked, "Where's the sheriff?" Maybe he would help her. After all, he had told her where to find the gate to the hall.

"Sheriff Howell is not on duty tonight," the male officer told her.

"But—but he pulled me over just a short while ago—near the hall," she said.

The officer's already small eyes narrowed. "He's not supposed to be out there. . . ." Something about his tone implied that it wasn't just because he hadn't been on duty but for another reason, something to do with that damn place.

"Why not?" she asked.

His jaw tightened momentarily before he replied, "It's a private facility, Miss. We have no jurisdiction there." As if that was enough of an explanation, he stepped away from the glass, through the door that must have led back to where the female officer had gone.

Rosemary could have hit the intercom button again, but she suspected that, just like at Halcyon Hall, nobody would answer her call for admittance. Nobody would help her. So she would have to figure out another way to get her sister out of that creepy place.

Connect with U(s)

Visit us online at
KensingtonBooks.com
to read more from your favorite authors, see books
by series, view reading group guides, and more.

Join us on social media

for sneak peeks, chances to win books and prize packs,
and to share your thoughts with other readers.

facebook.com/kensingtonpublishing
twitter.com/kensingtonbooks

Tell us what you think!

To share your thoughts, submit a review,
or sign up for our eNewsletters, please visit:
KensingtonBooks.com/TellUs.